A Million Miles from Yesterday

Maureen Connolly

Copyright © 2024 Maureen Connolly

All rights reserved. No part of this book may be reproduced or transmitted in any form or by any means, electronic or mechanical, including photocopying, recording or by any information storage and retrieval system without permission in writing from the publisher.

Slainte—Oak Park, IL
ISBN: 979-8-218-37812-7
Library of Congress Control Number: 2024905635
Title: *A Million Miles from Yesterday*
Author: Maureen Connolly
Digital distribution | 2024
Paperback | 2024

This is a work of fiction. The characters, names, incidents, places, and dialogue are products of the author's imagination, and are not to be construed as real.

Dedication

For my grandparents Michael and Sarah from Ireland, and my grandmother Alice from Canada.

Chapter 1

That spring a satellite in space went off orbit, news events could not be broadcast from England, pagers and cell phones in Chicago did not work, and it was hot in Alma.

It did not always feel like 1999 in Alma. More often it felt to Hank like the whole place was moving through an earlier time, a blend of the 1940's and a few selected decades since. No, there was little of a 'nineties feel to Alma. Most of the time he liked this, the way it played with his mind as he moved through his day. But not today.

The morning began as usual: the long climb out of sleep, out of Sarah's arms, into his own body in his own bed alone, in a small town in Wisconsin. At the clinic there was the familiar mix of pregnant women, asthmatics, heart patients, sore throats, back pain, sprained fingers. He coddled the eighty-nine-year-old who insisted on using udder balm for every ache in his bony body. He coaxed a five-year-old to sit still to get her ears checked by telling her a funny story.

By two o'clock, he was on his way out of Alma. The sun beat down on the town. Yellow wildflowers were poking up in the empty lot behind the general store. He bent his hand at the wrist, fingers up, in greeting to local workers resurfacing the gas station lot, their shirts off, exposing pale winter skin. He was making a house call.

Not a house call really, but a trailer call. On Mary Two-Rivers. The sky glowered as he turned onto the rutted back road leading to her place, and he felt like glowering back. He bumped his green pickup truck down the road, unable to find anything diverting on the radio.

His spirits sank.

Mary Two-Rivers' husband, who worked at the casino a hundred miles away, had disappeared a few months earlier. They couldn't find the body. What this meant for Mary, who was not sorry to see him go, was that she had to wait a year to claim his pension. In the meantime, she stayed in her run-down trailer on the reservation, watching television and eating. Mostly eating. By now she'd gained another twenty pounds. "Poor soul," Hank's mother would have said, "there but for the grace of God...."

It was as hot inside the trailer as it was outside. Mary – all three hundred pounds of her – was sitting in a large chair with an old telephone book under one corner, stuffing spilling out of the side. Her eyes were slits in the puffiness of her face. Bags of potato chips and cookies lay beside a small tobacco pipe on the counter. He cleared some space and sat down next to her.

He did not like to touch Mary Two-Rivers. He, who had touched the infected, addicted, unwashed, cancer-ridden, and obese so many times. So, he did an especially careful exam.

Pushing a ponderous breast out of the way, he listened to her heart. "How's it goin', Mary?"

"My grandson's such a bad kid," she mumbled.

"That's too bad." He noticed her legs were more swollen than usual. "Are you taking your blood pressure medicine?"

"Sure, Doc." She sat impassive. She only grunted when he said good-bye and climbed out of the trailer into the heavy afternoon air.

By evening Hank was down at Livy's Bar and Café having a few drinks.

"I had a piece of pecan pie down in Savannah one time that made my fillings ache," he said to Livy. "*Your* pecan pie is just right, not too sweet, the pecans are fresh, and it has a nice delicate crust."

"Thanks, Hank, I never heard anybody get so spiritual about my pecan pie before." She gave him a slightly lopsided smile and slapped him on the shoulder. He rocked on his swivel seat at the counter.

Livy doubled as a fire fighter for the county, and she was chunky but strong. She'd recently cut her dark hair short, so it was less in her way out on the fire truck. She was pushing forty, tired of looking for the right man to father a child for her and tired of providing condoms for the wrong men. She had an appointment set up at the beginning of the summer to have a baby planted in her womb, courtesy of the sperm clinic at the state university. Or at least what she hoped would be a baby, if the donor's sperm did what Hank described as the dance of life with one of her eggs.

The winter his wife had died, Hank began to stay late in the clinic, lights burning long after the last patient had left. Then about nine-thirty, a half-hour before Livy closed the café, he would pick his way across the street through the sludge and piles of snow and climb onto one of the seats at her counter.

"What'll it be, Doc?" Livy would say.

"A little whiskey for the inner man, Livy," he'd say, "and I'd better have something to eat with that so give me a piece of pie." He'd wink at her with a tired smile, over rhubarb pie, or cherry, or pecan, depending on what was in season or what Livy got the best buy on at the wholesale market.

"You work too much," she said tonight, "why don't you ever hang out with some of the other guys and go fishing, or shoot pool or something?"

"Well, that might be good, you know…but it seems like, just when I'm relaxing into their company, someone has a baby or breaks an arm and I just never get into the swing of what they're doing. Or the women for that matter."

Usually, their talk in the café came in fragments as she waited on customers. Other than the rare visits she made to his office like the time she cut her finger chopping celery, these scraps were the size and shape of their conversations. But tonight, Hank was the only one in the café. Livy pulled up a stool and sat down on the other side of the counter. Their conversation took winding turns down lanes they had not traveled before; they talked about baseball, wolves, opera, and politics, then they relaxed into quiet. The radio was on low. President Clinton was talking about democracy to the Chinese people, drought fires raged out of control in parts of Mexico and Florida, the prime minister of Japan had resigned over Japan's failing economy, Wisconsin was hoping for a bumper crop of corn and soybeans. After a while soft swing music began to play.

The screen door banged in the kitchen out back. Rufus ambled into the front room of the café.

"Hey Livy, I got you those CDs for the new player you got."

Rufus really was the most beautiful sixteen-year-old boy either of them had ever seen. It was as if nature knew his good-hearted parents were going to give him an impossible old family name and anticipated his rescue. He had thick black lashes, deep brown eyes, honey-colored skin, strong nose, well-shaped body parts; he moved with an unconscious grace charming everyone around him. This year he had added adolescent sinew and new muscle hauling boxes over at the recycling plant after school, but he still had a boy's smile— guileless.

"Thanks, Rufus, just leave them on the table near the stove." Livy smiled at him. "How's your mom?" Elrita Yazzi worked at the nursing home where Hank saw patients.

"Okay—she's in Madison for some kind of sculpting class today."

"Has your mother ever sculpted you?" Livy said, half-complimenting, half-teasing him.

"Nah, well…maybe once when I was little. I'm not much for holding still." He colored a little. "Gotta go, Liv, Dad's on the late shift at Harass this month."

"Right…wait, do you want an apple pie?"

"Uh…I don't have any money on me right now."

"That's okay. This one's from yesterday, take it home for the family. You'd be doing me a favor. It's still good though." She was wrapping the pie in plastic, slipping it into a brown paper bag.

"Yeah, Livy, thanks. Great, the kids'll love it." He turned towards Hank, "Bye, Doc." To Livy he said, "*Haagoinee*."

"*He'll* love it too," Hank said after Rufus rounded the corner onto the street. He looked up at Livy from his whiskey. "Was that pie really from yesterday?"

"Sure…what does it matter? I'm not going to go out of business giving away pies! I keep a good bottom line - *you*, for example, owe me $5.25 for the pie and the Jamesons." She tilted her head towards him, back of her hand on one hip, eyes dancing.

Hank was startled to realize it was ten o'clock. He'd almost forgotten he'd have to pay the bill, and leave. Now he was discomfited.

Livy began closing up. Still, he sat, elbow propped up on the counter, chin resting in his hand. He felt outside of himself. Like he was a half a beat off from the world. Or maybe that the world was a half-beat off from him.

Livy was walking towards the door, keys in her hand.

"Coming?"

The next morning when he woke up, Hank couldn't remember where he was. He'd sat on the porch in his old leather chair the night before, exhausted, watching a moth flap up against the inside of the frayed screens. He'd let himself have one more whiskey, then a cold beer, to wash down the whole long day. He'd finally gone to bed and fallen into a hard sleep.

Towards morning when the first clear bird calls sounded, he turned over and began dreaming. He was all over in his dreams: with his second cousins in Ireland, back in Chicago with Sarah, fishing in the North Woods of Wisconsin with his grandfather. He wanted to stay, to sit in the rowboat with his Irish-born grandfather in the immense quiet of the cool early morning lake, learning how to put a worm on a hook. But the sound of dogs barking pulled him into the middle of a Thursday morning. Yesterday's pants and shirt were draped over the back of a chair, his shoes and socks dropped where he'd taken them off. The same dust covered his bedroom furniture.

No medical emergencies during the night, and no office hours until one o'clock. Time to himself for a change. He wasn't sure he wanted it. Instead of being grateful, he felt a little crabby. His head ached, pre-coffee.

He stretched out his long body, felt the sheets rub against his skin. He could not will himself to get out of bed. He sensed that the layer of equanimity he'd wrapped around himself in the three years since Sarah died had a tear. That there might be things to glimpse through the tear that he did not want to see.

Chapter 2

Elrita and Joe Yazzi came to town the same year as Hank and Sarah, in 1993. They migrated to Alma from the poverty of the Navajo Nation hoping for a better life for themselves and their children.

They had been able to buy some farmland cheap a few miles out from Alma, including a ramshackle farmhouse in disrepair. Joe Yazzi built a hogan on the land that same summer.

He must have known the traditional home heated by wood fires would not work in the freezing winters of Wisconsin, but he built it anyway. It was a simple building: six sides made of logs slanting inward to form an opening in the roof for smoke to escape and, set back from the wood stove, a plywood floor as a concession to their northern environment. He built it in his time off from the auto assembly plant in Harass.

Elrita talked to him about it at first but, although he listened to her respectfully, he kept right on building the hogan. So, the five of them —Elrita, Joe, Rufus, Beulah, and baby Winona—lived in a tiny apartment in Alma that June. Elrita took the nursing job working with Dr. Cleary. She brought pitchers of cool tea, sandwiches, leftover stews, and fry bread out to Joe.

He took his time, working slow and steady. Their hogan in Arizona with its dirt floor had been there as long as they could remember, as long as their grandparents could remember. No one they knew had ever put up a new one. But Joe worked from some blueprint in his head, fitting pieces with the care of a cabinet-maker. In July when he finished, they invited their nearest neighbors, Doc Cleary and his wife, and Livy Reyna from the café in town to come over. By November, the cold had driven them out.

Today Joe sat in the shade of the hogan, making a toy for six-year-old Winona. He'd taken up carving and whittling since they came north to this state with all its trees. Elrita had gone to work after lunch, Rufus and Beulah were in school. Winona, home with a sore throat, was taking a nap in the old, restored farmhouse on the other side of the clearing from where Joe sat.

He was glad his group was laid off from the plant this week, glad to be sitting out of doors on an overly warm spring day.

"Are you the corn goddess?" he'd asked Winona as she settled in her bed, arms around her doll. "I'm *Winona,*" she said with delight, placing her small hands one on either side of his face. As soon as she fell asleep, he'd slipped outside into the open air.

He pulled a piece of maple out of his pocket and resumed fashioning a cradleboard for Winona's baby doll. A cradleboard just like the larger one Elrita had carried Winona herself upon in the early days of her life. "It's important to remember the old ways even when we're far from the *Diné,"* he'd said to Elrita.

And now they were talking about going home.

Not a plan to go home but a faint light through a door in his mind. "We have ties here," Elrita had said.

"I'm tired," Joe simply said. He was tired, and tired of the automobile plant. Five years of fluorescent lights and quotas. "I'm beginning to have the pain in my wrists, the tingling and numbness in my fingers," he told Elrita.

He smoothed the edges of the cradleboard with a piece of sandpaper. He hadn't started dropping things yet, but he could tell that before long he too would have to have a white doctor cut into his wrists so the pain would go away. People on the line younger than him, in their early thirties, had ugly scars on their wrists from the surgery, and were back doing the same job over and over again that led to the problem in the first place.

Elrita had given him a vitamin to help and massaged herbs into his wrists, but they were only getting worse. "Why don't you do a curing ceremony?" he'd asked her. She had not, and he began to see that to stop tightening bolts and rotating parts on the gleaming new cars coming off the assembly was curing she could not do. He made good money. Between his paycheck and hers from the clinic and the nursing home, they'd taken care of their family and even saved some. Soon maybe they could go home.

He concentrated on the beautiful wood in his hand, basking in his solitude. From above, a hawk cried, wheeling in the sky.

Along the curving road that led from Joe and Elrita's to Alma, before you reach the bookstore on the edge of town, was an old fruit and vegetable stand. The kind of small open stand you see in the Midwest countryside, abandoned for all but two-and-a-half months of the year, when it becomes laden with asparagus, radishes, carrots, beans, then tomatoes, peaches, corn, and squash. On this particular day, although the air was drowsy and insects were humming in the aspen trees, it was still too early for crops and the stand was empty.

But not entirely empty. Lonnie Two-Rivers sat on an old, rusted chair behind the stand waiting for Beulah Yazzi. He knew Beulah from high school, before he left to take the job at the Casino. He'd noticed her right away last year when she came to school – braid of thick black hair, shiny brown eyes, straight back, head held high. At first, he thought she was stuck-up, thought her Navajo self-better than the Menominee kids at Alma High School. After he finally got her to talk to him, he thought maybe he was right about that, but he liked the way she carried herself proud.

Beulah should be coming any time now walking home from school. He fixed his eyes on the bend in the road where it turned towards the stand out of Alma. He could wait.

When she rounded the bend, kicking some loose gravel as she walked, Lonnie continued to wait. He waited until she was even with the empty fruit stand, then he stood directly in her path.

"Hi, Beulah."

"Lonnie…you startled me." She stared at his lean muscular body, the tattoo on his arm, his even teeth. His skin gleamed in the sun.

He took her by the hand onto the path leading into a canopy of trees. He pulled her against him and kissed her hard, so hard it was almost painful and she could barely breathe. Beulah felt the heat pleasure rise up in her, like she was canoeing the rapids with a high fever. "I should never have let him kiss me that first time," she thought, but it was so delicious, and she kissed him back again and again.

This time he pulled her further back in the trees, began to rub his hands over the thin white blouse covering her breasts, over the back of her navy skirt. Then he reached under her skirt between her legs.

"No!" she grabbed his hand. He yanked the arm trying to restrain him and bent it behind her back. She groaned.

"What is it, you're too good for me?"

"No, Lonnie, I like you, I really do, but…." His fingers in her now, probing, thrilling, her legs weak and loose beneath her. She felt herself leave the canoe and the rapids and slide headlong over the waterfall. And Beulah Yazzi had her first orgasm, crying and shaking.

"You're mine now."

"But you hurt me!"

His face was dark with anger. "Come on, Beulah, you want it! If you tell anyone you'll be sorry...." He pressed his body into her, pinning her against a tree, but he'd loosened his grip.

Beulah slipped out from under him and ran. Flew away from him, over the creek behind the copse of trees, along the cow path next to the cornfields, then diagonally into the fields. Lonnie's feet stopped pounding behind her. Still, she ran, her breath raw in her chest, through the cornfields as the crow flies, past her father without him seeing her, straight up to her room with its slanted walls, and into her bed under her Navajo eye dazzler blanket. She curled up in a ball, her face hot. She begged the Great Spirit to help her. She promised she would be good if only He would make things the way they were before.

Chapter 3

The first thing Hank and Sarah saw when they happened onto Alma in the '70's was the census sign just outside of town. In their early twenties, they'd driven up from Chicago for a long weekend in Wisconsin, giddy with the freedom of time off, Sarah from her job as a photographer and Hank from school. They turned off the state highway on a whim, rode a few miles on a secondary road, down a soft hill, and there alongside Sarah's open car window was the white metal sign.

"Alma," the sign unmistakably read, "population 297." Not "295" or "300," but "297" which somehow pleased them both.

"Looks like there's another Alma near the Mississippi." Sarah studied the map. "I can't find this one."

"Here it is, though."

They almost missed the bookstore. They were nearly through Alma when they spotted the square lettering above an open door— "PIED-À-TERRE." A large yellow dog lay on the sidewalk in front of the door. The display window was filled with used books: slim volumes, thick tomes, pocket and oversized books, some with covers displayed, many resting in vertical or horizontal piles of various heights. A cat reclined along the oak ledge at the back of the display. If there was any theme to the piles, it was not evident to Hank or Sarah, except that books in some piles seemed to share similar colored bindings.

Inside Pied-à-Terre, dark wooden shelves were packed with books, and comfortable little spots were tucked away among the bookshelves to sink down and read.

A grandmother floor clock ticked softly in one corner. A photograph of Josephine Baker hung on the wall opposite the door next to a print of Monet's *Bridge at Argenteuil*. On the back wall was a framed newspaper clipping of Marlene Dietrich and a carved wooden clock in the shape of the state of Wisconsin. A voice Hank recognized as that of the tenor John McCormack soared from a 78-rpm record on a turntable lying on a cluttered glass cabinet desk near the front.

A tall angular woman with thick hair cut short on the sides and front and longer in the back stood next to the desk talking to a man in overalls. Her face could only be described as handsome, an epithet Hank remembered his mother using to describe certain female Irish relatives of his father's. "You can call it loving God if you want," the angular woman was saying, "I call it synchronicity with truth."

At the other end of the desk, a slender woman with lustrous red hair pulled back in a chignon, wearing a satin blouse the color of a ripe peach, was pouring hot tea into two china cups. She smiled, pointing to empty teacups and the filigreed teapot. "*Bonjour*," she said in an American accent, "please have some if you like."

Hank and Sarah roamed the aisles, picking up and putting down books, sipping tea. They startled each other, walking from opposite directions around a corner reading. He drew her behind a bookcase and kissed her deeply in front of a row of Victorian novels. They heard the elegant Alice's voice at the front of the store asking Alex if she wanted more tea. They couldn't hear an answer, but they heard a third voice speaking now.

They moved towards the front in time to hear Alex talking to someone about to leave. "Baths are the answer," Alex's voice boomed. "Showers are too fast." And then they both were sure they heard her say "Jane Austen" to the departing customer as he stepped out over the yellow dog.

Hank and Sarah came back to Pied-à-Terre countless times over the years, when they still lived in Chicago and after they moved to Alma. But they always remembered the first time in a special way, like you remember the first time of anything that you grow to love. They were in a part of their lives then that was full of first times. Those were their jug-wine days with friends, when they stayed up all night talking about their visions for the country. When status meant being able to give something of yours away on the spot if someone admired it. Those were the days before HMOs and corporations began to stir their toxic alphabet soups into the broth of medicine. Hank was excited about becoming a doctor, proud of his noble calling. They were happy.

For as long as he'd lived in Alma, Hank never heard anyone in the town refer to Alex and Alice as anything but the bookstore ladies. There were stories of course. About how Alex was a local, had been a strapping farm girl "from somewhere near Harass," how she had only gone as far away as the university in Madison. How when she came back, she brought with her a carful of books…and Alice. How Alice was from a little town somewhere up over the state line in Minnesota, that she came from money, had sung opera in St. Paul, been married once.

Alice had a certain élan. She wore her beautiful hair, colored the auburn of her youth, smoothed back from her face often in a snood. She wore styles popular when she was a child in the forties. She took pleasure in color and texture. On a December winter's day, with Alex in blue jeans stringing up colored lights in the window of the bookstore, Alice would be wearing a green gabardine suit or a dark blue velvet dress with lace cuffs, humming French tunes under her breath.

As for Alex, it wasn't so much that she did not have any sense of style, it was more that her presence was so strong people rarely noticed what she was wearing. Over the years, her hair turned iron gray. She remained plain. But at odd moments when she happened to look at Alice, an expression of such innocent delight played over her face that her features softened, and for a fleeting second, she looked like she was twenty instead of fifty-seven.

Alex and Alice both loved words, the sound and the weight of words, unusual words. Alex's speech was as full of color and texture as Alice's clothing. If a known word didn't suit her, she made a word up to suit the occasion, like "skedaddly" or "millennialize."

The bookstore ladies gave the individuals who came into Pied-à-Terre plenty of room to meander. But every once in a while, either Alex, or Alice, would look closely at a given one of the townspeople and utter a word or two – just this side of cryptic – to that person. It might be a single word or a quotation from a book. Or it could be the name of a book, or an author or a character. Usually, the person from Alma tried to remember the words from Alex or Alice, because— when he or she got home and sat down to think about it – the small gift of words often turned out, in an uncanny way, to be just what was needed.

At other times, the person minding the store—Alex, or Alice, or their assistant Margaret would be reading herself, deep into a book, and the store would be quiet. So that everyone who frequented Pied-à-Terre had experienced falling down a well of time, standing in the middle aisle or a corner reading surrounded by wood and stillness, then coming to, finding himself over near the back storeroom door or sitting next to a window.

The store had seats snuggled at intervals into corners and along walls, some allowing for only one person, hidden away so that they provided the most immense sense of privacy. You could not see the nooks until you were almost upon them, so that people in Alma were used to being startled by someone they knew blissfully settled in with a book.

After Sarah died, Hank would sometimes sit in an overstuffed chair towards the back of Pied-à-Terre along the same wall as the floor clock. The clock ticked and chimed in the corner so softly, when it was working, that—while he took in the good rich wood, the pearl face with black Roman numerals and brass pointers, the long pendulum—he only noticed its sound every once in a while. Like some distant reassuring sound from childhood. Like the scritching of a screen door, or an oven door opening and closing, that did not interrupt you from your play.

The big yellow dog was gone now but one of his descendants, who looked just like him, lay in the doorway of Pied-à-Terre. In good weather, Sam took his customary place directly in front of the door; in inclement weather he lolled just inside the threshold.

Either way, people had to clamber over his relaxed torso to gain entrance to the bookstore.

Hank felt the coolness of the interior before his eyes adjusted from the outdoor light. Like so many old buildings with thick walls, the bookstore was comfortable without air conditioning on all but the hottest days.

"It's a stare-y kind of day, eh?" Alice said. She gave her last syllable the Canadian inflection common in northern Wisconsin, so that it rhymed with "sleigh."

"What?" he said. He was pale, his expression confused.

"You know, one of those days when you catch yourself just staring off into space every so often. It's kind of relaxing actually."

Their eyes caught. She smiled sheepishly. He managed to give her a small smile back.

Pied-à-Terre had no coffee bar like the big bookstores in Madison or Chicago, although you could bring in your own coffee. The bookstore ladies had no interest in cappuccino or microwaves. If you wanted a cup of hot tea, you waited. While Alice rinsed the teapot with cold water, filled the kettle with fresh water and heated it on the little stove in the back room with its new boxes of old books, then brought the tea out steaming in the large china pot covered with roses and green trailing vines.

Hank took his cup of tea from Alice with gratitude. Today she wore a shirred lavender silk shift with folds of draping across the bodice. A piece of light amber hung from her neck. She had a Billie Holliday kind of camellia tucked behind her ear. As she handed him his tea, she touched his arm for a second.

My God, his heart lurched, *what am I going to do?* He took a swallow of tea. It made him think of the old country, of the countless cups of milky tea he had sipped with relatives and strangers throughout Ireland. He began to wander slowly through the shop.

Sarah... The slender curve of her. Her sweetness, her teasing. How she never let him win at cards. How she always stood by him.

Losing her was like losing a part of himself. Like he had the phantom limb of an amputee—the limb gone, the pain and numbness still present.

He heard Alex's voice coming from behind one of the bookcases. "...doctor...now there's an ego walking." Then the rich timbre of Livy's voice. "I know. You feel so sorry for some of them. It's like their egos take up so much space it's a wonder they can get into their clothes every morning!" Then soft chuckling.

Who were they talking about? Hank wondered. Alex would never talk about *him* like that, would she? *To Livy?*

Is this what they really think of me, 'an ego walking'? Maybe they mean the guy who does the medical at the auto plant. They couldn't be talking about *me*, could they? He moved quickly out of the vicinity of the two women.

Joe Yazzi was sitting near Marlene Dietrich reading about whales. When Hank walked by, he barely acknowledged Joe's greeting.

"What's wrong with Doc Cleary?" Joe said later to Alice.

"Peut-être, un homme agité," Alice said. "What?"

"I don't know."

Hank stood in the middle of the nonfiction aisle surrounded by the smell of old books. Books on every conceivable place...Russia, Egypt, Nigeria, New York Harlem, China, Finland, Oklahoma, Nairobi, Italy, Antarctica, New Zealand, Alaska.... Every conceivable place a person could choose to be, to spend a chunk or all of his life on this planet. He stood stock still, surrounded by the dreams and memories of real people who had chosen mountain-climbing, archeology, theatre, politics, commerce, agriculture, medicine, as a way to live. He could not move.

He tried to escape without seeing Alex or Livy, but as he headed towards the front of the shop he ran into Alex. There was no sign of Livy.

"Hey, Doc, that shirt looks like it could get up and walk away on its own," Alex said.

She was probably right. He'd been arrested by a glimpse of himself in the bedroom dresser mirror this morning as he was putting on his watch. "This," he'd said to himself in the mirror, "is what someone looks like who hasn't been kissed in a long time."

Alex had turned towards Hank now, studying his face. "Hey, Hank, did you read about the air force pilot in that small town in Ireland?" Her "about" sounded like "a boat." "Well, he was the only pilot in the town air force. Then he got married and had to leave off the job. So, then they had no air force!"

He had to laugh. It was such a convoluted story, such an incomprehensible, typically Irish story. He had to give her credit for trying.

Alex looked at Hank more intently. "Cut the crap, Doc. Get out of the set piece."

"What?" His jaw dropped. This was beyond vintage Alex. She'd never talked to him like this before.

"That's what you have to figure out."

Hank looked at her bleakly.

"You're a good man," she said. "I've never been too apt at the niceties. Now I'm in the homeward stretch of my life, it seems like I have even less time for them."

He felt like someone was shaking him by the shoulders but helping him stay upright at the same time.

Get off your duff, Cleary, he said to himself, you have to go home and change for work.

Alice was at his side. "Neruda," she whispered softly, placing her hand lightly on his back.

He lifted a leg up wearily to step over Sam. "Pirsig," Alex said, "the art of motorcycle maintenance."

Then he was gone. Alice looked at Alex.

"*Triste,*" she said. "Sad."

"Ruminant," Alex said.

Chapter 4

In Harass, disoriented seagulls circled above the parking lot of the town mall. There was a small mud-bottom lake part way between Alma and Harass, but the Great Lake connecting Chicago via the St. Lawrence Seaway to the Atlantic Ocean lay long miles to the east. Why these graceful birds had abandoned the blue waters of Lake Michigan for a small sea of concrete in Harass was not clear. They ought not to have been there.

The population of Harass was swelled by the auto assembly plant workers and management. Men and women whose fathers had raised dairy cows and cash crops had hired in to be 'associates' at the automobile factory. They were good people, solid Midwesterners, grateful for the jobs, especially jobs that paid so well. If they felt any heaviness at the end of the day, most of them just said they were tired.

The sun was brilliant. Its rays seemed unfiltered, so unmediated that the town looked like it was under a klieg light, its buildings standing out in bas-relief. The movie house was showing *The Annihilator*. The Deep Sleep Motel was running a special – *$49.99/nite plus 3 movies*.

As Hank passed through town, driving out to have lunch with the occupational medicine doctor at the auto plant, he caught a whiff of popcorn coming from the movie theatre. Outside Harass, he could see a farmer's wife bringing the midday meal out to the field for her husband. The smell of fertilizer came in through his open pickup window. He was deep in thought.

Hank was eleven or twelve, it was the holiday time, and he was waiting for his father to come home. He wanted to ask him for help with a gift he was making. Then his Da came in with some buddies, feeling no pain, the smell of whiskey pungent on his breath. Ebullient, over the top, he fell onto the couch and onto Hank, bouncing lightly and laughing. Only for a few seconds, but long enough for Hank's face to turn red and flatten, long enough for him to have an upside-down feeling in his stomach.

Ah, then, when his Da wasn't drinking—the charm of the man!

Reciting line after line of Yeats from memory. Telling marvelous bedtime stories about 7-Up rivers and blue mountains, stories filled with courage and valor.

Hank felt his arm burning from the sun where it lay exposed, resting on the window frame of the car. His fair Irish skin with its fine rusty hairs was pink. "I'll worry about melanomas another day," he said to himself.

Beyond the cornfields, he was startled to see what looked like acres of parked cars covered with snow. It might have been winter instead of early June. Driving closer, he realized the automobile hoods and fenders were all protected with white cloth blankets, probably new cars waiting to be bought or shipped. On the manicured grounds of the vast plant, signs were posted along the entrance drive: "Private Property," "24-hour Camera Surveillance," "Any Activity may be Investigated by Security."

Hank and Warren got their lunches in the company cafeteria, as big as the Grand Ballroom of the Chicago Marriott. At fifty-foot intervals up and down both sides of the cafeteria, television monitors were anchored high on the walls. Workers ate their lunches with a continuous stream of CNN. Captions of world and national events, and details of sports, entertainment, murders and deaths, were re-reported every half hour. No one could miss anything. "Let's eat in my office," Warren said.

They settled themselves in Warren's cubicle of an office buried within the bowels of the gleaming factory.

"How's it going?" Hank said.

"Oh…same old, same old. You know, futzin' around…." Warren's face was beefy under his straw-colored eyebrows. "I had a vertical motion injury this week. Some guy fell from a ladder up near the catwalk."

"Holy mackerel!" Hank said.

"Yeah, had to go out into the factory to get him in the emergency jeep, bells and whistles blowin'."

"Geesh."

"Head injury. Concussion, eccymoses, lacerations. No internal bleeds."

"Thank God."

"I guess."

They focused on their sandwiches for a minute.

"Well, here's something," Warren said. "The workers only rotate to a different work station every four hours now instead of every two." He was clearly irritated.

"Why?"

"Beats me. Some *wunderkind* in the company must've come up with it. No ergonomics guy, I'll tell you that."

"Boy, that's not gonna help."

"Nope."

Warren had left primary care to sign on as the occupational medicine doc, for the chance to have a regular schedule and see his family. Hank remembered when he'd taken down his shingle in Harass. In a way, he was one of the lucky ones. He bailed out of private practice before he'd sunk too much money into it or had too many dependent patients. His relief at leaving the seventy-hour workweeks behind had been palpable.

Initially, Oc Med must have seemed like a godsend. Little by little, Warren was caught between the bodies and health of the workers and the bottom line of the company. He began—at first singly, then by twos and threes—to make choices for diagnosis and treatment shaded toward the efficient, the practical outcome, the smoothest result for the company, and away from the messiness of human beings. The change happened in such a way he half-believed he was doing the right thing. He came home regularly in the evening to his wife and young children thinking most of the time that things were going well. He learned how to go by the book.

Hank felt a twinge of compassion for Warren, the double binds he must get in. Knees, hips, and ankles had to swivel hundreds of times a day to get in and out of cars. Shoulders, elbows, wrists, and hands bore the brunt of working with air power tools to put together a chassis. Back muscles *would* protest the same bend, stretch, pull, or lift over the years. Still Hank had given second opinions to workers with chronic pain or repetitive motion injuries, whom Warren had sent back to work or kept on the job. Some tried to make adjustments in the way they used their bodies. Others just accepted pain and multiple surgeries as a tradeoff for the good money and benefits.

Souls are like bodies, Hank thought, if we do things the same way over and over, maybe our souls become crippled too, lose their range of motion.

"Actually, Warren, I want to ask you a favor. I need to get away, go down to Chicago."

"Oh yeah?" The other man shifted in his chair.

"You think you could cover my practice in Alma for a few days?"

"We-ell." Warren's eyes narrowed. "I don't know," he hesitated, "depends on when."

"Oh....in the next couple weeks." Hank felt his gut tighten.

Warren pulled out a daybook. Hank wasn't quite sure why he had one since Warren's time at the auto plant was clearly circumscribed, weekdays 8 to 4 and – according to Warren's wife, who saw Hank as a patient – she and Warren had a meager personal life. Warren's wife had just been into the clinic to see Hank the week before. Berle was blond, their kids were blond, even their dogs were blond. She was like a robust Barbie doll. Usually cheerful, she came in with a complaint: "I can't feel my breasts," she said.

"That can happen when you get breast implants," he'd had to tell her.

He looked at Warren more closely. For someone with the analytical training of a physician, Warren was not astute. And if he ever had any verve for life, it had left him by the time he and Hank met. He reminded Hank of classmates from med school – wicked glints in Irish eyes, broad generous Polish fortitude, emotion-rich southern Italians—who had gone on to demanding successful practices. When he ran into them now their spirits were so hedged and trimmed, he suspected they were nearly devoid of personality in the examining room with a patient.

"I can do it the last weekend in June," Warren was saying, "I let Berle handle the social calendar, but unless you hear from me, you can plan on it."

No wonder this man's wife is fixated on her breasts, Hank thought. Out loud he said, "Thanks, Warren, I appreciate it."

It was that in-between time, past the shank of the day, not yet evening. A loon called by the little lake near Alma.

He thought of his wife, how her eyes lit up when he walked into a room. In the end he could not save her.

On the truck radio, Teresa Brewer sang "...*put another nickel in...in the nickelodeon...*"

The son of the U.S. president assassinated in the '60's had perished in a plane crash, continuing that family's long reenactment of their version of a Greek tragedy.

A white buffalo had been born that week in Wisconsin.

As the north end of Alma came into view, Hank's scalp muscles relaxed. He drove by the ravine. When he saw the red-lipsticked outline of the weathered Dairy Queen he almost stopped off for a root beer float.

He slowed the pickup to turn onto the woods road back to his cabin. The ginger smell of clover reached up to him from the grass. A soft rain was on the wind. He was considering the Zen of motorcycles.

Chapter 5

On Saturday Livy's Bar and Café was crowded. All the large wooden booths with their padded backs and big tables were occupied, and most seats at the counter and small tables. When Hank came in late afternoon, the smell of garlic and tomatoes wended into the main room from the kitchen, where a pot of pasta sauce bubbled on the stove. Fresh-baked cakes were displayed in a glass case near the front counter. Opposite the case, the carved oak rack where people hung their outer clothes in cold weather stood empty this summer day.

Small blackboards on the walls gave menu selections: *tacos, pesto chicken, meat loaf, catfish, guacamole, radiatore; soups—gazpacho, chicken with wild rice; pies—egg custard, pumpkin, blueberry.* Receipts piled up in the oval bowl on the front counter by the cash register.

Hank wore an undyed cotton shirt open at the neck and clean khakis. His thick reddish hair edged with grey was shaggy. He combed it with his fingers, making a mental note to get a haircut. He hadn't seen Livy since that day in Pied-à-Terre, or rather heard her, and what she'd said about him, or about someone, it could have been about him. He poured himself a glass of water from the pitcher on the counter in the dining room and sat down at a small table, looking around.

In the corner a couple of guys with bellies hanging over their belt buckles ate steadily and efficiently. One of the volunteers on the fire brigade with Livy came in, a good-looking guy who lived out on the lake road. He straddled a stool and sat down at the counter, facing the shiny bottles of whiskeys and liquors resting in alcoves on the wall. Two truckers, who met in Alma to switch loads—one driving down from Minneapolis, the other up from Milwaukee chowed down before heading back. A young girl had her face against the glass under the cash register, looking at the packages of Wrigley spearmint gum and a fanned-out pile of Hershey's chocolate bars.

The waitress who helped out on weekends waited tables nearby.

"Coffee's comin'," Hank heard her say, then "gotta go catch me a fish" to a table of customers as she headed back towards the kitchen to pick up an order. A new young waitress stood with pad and pencil at the front taking a carryout order, then turned towards the kitchen, the hem of her skirt flipping along with her ponytail. There was no sign of Livy.

The young waitress untied the café curtains drawn back on either side, letting them down to block the sun lowering in the western sky. She came over to Hank and handed him a printed menu.

"What's 'radiatore'?" he said.

"Pasta," the young waitress, just graduated from high school, said, "it's called that because it's shaped like a radiator." She blushed. "Are you ready?"

"I don't know what I want." He sat drinking a cup of coffee, treated himself by lightening it with half-and-half from one of the little individual containers on his table.

Snatches of conversation floated over to him...

"...they were having a real jawfest last night..."

"...the Brewers never should have traded that pitcher..."

"...now that you've burped maybe you'll have room for more..."

"huge bites this summer, brown spiders I bet..."

"... good seein' ya..."

He heard Livy in the dining area, talking back into the kitchen—"That sauce is *pleading* for more cilantro." She moved around the room, smiling her wayward smile, exchanging words with customers.

"The grilled cheese is great," a visitor said.

"That's because I stick with good Wisconsin cheese," she said, "real cheese, not that no-fat stuff. Eating that's a lot like chewing rubber bands, don't you think?"

Someone teased her about the chalk drawing on one of the blackboards—a yellow pie crust filled with blue heaps, steam squiggles coming off the top.

Her hair was growing longer again, Hank liked it. When she climbed on a stool to get a bottle from a shelf, the fabric of her blouse stretched over her breasts as she reached overhead. He noticed how well shaped and strong her legs and calf muscles were.

An old man from the nursing home came in with his daughter for his weekly dinner at the café. Over one shoulder he wore a navy canvas bag holding a canister of oxygen. Plastic tubing trickled oxygen up to him via nasal prongs. Livy sat down and talked with him about the joys of Jell-O and whipped cream, asked him what he liked.

"All kinds," he trembled, "I like all kinds."

Hank sipped his coffee, wondering when she'd see him. Finally, she came over, massaging lotion onto her hands.

"Hi, Hank, how you doing?"

"Okay," he said, "what's good tonight?"

"It's all good," she replied, "I used to be a chef in the big city, you know."

"Where was that?"

"In Chicago. I did middle prep at a restaurant called Chapulin – sauces and vegetables."

"I didn't know you lived in Chicago."

"Oh yeah. I liked the restaurant. But I decided to leave. The owner was a beautiful woman, but she always wanted her own way. And I never was a good second banana.

"So, I decided to find a place of my own. I bought a car and insured it with some fly-by-night auto insurance agency. I think a car had just crashed through *their* office window. You know the ones – staffed by greasy guys with skinny ties. The kind of auto insurance place that closes up the day after you take out your insurance!"

"So, then you came to Alma?"

"Yes."

The dinner service in the café was calming down. "I have relatives visiting," Livy said, "my aunt and uncle. Wait till you meet my Aunt Angie! The last three toes on both of her feet are duck webbed. She brings it up at various times, like when she wants to get out of something, or when things aren't going well, or when she's just bored. She met my uncle on the street in Chicago. He was handing out fliers to people passing, but with such courtesy – she said he asked each one's permission before handing them a flier – and such a gleam in his eyes, she was won over immediately. She says my uncle seemed familiar to her right away when they met…but now they have a new baby and they're not getting along so well." Livy paused. "Today Aunt Angie's got my neighbor kids out collecting dandelions so she can make dandelion wine." She shrugged her shoulders.

"I have some unusual relatives of my own," Hank said.

"Tell me about them."

"Well, there was my mother's great aunt who liked to sit in the attic of our old house on the West Side communing with the spirits. Then there's my sister. When she was about nine, she and her best friend were entranced with St. Rose of Lima, one of those saints into wearing a crown of thorns. So, my sister and her friend broke off stems from bramble bushes on the way home from school one day and tried to wear them under their chapel veils."

"*God*...what does she do now, your sister?"

"She's an actress." They laughed.

A couple came in the door of the café carrying a baby. "You keep the *niño* dressed like a gypsy," the man was saying.

"*Dios mio*," his wife said with a dose of crabbiness, "what do you expect from a woman with duck-webbed toes?"

Livy embraced them and kissed the baby's chubby cheeks. "This is my Aunt Angelina and Uncle Ramon."

"Hello," Hank said, "lovely baby."

"*Gracias*," Aunt Angie said, "really though he's too white – we're hoping he'll get darker. But my hair was just like his. I was light-haired until I was four." Her manner was so ingenuous that Hank was not the least bit offended.

Livy got her relatives settled over gazpacho and pasta. "Very good, *muy rico*," they said. It dawned on Hank that they were *both* speaking Spanish.

Livy stopped back at his table. "Are you going to eat?"

"Yes," he said. "Livy, I didn't know you were Latino."

She stared at him. "Chicana, on my father's side. What did you think I was?"

"I don't know...Polish maybe...with the name Olivia...." He felt like he was slogging through molasses.

Of course, the homemade salsa, guacamole, tamales, other Mexican dishes he hadn't even thought about, appearing on the menu regularly alongside the traditional Wisconsin choices like bratwurst soaked in beer.

What else didn't he know about her? *I always said physicians are like detectives, going from clues to a diagnosis or conclusion. What a joke! Here I am, a trained observer, and I never put it together.* He'd just accepted what Livy gave so freely, not really thought about who she was these years in Alma, never even asked her.

She gazed at him evenly, her brown eyes quiet. "While we're on the subject of names, how did an Irish boy like you ever get called

'Hank'?"

He was stung by his ignorance. He took a breath. "I know…here were all these little Pats and Mikes and Kevins running around at school, and there I was – Hank!" His voice rose as he was speaking—out of proportion to what he said which startled both of them. "The thing was my parents loved Country and Western, especially Hank Williams. I think it reminded them of Irish music somehow," he said, more subdued. "The kids were okay with it, but the nuns had a hard time. They wanted me to have some proper saint's name."

Mischief stirred in Livy's eyes. "Maybe Hank Williams was a saint."

"I don't think so, but then…you never know." He smiled.

"Well, you have the map of Ireland on your face anyhow," she said.

"I do?" he said, pleased. People had told him that all his life, but no one had said it to him in a while.

Then Livy stepped back from the table, glancing toward the kitchen. She seemed remote. "I've got something to take care of back there," she said and left abruptly.

Hank ordered a whiskey. *Why isn't she married? Maybe she doesn't even like men anymore.*

He took bites of meatloaf in between swallows of whiskey, watched her come back in from the kitchen and join her relatives. Livy, Aunt Angie, and Uncle Ramon all sat with their arms around each other talking and laughing, the baby snuggled between them. After a while, Livy walked over to get a pitcher of water. On her way back she tweaked the ear of the handsome fire fighter sitting at the counter.

A familiar grey haze hovered over Hank, ready to descend. Instead, he felt his hackles rising. He got up.

"Damn," he said to himself, "damn it to hell!"

Chapter 6

Old Harry was on his high horse. He had on his favorite clothes. He knew Dr. Cleary and his Indian nurse Mrs. Yazzi were coming to Alma County Nursing Home today. And he was ready.

"How do you do?" he said to Hank and Elrita, "You're both looking hunky-dory. *There'll be bluebirds over the white cliffs of Dover*...grand song, did I ever sing that one for you before?"

"I think you have," Hank said, smiling, "How are you, Harry?"

"Oh, fine, you know, I 'yam what I yam.'"

"Well, good."

"Did I ever tell you about the time I went to Carnegie Hall for the Benny Goodman concert? I'll never forget it – January 1938. The Duke was in the audience, so was Count Basie. And me. I was just taking it all in. The band playing those killer diller pieces that got people up out of their seats lookin' for a place to jitterbug, those plungers growling, that waa-waa muting! And that Benny Goodman clarinet solo! We were having more fun that the law allows. So, the piano player, I'm telling you, he was just noodling around, noodling around and then he found a groove and it was magic! I found out later the piece was called something like *Sing, Sing, Sing*, but then I didn't know the name—oh, the bite of it, the drive of it! Those were the days! Swing was king, and Benny Goodman was head of the pack."

"It sounds like a great night." Hank didn't appear as though he were on his high horse; in fact, he looked barely in the saddle.

Old Harry could see that the doc lacked his usual enthusiasm for jazz and swing. He looked glum, like he was only partly here talking to Harry in his room.

Harry knew about not being there for a few seconds or minutes, as though your mind stepped away briefly. It happened to lots of 'em in the Home, like the old coot in his 90's down the hall. Hell, it happened with *him* sometimes. He could lose something – say, a word – while he was gone. But most of the time, if he just said goodbye to whatever it was, thanked it for being with him as long as it had, then—doggone it—nine times out of ten, as soon as he let it go, the thing popped right back into his head.

Time, though. No, that would not come back, and the beautiful girls of his youth, slender, graceful and gracious in ways he could not see in the young women today.

Hank was talking to him. "Harry, man, your cholesterol!"

"Right, Doc, well…I'm getting on it, you know."

They both knew Old Harry was still sneaking a bowl of ice cream every night. Hank decided he could give him more time to modify his diet before starting medication.

"Didja ever think about time, Doc?" Old Harry continued, "how it passes. One minute you're havin' the time of your life, you know just what time you're in, and next minute twenty years have gone by, or forty, or fifty, and you're not sure what time it is. People like to keep track of time, then they say it drags on 'em or it flies by, like they have no say-so about it whatsoever. Time to go, time to stop, time to be on time…what d'ya think it all means, Doc?"

"I really don't know, Harry." Hank's face sagged.

Old Harry looked at him, then at Mrs. Yazzi. She was a handsome woman with her straight back and level gaze. When she told you something you always knew you were getting the straight skinny. She looked a little peaked today.

"Mrs. Yazzi, ma'am," he said, "did I ever tell you about the time I worked for the Armed Forces Radio Service during the big one, W.W.II? We broadcast music to three thousand marines and two thousand sailors in that harbor out there. Mostly jazz.

"They didn't let me talk much on the air but, boy, we played all the music for those guys. They were just kids, you know, all gung-ho, a little pale around the gills. They got transported on converted destroyers, tin cans we called 'em, bivouacked in with their duffel bags waiting to be deployed. They did their double-time marching, learned to quick salute anyone with wings on his uniform.

"We played 'em all on the radio for those troops: *Coming in on a Wing and a Prayer,* good ole Kate Smith singin' *The White Cliffs of Dover*, Glenn Miller, the Dorseys.

"Some of those guys ended up getting both legs blown off, or both arms gone. Some of 'em took the white cross in Europe."

"It was good they had your music, Harry," Elrita said.

"Yeah...." He looked over at Hank again who was sitting, somewhat slumped, on a folding chair opposite Old Harry's armchair.

"And *then* there was the Duke," he said, "there wasn't *nobody* like Duke Ellington. That Ellington band coming out of New York! Ellington in 2, Ellington in 4. That guy did everything."

Hank perked up at the mention of Duke Ellington. "*It Don't Mean A Thing If You Ain't Got That Swing*," he said.

"*Just Squeeze Me*," Old Harry said.

"*Mood Indigo.*"

"*Satin Doll*," Harry shot back. They grinned at each other.

"For my money," Old Harry said, "far and away the best was *Take the A Train*. It was on Victor. Now *that* was a piece of work."

"Superb...a classic...that 32 measure form!" Hank forgot himself for a moment. "First the reeds, then the trombones, then the trumpet solo by Ray Nance."

"Didja know *A train* was composed and arranged by Billy Strayhorn?"

"Yeah, I did."

"That guy was a soda jerk before he teamed up with Ellington. He was like a son to the man. Story was, he swung the other way, but who cares, look at the way he could write music. They said he was almost as good as the Duke, but he was the pure artist. Didn't travel with the band, liked to just stay home, make up tunes.

"The Duke," Old Harry continued, "towards the end of his life, he was lovin' God, was using all that talent to praise God...."

He paused. "They invited me to sit in with the band a few times, you know,"

Hank and Elrita smiled politely. They thought maybe Old Harry had made it to Carnegie Hall for the Goodman concert, they knew the World War II radio stint had happened. They weren't so sure about Old Harry sitting in with the Ellington band. But he *might* have, and *believed* he had, and neither Hank nor Elrita thought whether or not he had was a particularly important distinction.

"Well, those were the days, Harry," Hank said, getting up, "have to go."

"'Bye, Doc. *Row, row, row, your boat, gently down the stream, merrily, merrily, merrily, merrily, life is but a dream.*"

Hank stood near the doorway listening, then he left.

Elrita looked out the open window of Old Harry's room at Winona playing in the flower garden. A new cat who'd come to live at the Home wandered into the room. She was soft gray with cream-colored paws and a diamond on her forehead.

Elrita had been the one who convinced Hank to approve pets in the Home. A yellow, red, and tan cockatiel called Louie held court, and now a dynamic duo of cats luxuriated among the seniors – Molly, the orange tabby, and the feline who'd recently joined her, whom the residents had named Betty Grable.

Old Harry petted the cat distractedly. "Take Betty Grable down the hall to the new lady, the one who doesn't get around much. The rest of us are nattering away, and she's just sittin' there, not talkin'."

Elrita placed her hand on his shoulder. "*Ahyéheé*, Harry, thank you."

She rubbed cortisone cream over the pink blistered skin on his hands. The aides at the Home were supposed to remind him to do it himself when his eczema flared up, but they didn't always pick up on it. Old Harry seemed to fall into a reverie.

"Those *were* the days," he said, "We were all courtin' and sparkin.' It was just one great big sea of lovin.' On the one hand, you had this crazy man over in Germany, someone evil, you know. It took a long time, but we beat the hell out of 'im. Well maybe not out of him exactly, but out of what he was setting out to do.

"We were all on top of the world, buoyed up, everything good was comin'. We didn't know, we never could've known, it would get like this. Things did swing and sway for so long. Then, some time or so – when was it? – things started goin' down. It seems like there's a Hitler around somewhere, for sure, but we can't understand where."

"Harry," Elrita finally got in a word. "Harry," she said gently, "there's *no* Hitler any more. He's gone."

"I *know* that. I mean there's something *like* Hitler out there now, maybe crawlin' around lookin' pretty. I don't know...this is as far as I got...." He scratched his head.

When Elrita heard Old Harry out, usually she felt a smile inside. Today she shivered.

Her own Beulah was not happy. Something was very wrong with her older daughter. Beulah had become silent, taken on a closed injured look Elrita and Joe could not understand.

Elrita thought about her children. Rufus, her serious son with his beautiful face, and brown pools of eyes like his father's. Rufus was at odds sometimes with his schoolbooks, but he was on a true path.

And Winona. Elrita knew deep inside her that she'd never have words to describe her youngest child—how Winona saw right through into people from a clear space within her own self, how she knew about plants and animals without Joe or Rufus or any of them having to show her, how light played all its colors over Winona's little face like it played over the four sacred mountains at home in Navajo country.

Beulah's spirit was cloudy, and dark. Like the rose Winona had picked for Old Harry from the nursing home garden not long ago, a rose blooming red, soft petals still holding drops of dew. Cut off from its own soil and water, the red rose (which Old Harry had been reluctant to part with) by their next visit had darkened to black. Beulah felt to her mother like that black rose, the growing beauty in her somehow separated from what gave her strength.

In the past if Elrita wanted to help someone she loved, she would be around them, eyes and ears open, warming them with her presence, until the unhealed thing eventually would come to the surface, open up, and drain out, like a skin abscess responding to warm compresses. But it seemed Beulah's wound was too deep.

Elrita had brought it up to Livy. "She's spending a lot of time in bed, staying in her room."

"Maybe there's a boyfriend, Elrita, she's getting to be about the right age. Give her time," Livy had suggested. Elrita did not think Beulah looked like someone whose heart was calling to a first boyfriend.

Elrita Yazzi's father had been a Navajo medicine man, a *hataalli*. He knew how to perform thirty types of ceremonies for healing – blessing ceremonies, smoking ceremonies, even peyote to doctor things out of a person. Her father did charcoal gazing, stargazing, and hand trembling over someone to ask the Spirit for a diagnosis of their problem. He was gone now, but Elrita had asked him for his help.

She'd been waiting to speak to Hank Cleary when he was not so far away, biding her time until he came back into harmony with himself. But Hank was driving to Chicago on Friday, and she wanted to talk with him before he left.

This morning after he came by in his green pickup to get her and Winona, Elrita had waited until they stopped off at Dairy Queen, where she allowed Winona a cone, and they were well into the ten-mile drive out of town to the nursing home.

Winona was content in the back seat with her Reckless Rainbow pushup. "Is it true spinach is good for depression?" Elrita said.

"Yes, it does seem to be…who's depressed?"

"Well," Elrita lowered her voice out of Winona's range of hearing, "I think Joe is, just a bit…but something's not right with Beulah."

"Oh?"

"The light's gone out of her face. She spends a lot of time sleeping."

Hank thought about this. "Why don't you bring her in, and I'll check her over, make sure she's not anemic."

They were approaching the county nursing home, an old two-story red brick building set back from the county road by itself, amid dairy pastures and cultivated fields. Elrita knew this was the best Hank could do now. She was not satisfied with his reply.

Chapter 7

The cuts in Medicare funding, which drastically affected corporate nursing homes, did not make much difference at Alma County Nursing Home, where Hank served as medical director.

Surrounding farmers, no matter if crops were poor or price supports inadequate, still showed up at the back door of the nursing home with huge bushels of beans or corn. "Extra," they'd say, looking apologetically at their shoes, "thanks for taking it off my hands." The local people knew just about everyone in the Home, or knew one of their relatives, and so did the staff. Large pots of baked beans, homemade bread, cleaned and plucked chickens or even completely butchered pigs "just getting in the way anyhow" were delivered to the back doorstep of the Home on a regular basis.

Occasionally the pungent acid odor of urine escaped from a room where aides had not yet changed the sanitary garments of the incontinent, and there was a strong feeling of linoleum, but for the most part Alma Nursing Home was clean and not the worst place in the world for an old person to be.

After seeing Old Harry, Hank moved on to evaluate other residents with medical problems. He was abstracted.

While part of him attended to the old people, another part – lower down and turned inward – puzzled and obsessed over his life, new ideas and inklings of feelings buzzing around like baby bees. Somewhere off above and looking down on his doctor self and inward self was another part – a very angry self who did not countenance the other two.

If Hank's three atonal pitches had blended, they would have been like a Buddhist chant. But they did not.

He could see himself writing new prescriptions, remembering the skin hunger of the elderly, touching the small of someone's back while listening to his lungs, hands gentle on paper-thin skin, instilling eye drops, orienting a confused patient to time and place. And all the while the angry self-commented: *Who will orient you?* it asked darkly. *What about your skin hunger?* it mocked.

Somehow the residents of Alma County Nursing Home had gotten wind of *ginkgo biloboa,* extract of the ginkgo leaf, as an antidote to aging. Ambulatory, bedridden, healthy and sick alike stopped Hank for "a second opinion" about *ginkgo biloboa*. To whom he was adding a second professional opinion he wasn't sure, probably the milk truck driver or somebody's cousin. By the fourth or fifth inquiry, his angry self was suggesting nasty comebacks like *who the hell knows?* or *if I knew how to turn back the clock, you can damn well bet I'd do it!* His doctor self formed an answer that was quick and contained enough so he could keep working, with only brief delays from *ginkgo biloboa.*

Mr. Willy, who'd spent every clear day of the past couple months out working in the Home's vegetable garden, had a keratocanthoma on his arm. Hank removed the strange curlicued skin lesion under local anesthetic and placed it in a jar of preservative to be sent up to the hospital in Stevens Point for pathology. He wrote a note instructing the staff to have residents wear lightweight long-sleeved shirts and slacks when working in the gardens, and to avoid peak hours of sunshine.

Hank knew the specimen he'd excised was not skin cancer but still, he thought humorlessly, it would be too bad if we unwittingly gave the seniors squamous cell CA's by encouraging them to work outside in the garden. *Unwittingly, unwittingly...no wit,* the dark voice taunted. *That's me, all right,* the inner self moaned.

The angry self had reverted to the old black humor of medical training, the sick bizarre jokes that helped Hank Cleary and his fellows survive the surreal thirty-six hour work shifts without sleep, filled with absurd and impossible medical dilemmas. The doctor believed the black humor served no purpose now in this innocent setting. But the angry self challenged this opinion: *...things not so bad...what you always say...get real....*

It dawned on Hank that his nasty onlooker's anger was directed ruthlessly and mirthlessly at no other target except Hank himself, the hapless doctor on his rounds and his inward self keeping the good doctor company. *This is not good,* his inner and outer selves said to each other.

Hank was sweating. He leaned against the wall in the hallway outside one of the rooms. A recurring dream had visited him in recent weeks.

In the dream a baby is drying up from thirst. Hank searches for a bottle of water for the baby but cannot find it. The baby is flattening, becoming like a two-dimensional piece of cardboard. The dream is flooded with the smell of fear.

When Elrita caught up with him, carrying Betty Grable, he was relieved to see his nurse, grateful for her calm presence.

The new woman sat wrapped in a shawl gazing out her bedroom window at the mauve and blue clematis blossoms climbing the brick under the back porch. She looked up when Hank and Elrita entered. "What does it matter how beautiful it is when you're alone?" she said.

Her white hair was plaited into a soft braid and her skin was a delicate ivory, but her eyes were dull. "Each day takes care of itself, and then you're old," she said.

After Hank completed a physical exam and made some notes in her chart, Elrita slipped Betty Grable carefully onto the woman's lap. "Why don't you take care of her for a while?" Elrita said.

"Myswell," she said softly.

Out in the hall, Hank said, "Will you write for her to get primary protein included at each meal and at mid-meal snacks? Better check her renal function first. I'll sign the orders before we go."

Next were the Ms. Barries, 75 and 93 years old, respectively. The women were known in Alma as Miss Barrie and her mother. Old Harry, who was 81, called them "the Barrie girls". The aides addressed them by their first names but – whether out of deference to him or some misplaced political correctness – persisted in calling the women "Ms. Barrie" and "Ms. Barrie" to Hank. Every time he got a verbal report on one of the Ms. Barries from the staff, he had to say, "the mother?" and they would say "no, the daughter" or he'd say, "the daughter?" and they'd say "no, the mother." He didn't much mind ordinarily, in fact took a perverse existential pleasure in this minor conundrum. Today though he snapped at a practical nurse who was telling him about "Ms. Barrie's" dietary indiscretions: "Just tell me the full name, will you!"

When Hank first met the daughter, she confided in him about her mother. "She's, uh…," she pointed an index finger at her own head, "an old lady." Actually, Hank thought Ms. Barrie the elder had a lot on the ball and liked the way she smiled sweetly at him and said,

"Goodness…how nice to see you!" And he found Ms. Barrie the younger a bit coy.

The Ms. Barries would not relinquish the bowl of hard candies just inside the doorway of their double room although they were both borderline diabetics. They always offered Hank a sweet and he invariably refused. Today, while Elrita checked finger stick blood sugars on both women, he took a piece of toffee (*what the hell*, the dark voice said).

There was another thing the Ms. Barries had in common. They both had their eye on Old Harry.

The last stop for Hank and Elrita was the room of a married couple who had both fallen yesterday. The mister, usually able to get around, had taken a tumble. He was 108. His 85-year-old spouse had attempted to help him up and fallen on top of him. The x-rays were normal and both were unscathed from the accident. The LPN note however stated the man had developed nasal congestion and a sore throat.

"How are you?" Hank asked.

The ancient man did not answer for a minute. Then he said, "How do you think I am? I'm sick."

"How are you?" Hank asked the wife.

"I eat a banana every day," she said.

While Hank and Elrita were seeing patients, Winona was outside in the flower garden on this lovely June day. She admired the white morning glories wrapped around the back fence, studied an ant dragging another insect three times its size across a little plot of dirt. She looked at the tall fuzzy plants in the middle of the garden waving like feathers in the breeze. She stood completely still to watch four monarch butterflies flit around a large bush with droopy purple flowers.

When she got hungry, Winona came indoors, hoping to see Dr. Cleary and her mother coming around the corner towards her, all done seeing rezdnz so they could go eat. Instead, the first person she ran into, sitting in the living room, was Old Harry.

Winona liked Old Harry. She liked him best of all the rezdnz in the home. She liked the little white hairs that stuck up on his face, his baggy blue pants, his singing, and his stories. Especially she liked his stories.

She'd noticed that when Old Harry told Dr. Cleary and her mama stories, they seemed to start off just about anywhere, but when he told Winona stories he always began "Once upon a time...." Then she would feel herself go happy, and her ears pick up just like that baby fox she and Rufus found last week back in the woods where it was all tangly.

Old Harry gentled at the sight of Winona. He welcomed her with a little song – *"If I'd Known You Were Comin' I'd of Baked a Cake...."*

Winona smiled shyly. She did not curtsy, but there was the feeling of a curtsy between them.

"Good morning, little miss," Old Harry said, "well now, don't you just warm the cockles of my heart."

Winona glowed a little. She was wearing her pale green pinafore with ruffles at the shoulders and a sash that tied in back, the one she loved, that her mother had bought her at the resale store out by the highway. Her baby doll, whom she carried on the small cradleboard or in her pocket or tucked inside her shirt, rested today in the pocket of Winona's pinafore.

She looked at a froth of bubbles at one corner of Old Harry's mouth. He winked at her. "I have another song for you:"

Mares eat oats and does eat oats
and little lambs eat ivy.
A kid'll eat ivy too, wouldn't you?

What Winona heard was:
m*arzy doats in dozy doats*
in lid dell amzy divey
 akiddly divey two wood in you?

Then her face brightened. "We have lambs," she said, "but they eat grass. My father slaughtered one for Dr. Cleary."

"Whoa," Old Harry said, "yesirree, you are somethin', Miss Winona." Winona hugged the doll in her pocket with one hand and gave Old Harry a smile.

"Hmmm…yesirree," Old Harry said again, "you are one fine little girl. Here's lookin' at you, young miss."

Chapter 8

On the last Friday morning in June, Hank Cleary threw his duffel bag into the metal storage box on the bed of his pickup, on top of his extra medical kit, and hoisted himself into the driver's seat. He drove past the two-pump gas station, the general store, Pied-á-Terre, the Café, and up the hill onto the secondary road. A farm tractor moved slowly along the side of the road, followed by a huge combine. A porcupine lay dead, its quills sticking up around it.

Usually, Hank is breathing slow and deep as he comes back into Alma. It happened the same way every time, so he never thought about it until he felt inhabited by ease, and realized he's just coasted down into town.

This day Hank breathed deeper when he got out to the highway. He blew noisy breaths out through his mouth, opened up the side and back windows of his pickup as far as they would go. He put his foot to the accelerator.

Fifteen thousand years earlier the Wisconsin glacier, the last advance of the continental ice sheet, covered most of the state. The glacier rerouted ancient rivers, left abandoned valleys where rivers had been, deposited dams of rocks and earths creating thousands of lakes across the state. Glacial melt water carved weird shapes into soft sandstone. All around Hank are wetlands and woodlands, bluffs with yellow birches, mountain maple, and red elder; deer, muskrats, coyotes; black-and-white warblers, wrens, and a hundred other species of birds. Deep below, the aquifer gives water to the springs which feed the lakes.

But Hank was fleeing, oblivious to all this beauty. Heading for Chicago. He skirted the port of Green Bay, wove in and out of traffic, driving south. His truck moved him fast, through places, through time, taking his body away from the time he was in.

Near the Interstate-94 interchange, traffic slowed to a crawl detouring around an overturned semi on the road. The smell of a cigar drifted over from a nearby car. Hank flashed on summers of his childhood, traveling the other way up to Wisconsin, with his grandfather's cigar smoke filling the old Plymouth.

They'd start out early, his father driving, his mother quiet in the front seat. In the back, his grandfather by one window, Hank and Tara fighting over who had to sit in the middle with feet pushed up by the hump of the car floor and who got to have the other window. Everyone already gasping in the humid Chicago air, Hank's and his sister's empty stomachs churning from hunger. "We'll stop for breakfast once we're on the road," his father always said. When they finally ate, they had sweet rolls and juice, guaranteed, along with the cigar smoke, to bring on more nausea.

Hours later they'd stop at some farmhouse restaurant for homemade fried chicken, corn-on-the-cob, mashed potatoes, and cold beer for the grownups, and they'd all feel better. Da would stop the car by a field, and have Hank and Tara climb under the fence to pick up loose ears of corn. By late afternoon, the Plymouth would be on the rolling roads of northern Wisconsin. The heat would shimmer off the asphalt hills on the horizon, creating mirages of water. "The lake! the lake!" he and Tara would shout, then beg, as the day lengthened.

Finally, the cottage. Those rented summer cottages! Once they had a cottage vertically divided with thin wood partitions, which stopped a foot and a half below the ceiling, separating them from the people on the other side. In another cottage Hank found a pile of arrowheads under the lumpy-mattressed attic bed where he slept. Those vacation cottages by little lakes, braced by stands of northern spruces and pines! All those cottages, weather-beaten and run down. To Hank every single one had been glorious.

Gone, he says to himself, *what was it? that quality...it had something to do with the glory of the cottages.*

The semi off the road now, cars were picking up speed. A sports utility vehicle, big as a small bread truck, cut in front of Hank's pickup, obstructing his view for miles. "Jerk!" Hank said to his front windshield. He gunned his engine, wished he could have it out with the driver. The way greenhorns from the old country did. Immigrant Irish men with a quarrel spit on their hands and took to fisticuffs to settle the matter. He'd like that – to challenge rudeness, assuage anger, have it be over. He was hot, sweaty, tired of engine noises.

One time, coming home to Chicago from a vacation in Wisconsin, Hank had heat stroke. "I'm thirsty, Da," he'd said. His father said,

"Quit your blathering, now," and drove on. When they stopped for gas, the attendant stared at Hank wedged between Tara and his grandfather in the back seat, his face red with mottled white edges near his scalp. After they got home, he had to be put on a cot in the cool basement with wet cloths on his skin, and long weak days to follow.

Hank gave up on not using his air conditioner, closed the windows in the cab of the pickup, adding his own small contribution to the ozone hole in the atmosphere.

Near Kenosha the pickup's oil light went on. Off to one side of the expressway a Wal-Mart store, covering acres of land, came into view. In Wal-Mart, he purchased a quart of oil and new windshield wipers in the automotive department, passed a large gun display across the aisle from the toy section.

Hank wandered vaguely towards the grocery area, his stomach rumbling. He bought cheese, fruit, then was stopped in his tracks by a neon sign in bread and pastries: "90,000 donuts/hour." *How many people can eat how many donuts in any given locale? Where do all the donuts go? Do human hands ever touch the batter, or does it move from metal vats in and out of metal templates in an unending production of donuts?*

Back on the road he sped up, slowed down, steered without thinking. Some Chautauqua this was turning out to be, he mumbled. He pictured himself on a well-tuned motorcycle skimming over an open road in the crisp air, just barely tied to the road by gravity.

The radio picked up a Chicago station. Some blues singer wailed "*...I'd rather be sloppy drunk...than anything,*" then hip-hop music played. A billboard alongside the Expressway read *WHO'S THE FATHER? 1-800-DNA-TYPE.* So many people got pregnant so easily.

He thought about Sarah, the child they never had.

They'd married late. When he finally finished medical training, Sarah's career in photography was taking off. They waited to have a baby. In 1995 came the diagnosis of ovarian cancer. Within a year the cancer took one of Sarah's ovaries, and the chemotherapy destroyed the other one.

She'd been buried in Chicago, at the request of her mother who was elderly and frail.

His wife's body was shipped from Wisconsin by rail; Hank followed, one car back on the train, dazed, too shaky to drive. The wake was in the old neighborhood on the far West Side, the funeral at her childhood parish. It had been strange to be with Chicago friends again, people he liked, noting changes in their appearances, unable to care anything about them. With many, the common bond had been time with Sarah.

And of Sarah he could not safely speak.

A red Chevrolet passed him on the right going 80 mph, cutting across three lanes of traffic without signaling. Hank was jolted into awareness. As the Interstate curved towards Chicago, drivers seemed to be more erratic and bizarre in their vehicles than he remembered. Hundreds of cars hurtled towards the center of the city, scant feet between them, all going twenty miles over the speed limit. Another red sedan sped by, rap music trailing out its window: "Duh *duh duh duh d-u-h, d-u-h d-u-h, duh duh duh duh d-u-h, d-u-h d-u-h motherfucker says, d-u-h d-u-h....*" A traffic helicopter hovered above. It was two o'clock in the afternoon.

Ahead he suddenly saw the tops of the John Hancock Building and the Sears Tower, the giants of the Chicago architectural skyline. No tinge of pollution hung over the city today. His heart lifted.

After I-94 merged with the Kennedy in Chicago, combining two multi-lane expressways, Hank had enough. He exited onto local streets to go the last couple miles to James' and La Shondra's place.

Ruben Baby Factory Store said a sign on a corner building. Maybe Livy can get a baby there, he mused.

City buses had mural-sized advertisements for plays and entertainments in vivid colors the entire length of both sides. Riders looked out through mesh-like grids on the windows, the infrastructure for the murals.

Milwaukee Avenue was a whirlwind of activity. Cars continued on through every red light, blocked moving lanes of traffic anywhere in order to get across the street. Driving etiquette seemed to have become a quaint anachronism. Yet as Milwaukee angled its way south and east into Bucktown, its familiar chaos somehow reassured Hank. The desperado drivers. Young women in shorts and halter tops with toddlers slung on one hip. A car sitting in an alley idling its engine. Push carts with *aguas de mango, de fresa, de limón*. A bicyclist claiming his narrow space between car and curb, cigarette dangling from his lips.

Hank passed the old Charleston bar, turned onto Leavitt, pulled up in front of James' and LaShondra's. He turned off the engine and leaned back against the seat. He tried to recall the moment in front of his cabin when he stepped up into his pickup in the early morning woods of Alma.

Chapter 9

The hickory smell of barbecuing chicken wafted through the narrow gangway between James' and LaShondra's brownstone and the house next door. In their back yard a localized cloud of smoke hung over the grill next to a rickety fence adorned with pink tea roses. Non-localized music came from their tape player. LaShondra spotted Hank first and gave a whoop.

"Honey," she said, stretching her arms wide, "it's been so *long*!" She strode across the yard and gave him a big-bosomed embrace.

"Hey, LaShondra," he said, grinning at her. James put down the barbecue tongs and he and Hank grabbed each other in a bear hug. "Brought you some Point beer," Hank said.

Hank and James had done Family Practice training together at Cook County Hospital, the institution serving the underclass of Chicago. After Residency, James could have been on the fast track at any university medical center. Instead, he'd elected to stay at County, attended dozens of patients each day at the hospital or in the maze-like outpatient clinic Fantus.

LaShondra was a trauma nurse in the emergency room at County. They'd ended up working not far from the project where they'd grown up.

"How was the trip?" James said.

"Not too bad. I could do without S.U.V. s though. It seems like they're all over the place, clogging up the streets. I'll bet the people who own those things don't even take them out of the city, much less use them for sports, *and* they pollute like crazy! Plus S.U.V. people are lousy drivers, but they think they own the road because they're in something big."

"So, not a good time with the S.U.V.s, huh?" James said.

"Another thing, what is it with red cars? Every time someone tried to run me off the road they were in a damn red car!"

James and LaShondra exchanged glances.

"Well," James said, "the expressways are crazier than they used to be. You know teenagers sometimes throw things off the overpasses."

"Hard head, soft behind, my mama used to say." LaShondra put a plate of cheese and crackers on the picnic table. "If we didn't do what we were supposed to we got paddled. I know that's not politically correct these days, but it worked for us comin' up."

"As if that's not bad enough," James continued, "this morning on the news there was a story about a road crew member getting shot at. They were working on repaving the Ryan last night, and all of a sudden someone's taking pot shots at the flagger. He couldn't move because bullets were flying on both sides of him."

"I heard about the bottles and cans but this…." Hank felt a surge of protection and fierce love for Chicago, this city of his birth, and the people who made a living here.

James turned the chicken over on the grill. The cold beer felt good going down Hank's throat in the warmth of the afternoon. He leaned back in the lawn chair. "So, leaving that aside, how are things in Chi-town?"

"Well, there's a kind of pre-millennium thing going down – some people believe the world's going to end the last day of the year."

"You're kidding."

"No. But other than the world ending, things here are good." James grinned.

The chicken done, LaShondra brought out crusty sourdough bread and James's special potato salad from the kitchen. They sat at the picnic table to eat.

"County just keeps on going," James said. "More infectious disease than ever. The same women whose husbands beat them just a little, but they can't leave them yet, so they bring their kids into the clinic every few weeks for some minor physical ailment.

"Do you know they still call it fantasy clinic? More than one hundred thousand patients come through in a year. Thousands of patients can't be wrong," he chortled. "All those people with bullet holes, burns, bronchitis, allergies, out-of-control diabetes—every last one of them has a fantasy we'll get 'em pulled together, make a new man or woman out of 'em!"

James and LaShondra told the same types of nihilistic jokes James and Hank used to tell each other to get through the crucible of medical school and residency. Now his friends admitted the constancy of need they encountered every day.

"It's a lot, man," James said, "but we just keep laughing. Shondra and me, we still go to the Baptist church on 47th Street. And on our days off we get together with her brothers and sisters, and we *laugh* and *laugh*, sometimes we laugh *and* cry!"

James had kept the stubborn gleam of his roots, Hank thought, maybe in part because he worked daily with his own, saw his parents, grandparents, aunts, uncles and cousins reflected back into his face.

"Remember 'KISS'?" Hank said, "'Keep it simple, stupid'?"

"The loving acronym the seniors threw at us the first week of med school? Sure."

"And we thought we already knew everything there was to know about what 'kiss' meant." Hank winked at LaShondra.

"Don't you two start, now," she said in mock warning.

"How's the ER these days, LaShondra?" Hank asked.

"Oh, the usual – gunshot wounds, multi-vehicle injuries. Some guy came in DOA yesterday. He'd pissed on the third rail of the L tracks, and the urine bounced back and electrocuted him." They were solemn for a second or two. Then La Shondra let out a high cackling laugh, so contagious the men had to join in.

"We had an unusual case last week," she said, recovering. "A man came in comatose. We thought, oh, another druggie, some poor guy stroked out on cocaine. You know, one more precious black male squandered on drugs. But it turns out to be West Nile encephalitis. Seems he'd been in New York and they think that's where he contracted it. Encephalitis – death by mosquito."

"Mosquitoes coming further and further north now. It's the weather," James said. He got up from the table and settled himself in a lawn chair, his feet up on the picnic bench. "How about you," he said to Hank, "what's new with you?"

"We have more Lyme disease than last year. And I have a patient with five children who got pregnant because of St. John's Wort."

"Say what?" James said.

"That's not the usual way," said LaShondra.

"I mean the St. John's Wort interfered with her oral contraceptive."

"That could cause you to be depressed," LaShondra said, handing him a plate of brownies.

"You still delivering babies?" Hank said to James. "Yeah, every so often. Remember OB, the Labor Line?"

"How could I forget." Hank and James had done their obstetrics training at Cook County, twelve hours on and twelve hours off for the entire rotation. Women arrived at the Labor Room, on the fifth floor of the old yellow brick hospital, fully dilated and ready to deliver, many with no prenatal care. They all labored together in one large room, on hospital beds separated by cotton draw curtains. The beds rolled on casters down a long narrow hall for deliveries. Only sometimes there'd be a traffic jam, one or two beds lined up, moving towards the delivery rooms, a bed coming back, no space to pass.

"The Labor Line," James was saying, "I delivered as many babies in the hallway, or in the Labor Room, as in a delivery room!"

"Those babies came when they were ready!" Hank agreed. He could remember standing in that hallway as if it were yesterday, his shoulders close to the painted walls, bending towards a moaning woman to catch her baby as it charged into life. Day in and day out, Hank and the other young doctors saw all the vagaries of reproductive anatomy, their own sexuality modulating and modulated by their care for the laboring women.

Sometimes Hank slept so exhausted his body dropped into a deep dreamless underwater. Towards the last few weeks of the rotation, he peered at a sea of female genitalia in his dreams, swollen vulvas, gaping vaginas, with rounded tops of little downy heads pushing apart their lips.

Once, when the obstetrics resident could not be spared from the hospital, he rode high in the cab of an enormous ambulance, to a rundown clinic on the South Side to assess the health of the fetus in a seven-and-a-half-month pregnant woman. He'd felt a little inflated by the charge, scared by the responsibility, in awe of the potential. To his relief, the woman and unborn baby were stable.

"At least mothers and newborns get to stay in the hospital past twenty-four hours again," James was saying, "*and* Congress just passed a law requiring HMOs to allow women to stay in the hospital more than two days following a mastectomy."

"Hey," Hank said, "piecemeal medicine by non-medical legislators—what more could you ask for? Of course, they only see the tips of the icebergs, but hey."

"Considering that corporate medicine has most politicians in its hip pocket," James said, "it's surprising that *anything* is happening in the U.S. Legislature."

Our Lady of Hope, in Hank's old neighborhood—which really

needed a good hospital—was being milked dry by a corporation from another part of the country. He asked if they'd read about the woman whose orthopedist said he could save her leg, but the HMO said that wasn't cost-effective, and they'd only pay if he amputated. The CEOs wouldn't want things like that to chip away at their take-home, James said, hard to get by on $5 – 20 million a year.

Hank grimaced. "Hippocrates must be turning over in his grave."

"Then there's those bad-ass lawyers," James added. "They don't get it. It's partly the way they're trained. They move from general precedents to cases, use deductive reasoning. We go from the opposite end, use the inductive method, from particulars to diagnoses. We *never* go from page 1132 of *Cecil's Textbook of Medicine* to a conclusion about a patient, it's always the other way around."

"If physicians can understand lawyers, why can't lawyers understand physicians?" LaShondra said.

"There's no money in understanding."

James said their old classmates in the suburbs felt like they practiced with their backs to the wall, and an elephant on their shoulders. Not so bad for him at County because they took all comers. Most of the patients were on Medicaid or didn't have any insurance, and County wanted his clinical skills. In Alma, his patients paid cash or sometimes goods, Hank said. If someone couldn't pay, he cared for him anyway. It worked out, and he was able to sidestep the big mess too. One of LaShondra's ER docs was trying to get out. One of the best emergency physicians she'd ever worked with, only in her thirties, looking for another job, fed up with subpoenas from attorneys. She could hardly see patients she spent so much time testifying – not like the cases were her liabilities, but they siphoned off her time. Too bad, the doc was damn good at what she did and she cared! In his opinion, Hank stated, American medicine was a ship on fire about to ride over the top of a waterfall.

"There are some bright lights," James offered, "Quentin Young's still going strong, pushing for reform. And Shondra's circulating a petition to have the Bernadin Amendment considered on the next ballot in Illinois – to have universal health care in the state."

"My cousin who's a lawyer says he thinks health care is a privilege, not a right," La Shondra said.

"A *brother*, a *home boy*," James interjected.

"I'll bet he wouldn't have said that when he was barely making it in his twenties, eating mustard sandwiches in a walkup," she continued. "There was another guy, a white guy, supposedly a former sixties radical. He wouldn't sign the petition because he said his kids' college education was tied to pharmaceutical company stock profits. No matter what kind of a society they're educated for, I guess!"

"Take it easy, baby."

"Well, it busts my ass. It's not like the ballot initiative even spells out any specifics, it just says 'let's discuss decent health care for everyone.' Where are these people coming from?"

"Here's a little Irish prayer for the villains," Hank said. "In return for paint-by-number medicine and fuzzy warm lies, may they wake up sweating at night and spend days waiting on the phone to talk to themselves."

"To the fucking success of the dispassionate!" he said, lifting his beer glass into the air.

He did not tip the glass to his mouth. "The hell with that," James said.

They finished the plate of brownies and stretched out in lounge chairs with their sandals kicked off. A rabbit, without any natural predators, basked in the late afternoon sun near the back fence. A fresh breeze stirred in the little yard. Hank helped himself to another beer.

James rolled his head to one side on the cushioned backrest of his lounge chair and looked at Hank. "Are you okay?"

Hank took a sip of cold beer. "There's someone…a woman…"

"How you feeling?" LaShondra said.

"Like it's a terrible amazing mess."

"I'm not sure that's a feeling but we'll go with it for now," James said. "So, this is more than just a red car syndrome, huh?"

"But how are you feeling about *her*," LaShondra persisted.

"I don't know…maybe…I feel…good around her. But I'm not sure what she thinks of me. There's a chance she thinks I'm a jerk."

"What?"

"She's so easy and warm, everyone likes her, and I… haven't been too connected…."

"Cut yourself some slack, man, look what you been through," James said.

"Yeah, well, that's part of it." He took a long swallow of beer. "It's been three years since Sarah died, I thought I'd never get over her, now something's changing…I don't want Sarah to leave me, become someone I used to know."

"But she is, Hank," James said.

"What?"

"Someone you used to know. That doesn't mean you'll forget how it was to love her."

Hank leaned forward in the lawn chair, bare feet on the grass, his head in his hands. He rubbed his eyes and face with his fingers. "You know that saying 'roll with the punches'? I'm not good at that. Sometimes I think I am, because you get so beat up in medical training, you get used to it. But then punches start to bunch up on you, and you try to stop them. You forget how to roll with them if you even knew in the first place. *Then* there's a knockout punch, and all you want is to not ever see a big punch again."

James and LaShondra were silent. It was dark out now. Then James said softly: "Maybe don't think about it so much, just go with it."

That evening Hank was tired but could not sleep. He lay awake in the second-floor bedroom of James' and LaShondra's Chicago brownstone, watching the green of summertime trees sway against the light of street lamps. Trains clicked on the tracks near Western Avenue. Sirens moved up and down the same five notes, like a crazed soprano doomed to sing the same part of the musical scale over and over.

When he finally fell asleep, Hank saw interconnecting biochemical symbols. *It's the Krebs energy cycle*, he said to himself in the dream and, *knowing* he was in a dream, commented further— *how strange*. He slept deeply then. When he dreamed again, he saw two serpents winding together on a cross, forming helices. Up close, he saw, embedded and contained within the serpents, bright pairs of corresponding genes.

Chapter 10

Hank was on his own Saturday. Both James and LaShondra had gone to work. The morning already warm he walked the few blocks from Bucktown to Wicker Park. Air coming up through the sidewalk grates on Milwaukee Avenue felt cooler than the ambient air. City birds seemed bigger and noisier as though trying to hear each other over all three million people living in Chicago.

When he and Sarah lived in Wicker Park, it was raw. A heady mix of Polish, Ukrainians, artists, and gangbangers. Eventually realtors moved in and raised rents, and artists moved out except for the ones with family trust funds. The community was still eclectic, but not in the same anything-can-happen way.

Hank detoured to walk past his and Sarah's old apartment on Wood Street. On Saturdays they used to go to the Busy Bee and fill up on dumplings and pork and sauerkraut, or they'd buy a chunk of the best liver sausage in the world at Lottie's Delicatessen, take it home and slather it onto rye bread, eat it with bitingly Kosher pickles. After a nap, they'd make love for hours. *We were living the life of Riley then.* The corners of his mouth go up.

The service garage on Damen Avenue had become a trendy café. On the former apron of the garage, tables were set up, and both wide garage doors on either side of the doorway were intact, raised today to bring the al fresco effect indoors. The cut-rate grocery across the street was gone, replaced by a video store.

A warm wind made the long grass in the park ripple like loose fat rolls on a flabby body. But the fieldhouse had been sandblasted, and the park cleaned up. Someone's sleeping bag was stashed in the bushes near the new black wrought-iron fence. Hank stood near a weathered tree. He leaned back carefully until his upper body and head released against the thick trunk.

A young woman with magenta hair and male friends played multiple games of Frisbee, sailing the hard plastic discs crisscrossing through the air. The dog people were out, making doggy comments to each other, watching their animals gambol on the grass. Homeless guys sat in the middle of the park passed the bottle in a brown paper bag. Babies were crying, fat babies conceived with ease last year in the cold Chicago night.

Hank sat down on a bench. An elderly woman threw whole walnuts in the shell towards the squirrels. A man wiggled one foot at the ankle, playing a game of solitaire. A child balanced, walking on a low stone border.

Tiny anonymous insects crawled across Hank's *Sun-Times*. When he brushed them away without thinking, they turned into small commas of blood against the page. A lone man drinking out of a paper bag moved to a bench closer to Hank.

Hank edged away. The sun was climbing into his face. He scooched back into the shade, stretched out his long legs. Then he got up and walked across Damen Avenue to the L.

The elevated trains in Chicago, called "L's" for the shape of their route downtown, no longer had real names. The Lake Street L to Austin on the far West Side had become the Green Line. For people moving so fast they only had time for a flash of color to know where they're going. The trains came every eleven minutes now according to the schedule, but Hank still heard old people asking, "How often does it come?"

He transferred from the Blue Line to the Green Line downtown. The L didn't squeal any more making the sharp turn around the last office building on its way out of the Loop. It crossed the Chicago River and headed west. Large tracts of razed land on the West Side lay bare from the riots of the sixties. Through the window he glimpses what appears to be a drug deal going down in Garfield Park. Below a powder blue van with the inscription *Fr. Roy and the Jubilee Travelers,* sits in a lot full of wrecked cars.

Inside the train an unsteady man talked to his friend. "She's rough, my auntie, she starts talkin', you'll never stop listenin'. She's so rough, mean and evil, my auntie, I love her. I come to be with her. I got to deal with it."

"There ain't nothin' that's that bad."

"I wouldn't put it on someone else, wouldn't be fair. She's rough. I still love her, the only one I got. Hey, man, can I come in your place?"

"Ain't nobody can come in somebody else's place, man."

Hank shifts in his seat. *Maybe all the guy in the park wanted was the feeling of another human being nearby.*

At the Laramie stop, beady-eyed pigeons strutted around his ankles on the platform. Exiting riders were courteous of each other's space but didn't allow their eyes to meet. The woman ahead of Hank wore open sandals, a short orange top and brown tights the exact color of her skin, giving the startling impression she was naked from the waist down. On the street, a man walked through the dispersing passengers puffing on a cigarette. In between drags, he took the purse-lipped slightly gasping breaths of someone with chronic air hunger. Small birds flew in and out of a nest tucked up above the empty railing of an abandoned storefront awning.

The little corner store building down the block from his family's old house was still there, but it no longer sold penny candy. A sign on the outside read "God's Love C.O.G.I.C." (*Church of God in Christ?*). Girls played Double Dutch on the sidewalk, swinging two long ropes back and forth under the jumper. A knife grinder in a dull red truck sharpened switchblades for guys in dark sunglasses. The tune "Pop Goes the Weasel" trailed down the block from an ice cream truck.

On Hank's old block a woman left her house, took a quick look around and tucked a key in her bra. A blue chalk outline for hopscotch was drawn in a childish hand on the sidewalk – squares numbering one through eight. If you hopped all the squares without losing your balance, you made it to the half-dome at the top called "Heaven." *Do you now?*

The Clearys were among the last of Chicago's West Side Irish. Their brick bungalow was typical of others in the neighborhood. Coal, already an anachronism, was delivered into the basement when he was a kid, through a two-foot square chute at ground level off the gangway.

In those days, flowers were lush, and children played without fear. Peonies crawled with ants along old Mrs. Cassidy's fence, and it seemed there were lilacs everywhere. Hank and his friends played marbles near the lavender lilac bushes, on the bungalow's stone steps, huge and rough and solid like walls and tables for young bodies.

The crawl space under the front porch was a place to hide. Thin latticed wood on either side allowed patterned light in along the edges of the space. It was musty, slightly cool in summer, a place people forgot about even though they knew it was there.

The house next door where the Greek family lived has an iron security door over its front door now. In summertime Hank sat on their back porch having a second bigger breakfast with their whole family, something substantial like porridge. When it rained, he and the son went to the third floor of the graceful frame home, where the artist-father let them paint at easels.

In the alley, the tall skinny garage Hank jumped from one heart-stopping day when he was nine, stands upright. Other wooden garages and sheds looked about to topple over and bore the marks of graffiti. The bench remained in the back yard where Tara, languid among old satins and chiffons, played the Lady of the Lake in the annual tableau put on by the neighborhood kids. Many yards had debris, but their back yard had grass and the tulip garden they planted remained. How Hank and Tara loved those red and yellow tulips waving bright in the cool springs of their childhood! The tulips have gone topless now, only their green stems and leaves scraggling in the air.

The front windows of the bungalow were open. For a moment, the day became so still Hank could hear a small plane pass overhead, see the flicker of shade it cast as it came between him and the sun high in the western sky. He could almost hear his parents inviting relatives into the little front room of the bungalow.

Suigh síos, sit down, they'd say in Irish.

When his uncles, aunts and cousins from the Old Country spoke in English, he was perplexed by their use of qualifiers in conversation. "The weather's not bad at all," they'd say, or "I've only a small bit more to tell." Later, when he was grown and had studied Gaelic, he realized the qualifying was built into the syntax of the Irish language. And maybe into the spirit of the people too, after centuries of enduring hardship.

The people from the west of Ireland, for all they loved to talk and tell stories, had a habit of taking a delicate suck of breath in through their mouths every so often as they spoke, almost like a punctuation mark. Sometimes he imagined they held their breaths while they spoke (the risk of it) and needed a quick draft of air (not *too* long, not *too* deep) to continue.

Hank felt the hard wood under his knees in the front room, where the Clearys knelt to say the rosary. The smell of his mother's perfume came back. He saw her face light up looking at his father, heard her saying, "Isn't that grand?"

He could smell soda bread she made, the warm buttermilk fragrance of the loaves coming out of the oven. He remembered the glare in his eyes, on good mornings when his father hadn't been drinking. Da would open the curtains letting in the early sun. "Rise and shine," he'd say, rousting Hank out of bed for school.

By the time he was in his late twenties, his father's binges had scattered out, become less extended, lasting a long evening for his mother instead of a few days. Hank had finished medical school by then, was out of the house.

"It's himself," his mother said one day when he'd come to visit. She was standing in the middle of the tiny front room of the bungalow, the lace curtains lifting in the breeze from the windows. "Cirrhosis."

So, it's come to this, he'd thought. He didn't feel much of anything.

"Aw, ma." He walked over to his mother, gathered her into his arms. He felt the pale skin of her arms, smooth and cool, her back and neck firm. Then her body loosened, and she crumpled against him.

He could still see his father's face, with tears of laughter from some wild, hilarious story, or the sad tears of being in his cups. He could see his mother, gentle, waiting. They were both gone now. He stood a minute longer on the cracked sidewalk in front of the bungalow. Then he left.

On the way back to the L, Hank heard the carillon ring four times in the spired tower rising above the roof of St. Michael's.

All the old-time nuns were probably gone by now. They were eccentric and sadistic. Sister Alphonsus who sewed lace on the bottom of boys' shirts who couldn't keep their shirttails tucked in. Sister Mary Joseph who gave them a baby bottle in front of the classroom as punishment. And Father Roarty, who managed to keep the parish financially afloat, and said he hoped someday to be the patron saint of wheelers and dealers.

Something made him redirect his steps towards St. Michael's. Years, maybe decades, since he's done this, stopped off at church for a "visit" in the middle of the day. As he walked, he anticipated the dark quiet, sitting immobile in the pew.

The church was locked. For a second, he was stunned. *Of course…thieves, vandals. Churches in the city haven't been left open for prayer in a long time.* His body sagged. "Anyone can go into a church any time when they need to," his mother had said. He'd liked that – the idea of a holy place, a building set aside to be with God.

Teilhard or Rahner would say we carry the place around inside ourselves too, but still....

When Hank got off the L in Wicker Park, it was still light out. The sky was robin's egg blue with clouds in a vast foldout like a white fan. Music came from the Flat Iron Building, a place he'd been to many times with Sarah, a place full of memories. He started to turn away, then turned back.

An old man stood just inside the Flat Iron, playing the violin. People streamed past him going to the art galleries on the floors above. His open violin case lay on the floor beside him. The man wore clean trousers and buttoned shirt, but his shoes had open strips in the tops of the forefoot sections. Probably left over from when Wicker Park still had a lot of working-class Europeans, Hank thought. He smiled at the man.

"When they go past me like I'm a bum," he said to Hank, "then I can't feel it to play."

"I know," Hank said. The man studied him for a minute, then played a lively jig on the violin. Hank slipped a bill into the violin case, and the musician tipped his stringed bow.

Out of doors again, Hank stood near the park. He saw that the empty nest, which earlier in the day appeared to be sitting in the branch of a tree, was actually woven into the top of a street lamp in front of the tree. If you move a foot to the left or the right, or walk on the other side of the street, he thought, all of a sudden you see things differently.

If your steps were off just a little, what happened? Maybe you don't see, maybe you wander around in a circle the rest of your life.

Chapter 11

On Saturday evening Hank went with James and LaShondra to Grant Park for a blues concert. They spread a blanket on the grass, out beyond the chairs facing the band shell. Hank lay on his back, hands under his head, watching one of the hawks placed in the city to weed out undesirables, swoop between tall Loop buildings.

It was a balmy evening. Warm wind blowing off Lake Michigan gave a tropical feel to the park. The Chicago blues crowd, funky and laid back, was eager for the music. The scent of marijuana smoke drifted up to their blanket. "How'd the Cubs do today?" someone said. Being with James and LaShondra felt like putting on a worn, comfortable shirt.

"Man, it is some kind of beautiful night," James said, "…how was your day?"

"I didn't actually have too bad of a day," Hank said. "Someone said 'Hi ya, handsome' to me in Wicker Park." He cocked an eyebrow at them. "'Course it was a woman walking through the park who was also talking to the birds and squirrels."

"Well, so?" LaShondra said, "May *be*, she knew what she was talking 'bout, to all of you."

He ran his fingers through his unruly red hair streaked with gray. "May *be*," he grinned.

As they talked a mass of bruised color appeared overhead, coming from the North, above Michigan Avenue, then Columbus Drive, like a bowl closing over the sky. No rain, just the dark edge sliding steady and fast into the still light rim of sky. Then it cleared.

"The Queen of the Blues…" the announcer shouted. The crowd roared, and Koko Taylor took the stage, launched into her trademark *Wang Dang Doodle*. Halfway through the set, Buddy Guy joined her on stage, and they traded the spotlight, singing the blues. Hank and James and LaShondra were on their feet, clapping and swaying with everyone around them.

A slim woman passed in front of their blanket, in a form-fitting blue shirt and a pencil—style black skirt with blue flowers. Her buttocks moved rhythmically beneath the thin material of her skirt. Hank felt a stirring in his body, a stab of longing.

"I'm going to take a walk over to Buckingham Fountain," he said.

"Sure, honey, take your time," LaShondra said, "it's a great night for it." She and James were sitting on the blanket again, holding hands.

Hank walked through the rose garden leading to the fountain, inhaled the perfume of the roses in the cooling air, Lake Michigan glimmering off to his left. The wind blowing off the lake felt good on his skin. Like the wind must have felt blowing off the Atlantic, over Galway Bay where his grandfather fished for salmon and mackerel, onto the cottages and bogs of Connemara.

It was Lake Michigan he missed, the water, the expanse of it, changing from blue to green to aqua to pewter, its sound slapping against the shore, the *feel* of it nearby.

"The waves are running tonight," his father would have said.

Da loved to speak of Lake Michigan that way. The same words Hank's grandfather had used about the ocean dashing up against the Galway cliffs. "*In Iarthar na nEireann*, in the West of Ireland," his grandfather would say, "*cois farraige*, by the sea. The waves were running and the salmon were leaping."

A pregnant woman and her husband strolled nearby on the promenade.

In his parents' circle, being pregnant was known as "having a bun in the oven." He thought the nurturance of the image vied with the objectification of the woman and her womb. An Irish biddy from the South Side had once volunteered to him, about young women she knew who kept getting pregnant every eleven or twelve months, "They wouldn't keep coming on with the babies if they'd just keep a nickel between their legs!" The comment had flummoxed him, taxed his imagination as to its moral and gravitational perspective.

A woman with dark exotic features walked near Hank in the rose garden. Her breasts were full and loose under a summer top. He envisioned himself cupping her breasts in his hands, stroking their soft curving skin, touching the nipples. He could smell his own musk in his nostrils...as though the black-skirted woman by the blanket had knocked down a dam holding back his sexual desire, and now he was flooded with it.

He approached the fountain. *What was Livy doing tonight?* She'd had her appointment at the fertility clinic today. He saw her face, flushed and warm, the brown shine of her eyes.

Was she hopeful? Afraid? Even now, the strongest sperm swimmer may be drawing near to one of her eggs, poised to coalesce, to form a tiny zygote, incipient precursor of the child she wanted.

Darkness fell. The illuminated water in Buckingham Fountain changed from red to blue to yellow as it splashed over central tiers and arced from the mouths of stone sea serpents around the periphery. A young couple lingered at the railing, sharing soft shrieks of delight when the breeze sprayed them with cool water. They embraced in a kiss. With a pang, Hank recalled holding Sarah the same way, lost in each other, coming back to themselves in the glow of the fountain. He saw her face, soft with love, as she had looked that night.

Lines from Neruda came to him:
> *All must be remembered...*
> *yard after yard of all we inhabited,*
> *the train's long trajectory,*
> *and the trappings of sorrow.*

Chapter 12

Livy Reyna took Saturday off to go to the fertility clinic at the University of Wisconsin in Madison. She got up early to bake and make soups, left Livy's Bar and Cafe in the hands of her waitresses, and drove to Madison for an artificial insemination procedure. When she returned to Alma, she gathered the dirty laundry from the cafe and started it washing, then walked over to Pied-á-Terre.

"They call it assisted reproductive technologies," she said to Alex, who sat on a stool beside the cluttered glass desk.

Livy had changed clothes after she got home from Madison, and she had on one navy sock and one purple sock. She felt tired. "They say I ovulate, so...we'll see if my little ova reach out their loving arms to some lucky sperm!"

"I wish you the best, Livy," Alex said, a warm smile across her plain face, "may you become pregnant forthwith."

Alice had been reading a book on Provence, absorbed, twisting a strand of auburn hair between her fingers. Now she looked up. "*Bonne chance!*"

"I'm praying to the *Virgen de Guadalupe*. And to Inanna, just to be on the safe side."

"Ah," Alice said, "the *Grande-Mere*."

"How was it?" Alex asked.

"Okay." Livy, who handled most situations with aplomb, had felt somewhat out of her element at the clinic. "I had to keep my legs up for a couple hours afterward. The fertility specialist himself was gentle. He only patronized me a little."

"Blackguard!" Alex said.

"He didn't seem to know it. I started to simmer, then I said to myself, 'It's not worth it.'"

"Perhaps the better part of valor."

"*Now* I'm feeling it!" Livy's beautiful voice cracked a little. "The procedure was all right. What got to me was the clerk. She says to me 'Are you an HMO?' not 'do you have an HMO or a PPO, or 'what insurance do you have?' but '*are* you an HMO?' ¡*Hijole*! I felt like decking her."

Alice rose gracefully and walked over to Livy. She put her arms around her. "*Chére* Livy."

Livy poured herself a cup of strong black tea from the china pot embellished with roses and vines and sank gratefully into a comfortable chair.

"Mexico," she said to the bookstore ladies, flashing a white smile, "means to be in the navel of the moon. I like that. I know what it means to be Mexican. I don't understand what it means to be Irish."

"Maybe Hank can help elucidate that," Alice said.

"I don't think he knows what it means."

"Hank knows more than you think, more than *he* thinks," Alex said.

"He acted strange the last time he was in the café. He just got up and left, bolted, without saying goodbye."

"Hank's a Celt all right," Alex said.

"Hank," said Alice, "is the *crème de la crème*. He's only looking for his *juste-milieu*."

Livy accepted a fresh cup of tea, cinnamon this time, and walked back to the bookshelves. She wanted to explore her roots.

Livy Reyna had grown up in the Pilsen community in Chicago. Her mother had been born in Mexico, as had her mother and father before her, but not her mother's grandfather. He had been born in Ireland. Livy's great-grandfather was one of the Irish soldiers who left the United States Army to fight with the Mexicans in the U.S.-Mexican War of 1846.

Livy didn't know much about her great-grandfather. Her mother had been a small child when he was an old man. Her mother remembered him as tall and broad-shouldered, blue-eyed, with scars on his face, but remembered more clearly the stories she had heard.

His name was John Riley. He left Ireland before *An Gorta Mor*, the Great Hunger, one of many who emigrated from a pre-famine Ireland itself full of want and misery. Because of high prices charged by British ships bound for the United States, he'd traveled first to Canada in the leaky hold of a returning timber ship. From there he made his way to the United States, then Mexico, where he led the St. Patrick's Brigade. When Mexico lost the war ("half our country taken from us," her mother said), John Riley was spared from hanging. Because he'd deserted before war was declared, he was flogged and branded instead. A handsome man, his cheeks had been branded twice, because the letter "D" for deserter was placed backwards the first time. His entire back was scarred from the whiplashes.

Livy found a book on Mexican history and settled in with her cup of tea.

The San Patricios were honored every year in the square in Mexico City for their bravery, she discovered. The name of each San Patricio who died was called out, followed by the chant of the crowd: *Murio por Mexico*, He died for Mexico.

The Irish in the United States military in the mid-1800's, Livy read, were treated with cruelty and contempt by the Anglo-American officers. Nearly 250 Irish soldiers deserted to the Mexican Army at the promise of better pay, land, and for what many saw as a just cause. Polk started the war, Grant and Lincoln both opposed it. Many Americans thought it was a simple land grab.

The St. Patrick's Battalion marched in the lead column of the Mexican General Santa Anna's army. Santa Anna said later if he'd had a few hundred more like them he might have won the war. They defended Monterrey, Buena Vista, and finally Mexico City where over half the Irish brigade died in battle. The battle at Chapultepec Castle in Mexico City lasted two days. When Chapultepec fell, the war was over, the U.S. flag was raised, and thirty San Patricios were hanged.

John Riley, her mother had told her, helped bury his companions under the gallows.

Livy thought about what the life of her great-grandfather must have been like, and about the new life she hoped would form within her. "*Niña*," she said softly, touching her flat belly, "or *niño*, may you be as strong as your ancestors."

On her way out of Pied-á-Terre, she spoke again to Alex and Alice. "Those Irish soldiers who fought with Mexico in the U.S.-Mexican War," she said, crouching down to pet Sam, "the ones *en solidaridad* with Mexico, had *compasión*." She caressed the silk of Sam's head who stood transfixed, rapt with pleasure. "Those Irish men were *valiente*."

Chapter 13

On Sunday, Alma rested. Even Livy. By the time the breakfast crowd in the café thinned out she'd already prepared the dinner entrees, and it was quiet enough for her to slip away to Yazzi's for a few hours.

Their home was a simple ample farmhouse. Lilacs surrounded it on three sides in the spring. A majestic blue spruce towered over the gables, of a color blue tinged so exactly right with black that, when people looked at it, all they could do was be grateful.

Livy and Elrita sat on a swing in the garden drinking lemonade under the arbor. Beside them roses climbed a wooden trellis. On the other side of the garden a life-sized statue of St. Francis of Assisi stood in the clear sunshine. Near him Winona played with her doll.

Winona sat on the ground with her legs bent under her, red flowers spread in a semicircle around her. Her dark hair fell loose over her round little-girl head. She held a leaf that grew off both sides of its stem, like a tiny flat Christmas tree. She absentmindedly stroked her face with the dark side of the leaf, the smooth unveiny side. Her mother had allowed her to wear her turquoise necklace today, because it was Sunday and Livy was visiting. But Winona felt contrary. Rufus was away somewhere. And Beulah! Beulah never took her on butterfly hunts any more or sat brushing Winona's black hair and tying it with colored ribbons out by the hogan.

Usually, Beulah felt to Winona like a full-grown lamb, bright and wooly-warm, ready to leap. Now Beulah had changed, like something cold had gotten inside her, and she felt jumpy, like a jack-rabbit.

Last night Beulah had sat on the edge of Winona's bed at bedtime. "I have four animals that guard me at night," she said, "one at each corner of my bed."

"Why?" she'd asked. But Beulah only drew her lips together in a line, then hugged her extra hard before she went to her own room.

Winona liked dreaming stories, but Beulah's story scared her. What monster would want to harm her sister?

She scooted over to her doll. Scrubby grass and stems of daisies rose like a forest around Carmelita, forming a canopy over her head. Nearby was a sculpture of children holding a large shell, tipping it towards another shell that formed a basin. "There's a fairy in every flower," she told her doll. "They take baths in mother's sculpture for the birds."

A robin plumped its red breast and flew away, the white tips of its tail feathers flashing in the sun. "What if you could ride on a robin, Carmelita, way high in the sky? You could hear what the tall trees are saying and the music of the wind."

From the next field over, a rivulet of water flowed out from between rows of corn, forming a puddle. Winona set her doll on a piece of birch bark, attached to an old shoelace, and carefully pulled the small raft across the puddle lake.

She lay Carmelita down on a scrap of flannel beside a clump of lavender flowers with gold centers. Doc Cleary has a heart of gold, she told her, and so do you.

A pale green butterfly with brown spots flitted among the Queen Anne's lace. "Butterflies love fairies," Winona whispered. "They stop off at the flowers to see if a fairy wants a ride. Shh, can you hear? – fairy sounds." And indeed, deep under the quiet, was a faint hum like miniscule tinkly chimes.

Drowsy in the grass, she watched her mother and Livy rock in the swing.

"That contraption of a table," Livy said to Elrita, wrinkling her brow. "It's like a medieval torture rack! And those metal stirrups are so cold on your feet. You have to be in superb athletic condition, a contortionist, to get in position for the exam," A slow melodic laugh rose out of her chest. "There's only one other thing I've spread my legs that wide for, and *that* was something I wanted."

Elrita blushed, but kept listening, eyes focused on Livy.

"Sorry, it's the Chicago girl in me coming out." Livy paused. "Although it's nice not to have to deal with a man for this – all their *requirements*."

"Men," Elrita said. "It's hard for them to live up to what we want them to be. The Navajo people know this."

They rocked in the swing. Livy regarded Winona playing. She

could smell the viney odor of the tomato plants, hear the hum of insects. A tear slipped down her cheek.

"The baby…it's my *sueno*, my dream."

Elrita squeezed her hand. "I know."

Livy gazed out at the barns, the one for the animals and the one closer to the house which Joe had fixed up as a sculpture studio for Elrita. A wood sorrel rested in a glass jar on the windowsill of Elrita's barn.

"How's Beulah? I brought her some clothes."

"Beulah's the same. She's been walking beans for the farmer two fields over."

"The same?"

"Yes, *Oh*," Elrita spoke in Navajo.

"And Rufus?"

"Lonnie Two-Rivers invited him to go fishing. He's going to show him how the Menominee used to spear fish by torchlight in the dark." She paused. "Rufus is searching for his umbilical cord."

"What do you mean?"

"In Navajo country we bury the umbilical cord after it dries. Under the corral when a male baby is born so he'll have many horses. The *Diné* believe that if you do not bury the cord, the boy will search for it. I think we forgot to bury Rufus's cord. He's becoming a man now, and he is searching for his umbilical cord. He's trying to find his tie to the land. I decided to let him go with Lonnie Two-Rivers."

This was a lot of words for Elrita, and she fell quiet. A blue jay squawked. The trees rustled in the breeze.

Livy lifted the hair off the nape of her neck. She thought about children, how they occupied your thoughts and filled your heart.

Chapter 14

Hank woke up to the smell of bacon frying. Downstairs in the kitchen, he and James and LaShondra polished off a big breakfast of bacon and pancakes. Hank helped with the dishes.

"*We* are going to church," La Shondra said. "*You*," she waggled her finger at him, "are going to lie on the lounge chair in the back yard and do a whole lot of nothin'!"

So, he stretched out on their chaise lounge in the sun, groggy and full, and did nothing. Or almost nothing. He drank hot black coffee out of a stoneware mug and observed an insect the size of a pencil point crawl upside down on the underside of a glass table.

When they got back, James said, "Don't be a stranger," and La Shondra hugged him an extra minute before she lets him go.

Hank left their place in Bucktown, detoured south on Damon to 290, then drove east. He crossed the Chicago River, reversed in its flow at the turn of the last century, a colossal feat of engineering. By the mid-1900's the river, via the St. Lawrence Seaway, linked the Great Lakes and the North Atlantic with the Mississippi River. The river had been neglected for a long time, but he'd heard it was being reclaimed, cleaner than when he and Sarah lived in Chicago.

Downtown he managed a run of green lights, past the Library with its archetypal exterior, and Buckingham Fountain shooting plumes of water and headed north out of the city along the lake. He crossed the river again on Lake Shore Drive, and rounded the curve at Navy Pier, watching the sailboats scattered on Lake Michigan, anticipating the panoply of boats in Belmont Harbor. But traffic, ordinarily smooth on the Drive, backed up and he got off in Lakeview to cut over to the expressway.

He was stopped in his tracks by a huge parade on Halsted Street. Floats and marchers, decked out in primary colors, rolled and pranced down the street. Elaborate glamorous costumes, bare-chested women, men with semi-bare backsides, drew whoops and cheers. A police officer in a blue shirt and black shorts rode by on a bicycle. Couples stood with arms around each other enjoying the day. Hank tried to imagine the bookstore ladies or anyone he knew from Alma with chest thrust out marching down Halsted.

A young woman in her twenties, with a metal stud through her tongue, told him that further up he could get across to the expressway. "Halsted's blocked off to cars all the way up to Montrose."

"Thanks."

"No problem." She handed him a card.

He read the card, bemused. *YOU HAVE BEEN ASSISTED BY A LESBIAN HELPER.*

In the lower left corner were the words *Think globally,* in the lower right corner *Act locally.* He looked up and she was gone.

Hank got across at Montrose as promised, drove through Uptown past a sign in a grill window boasting "only a rooster can get a better piece of chicken than Jake's." He simultaneously winced and grinned. This too was Chicago.

On the spur of the moment, he took a meandering old highway north towards Wisconsin instead of the interstate. Going up to Wisconsin. Or *down* to Wisconsin, as Da used to say about the Cleary vacation trips. Hank had a conversation with Alex about this once.

"In Da's opinion, there was no reason to say 'up' to Wisconsin, Alex," he'd told her. Deep in his cups or on the wagon, his father was consistent about one thing—once he got an idea into his head, he wasn't likely to change it. "There was no telling him. Even though it makes sense to say 'up' when you're going north."

"Does it?" Alex replied. "Considering you're traveling over the curve of the Earth, I'd say you're going over."

Across the Wisconsin state line, he stopped off at a Piggly Wiggly grocery. He bought a gallon of drinking water, sipped water from his coffee mug in the pickup as he drove. Geesh, was he going to become like all those people in the city carting around bottles of Perrier, La Crosse, waters of every persuasion, wherever they go?

A familiar song played on the truck radio: *"...a kiss is still a kiss...a sigh is still a sigh... the world will always welcome lovers...."*

Not always, Hank thought. The world welcomed lovers of youth and beauty, unblemished, the strong arm of the male around the curve of the female. Some pairs of lovers do not conform to this vision. He wondered what it's like to not be able to hold hands in public. How was it when you cannot say to people – like Elrita did when Joe had pneumonia last year – "We almost lost him." And know the listener completely understood that what she was really saying was *Elrita* almost lost her *other*, the human being with whom she is mated, whose drawing in and out of breath matters more to her than anyone else's in the world, as much to her as her own.

Yet they did not look unhappy, those marchers.

Hank fell into a kind of daydream. Traveling, we're all travelers. Like the tinkers in Ireland who roam the land—sad how their numbers had dwindled compared to twenty years ago.

We're all travelers. It's just some of us are roaming the land slower than the rest. Like I've been in Alma the last six years, roaming, roaming, in a slowed-down way, in Alma, in this time, that it seems I'm living there. Maybe death is that you move so slow, you stop. If you move slow enough in time, you die.

He took a sip of water.

Sarah was delicate, more ethereal than Livy. Not so of the earth as Livy. But he laughed with Sarah, and he can laugh with Livy. That part was the same. There's something loose and wild in Livy. She's a little crazy, but then so am I.

Bodies, bone, blood, muscle, sinew, appendages, secretions, all the internal organs. How strange and wonderful we are.

Hank reached the hills of northern Wisconsin, lowered the side windows to catch the scent of firs. Tiny insect corpses spread out over the pickup windshield. The trip home to Alma seemed shorter than the trip leaving.

He needed to recheck Beulah Yazzi, get her back in to the clinic to find out why her face had taken on a pinched look when he examined her for her school physical. See if she'd let him in behind the door she'd closed to Elrita and Joe.

And Mary Two-Rivers—a rough piece of work, as James would say. Elrita had paid Mary a nurse visit last week to check her blood pressure and glucose level. "She doesn't look so good, Hank," Elrita reported. "She's sluggish. I gave her some Eucerin cream because her skin is like sandpaper." His thoughts skittered over Mary Two-Rivers, skirted her bulk, started to move away as usual, then paused. What *was* it? The gluttony, yes. But not only the unbridled eating. It had to do with her sitting around and not doing anything, her inertia. Something else flickered at the edge of his mind.

Approaching Alma, Hank whistled softly through his teeth. He unconsciously dropped his vehicular speed another ten miles per hour. He raised his fingers off the steering wheel in greeting to a man walking by the side of the road.

He saw embankments of clouds in his rear view mirror; the weather was at his back. He sang along with music on the radio.

"Oh my God!" He almost slammed on the brakes. "I've been seeing Mary Two-Rivers for a year, and I missed it! The dry skin, the lethargy, the weight gain – she's probably massively hypothyroid. The diabetes, the obesity – a multiple endocrinopathy syndrome if I ever saw one." He tried to remember if the thyroid gland in her fleshy neck with its rolls of fat is enlarged. He didn't think so. Still, he'd bet money her thyroid had pooped out, was putting out next to no hormone.

Damn! he said to himself, *you see one thing, you don't see the other*. A line came to him from the Hippocratic oath – "The health of my patient will be my first consideration." *Maybe if I'd given the woman more than an aliquot of my medical attention.*

Fog covered the secondary road into Alma. Hank took a swig of water from the gallon jug. And then. He made a mental note to order a thyroid profile on Mary Two-Rivers in the morning. And then. He forgave himself. A small pebble lifted off his heart.

A bushy tree rose up out of the fog on the edge of town, like dark flames against the gray milky air. At seven o'clock postmeridian, central daylight savings time, he coasted down the hill into Alma. The street was cocooned in fog. At the far end of town, the tin sign by the gas station, with its camel astride the words *pleasure to burn*, jumped into his headlights in the fog.

Hank turned onto the road to his cabin. Slender white birches appeared and vanished in the fog. He breathed a deep and easy breath.

Chapter 15

Beulah Yazzi signed up to detassel seed corn in July. Before dawn she got on an old bus belonging to the Alma County farm bureau, with a dozen other high school students, and rode out to the scattered local cornfields.

"More corn is being grown up north with the warmer summers," the Ag worker told them. "The gold-green tassels at the top look like tightly woven leaves—they're the male flowers. Below are the kernels on the cob or the female part, further down the silks that catch the pollen. In every fifth row, leave the strong plants intact, so their tassels can pollinate the detasseled plants in neighboring rows." He added, "Be sure to bring two gallons of drinking water every day."

From five in the morning until three in the afternoon, the teenagers walked among the rows of corn removing tassels. The tassels popped out easily from the tops of the corn plants, and machines had already made a first pass through the fields. But the work was wearisome. The sun beat down on the Earth's equator and the warmed air spiraling towards the poles brought intense heat to the Midwest. Bugs stuck to sweaty skin and sharp-edged corn leaves made scratches like fine paper cuts all over their arms. The young workers were paid seven dollars an hour.

Beulah did not enjoy the bus rides to and from the fields, with their light-hearted socializing, especially the banter of the boys with the girls. "Hey, Beulah," they'd say, "what's with you?" She was grateful for the company, though, because when she was not alone, she felt safe. She took rides from her mother and father now when she went out or walked with Rufus.

She liked the detasseling. Moving single file along the corn rows, everyone was working too hard to talk much. She could settle into herself, not have to pretend like everything was okay.

The first day on the job they'd worked the cornfield adjacent to Yazzis' land. She'd had a bad time. Her heart pounded, remembering running from Lonnie through the same field in the spring. And sometimes now, in the middle of detasseling, she seemed to forget where she was for a moment. So, she was glad that if you missed a tassel, the person behind you was supposed to get it.

Rufus knew something was wrong, did special Rufus things like bringing her berries from the woods. But he was her brother, she couldn't talk about it with him. When Lonnie invited Rufus to go fishing, she was shocked. When he accepted Beulah felt betrayed, sorry she hadn't told him.

She could not tell anyone about what had happened with Lonnie Two-Rivers. She had brought dishonor to her family.

Beulah didn't mind the strenuous work, the sweat in her eyes, the scratches on her skin. It suited her. During the ten hours in the cornfields, she found an energy that eluded her in the rest of her life.

The week after he got home Hank was busy with patients in the clinic. He smoothed the ruffled feathers of patients whom Warren had treated brusquely. Once the offended were mollified, his waiting room had filled up with people needing medical attention. One right after the other, they came in with a variety of time-consuming problems.

He listened to the immensely personal stories individuals tell a doctor in the privacy of an examining room.

He heard the painful confession of a sexual dalliance, followed by a painful sexually transmitted disease, and dispensed antibiotic absolution. An old woman told him her head felt so tight she worried she might have a tumor. It turned out she'd gotten carried away with her hairspray. The sparse strands of hair and her reddened scalp appeared to be shellacked. Hank reassured her and sent her on her way, counseling gentle shampoo, soothing oil, and to spray no more. A patient came in with a mink bite on his thumb, another with a tick bite on his scrotum. He saw five variations on the dizzies. One of his healthy patients, who'd recently joined the Kick in for Christ Karate School, came to be rechecked for bloodshot eyes and a fast heartbeat. Then she admitted taking over-the-counter diet pills, in an attempt apparently to get slim for Christ.

Mary Two-Rivers had a grossly underactive thyroid. When her blood tests came back, they confirmed his diagnosis.

"I don't want to take no more pills," she protested.

"You need to take what your body can't make," he said, persuading her to take thyroid replacement. Then he discovered she'd been filling up on cabbage to stretch her money. "All that cabbage is causing you to put out even less thyroid," he told her, finally convincing her the cabbage interfered with her already meager production of the hormone.

That week Hank got over to the cafe after work, tired but buoyed up at the prospect of seeing Livy.

"Hi Livy," he called to her.

"Hey Hank." She smiled in his direction but didn't come over. Wrapped up with customers, she appeared too busy to interrupt.

Chapter 16

On Independence Day, red-white-and-blue bunting hung from porches of small frame houses in Alma. He spotted Livy riding atop the volunteer fire truck in the parade. But he got called away to attend to an elderly man whose asthma, worse with the hot weather, had tipped him over into congestive heart failure. By the time Hank got him hospitalized, the post-parade picnic supper was long over.

That evening he sat in a Harass bar having a few drinks. A down-at-the mouth place full of losers. A comforting dark place. He sat at a grimy table, its wood pockmarked with nicks, his head hanging, eyes almost closed. Warren covered his calls.

Hank took a long swallow of whiskey. He'd spent time in a bar like this when he and Sarah broke off their first engagement.

Sarah...Sarah... he'd been afraid to go in deep. He emptied his glass and ordered another.

He slipped into a slough of despond. What if Livy turned him down? What if he told her how he felt, and she didn't feel the same? Could she love a man like him?

Danger. I'm flirting with danger.

Hank slept fitfully that week, restless in his dreams. Then he went again in search of Livy.

In Pied-à-Terre, the cat roamed the window ledges and Sam lay on the cool wooden floor—both animals knew to be out of the heat on a day like this. Hank bent over to pat Sam's yellow head. He wore a new blue shirt he'd bought in Chicago and summer shorts.

Rufus Yazzi sat with his legs comfortably stretched out, handsome face intent, pouring over the glossy pages of a book of nineteenth century Impressionist paintings.

"You just missed her, Doc," Rufus said, when Hank inquired about Livy.

"She's not at the cafe. They said she'd been cooking up a storm, then left. That's the third time I've tried...."

"She might be at our place. I think that's where she was going." Rufus' eyes strayed to the open book in his lap. Then he looked up at Hank and smiled. "Cool shirt."

Silent Margaret, taking care of the bookstore today, sat reading. She wore salmon-colored culottes, a green shirt, white knee-highs, and oxford shoes. She was pale and her lower lip protruded which lent her an expressionless look, like a fish in water. How far under the water was difficult to tell. She smelled of tobacco. She started when Hank came in but again became engrossed in her book.

When Hank first saw Silent Margaret years ago, meticulously sorting books on a shelf, he knew she was one of the marginal people—like the ones walking the streets of every city in America—who somehow came to be found in Alma.

She was exquisitely sensitive to sound. If someone closed the door to Pied-a-Terre, with its jingling bell, a little too firmly she would jump. She felt bruised to Hank, like there was discoloration of her nerve endings. Or her neurological system had too many synapses. She didn't avert her eyes so much as she had a kind of inward-turning gaze, as though she were looking at something deep within herself. She felt oblique, like an actor in a film, as though she were turned towards a reality more real than that of every day. At the rare times Silent Margaret spoke, her voice came out in a curious chant, all on one note, which was distancing and engaging at the same time.

Once Alice said of her, "Margaret is *une personne interessante.*"

Hank had not considered Margaret that way. He assigned her a few diagnostic labels if he thought about her at all. *Extreme introvert with obsessive-compulsive features...addiction to nicotine...no probable danger.* In the colloquial part of his mind, he just thought of her as "off." He realized then that some "off" people were intriguing, and others were not, not unlike the rest of the population. Alice evidently found Margaret intriguing.

"Margaret," he said. She jumped at the sound of his voice. But she took his money for the book he'd chosen. She counted his change three times.

She was someone's little girl once, until something caught up with her. *A shyness damaged by time. The wrong kind of love, or none at all. Or an aberration of genes sending chemicals sluicing through her blood.*

In Alma, people let Silent Margaret be. Because, for all her strangeness, she was not a stranger.

Chapter 17

Alex and Alice believed in fully operational sexuality for Sam. He had kept his male ways, but tempered with such gentleness that small children grabbed his neck or lay their heads along his warm back. Nevertheless, he had sired many a litter.

The yellow lab had not been in his usual spot in front of Pied-a-Terre for three days.

The bookstore ladies were worried. He'd gone missing before for a night or two—some romantic escapade they always assumed—but he'd never been gone this long. They asked Joe Yazzi for help.

Joe took Winona with him to the woods. They searched along green leafy paths, near the creek with its speckled stones dappling clear water, and in out-of-the-way places by the little lake. In a thicket well off the main path, they found him.

Standing erect, instead of reclining, Sam appeared bigger. From behind him came faint mewling.

Joe extended his hand, talking in a low familiar tone. Usually so accommodating, the dog stood his ground. Winona took a few steps and reached out her arms, looking at Sam lovingly. In the end, her child's form and sweetness won him over. Sam relented.

He had sired four pups. By their size, he'd found a willing female some time in spring. Clearly Sam's, with the same patient eyes and shapely head, their slanted pupils bespoke an exotic mother. Their eyes seemed to refract light like a prism, as well as gather it in to bring them pictures of their new world. The mother was nowhere around.

The pups tumbled together. Their little ears stuck straight up and their paws were large for their bodies. A stripe of coal black extended from their heads down to their noses. They had grayish brown coats except for one who was buttercup yellow.

"Look at the little one, she looks like Sam!" Winona bent to pick her up.

"Stay back!" her father said. "The mother is a wolf. Wolves don't attack humans, but they will if you come too close to their dens."

"He had himself the *bon plaisir*," Alex said, when she and Alice came to see Sam's offspring. "He became enamored with a wild one."

"Wolves usually don't let dogs get anywhere near," said Joe, "Sam must have been persuasive."

Like Winona, they melted at the sight of the little yellow wolf-dog. "She has Sam's cachet," Alice said, "let's bring her home."

He put out his arm when they stooped to cuddle the pups. "No. Who knows where the wolf is now? She may be back, and it may not go well if they carry our scent."

"Do you think she's around?" He shrugged.

"*Bien*," Alex said. "The *qualité* of their *papa* is known. Clearly *la maman* is of noble lineage. In that we shall trust."

Winona knew a secret about the Home. In the bottom of the garden under the trellis, hidden in the hanging vines at the back of the arbor, was a little white gate. You could go through the gate into *another* garden.

She was the only one who visited it, climbing into the tangled other side. Maybe the *rezdens* knew about the hidden garden a long time ago but they forgot.

"Stay away from the jungly part, Carmelita," she told her doll, near the milkweeds where woodchucks and cats got in. "The animals will not harm you on purpose, but they are *e nor miss* and could step on you."

She knelt to examine stalks the color of milk with brown black caps. "A mushroom village – don't bump into it! But here's a mushroom table, just the right size for you, and the kind that's good, so you can take a bite if you get hungry."

She ducked under a spider web woven into the light and air. "Spider woman taught the Navajo how to weave. This is why we never kill spiders, and they help us by catching flies and mosquitoes." Carmelita stared back at her with shiny black eyes and smooth brown skin not unlike Winona's.

"You understand," Winona said, "you're bigger now. *I* think spiders are spinning dream webs to catch food for their babies."

"Look!" The girl turned her doll so her black button eyes faced upwards into a Hawthorne tree, then she stretched out on tiptoe craning her neck to look at a yellow and green finch on the lowest branch.

Ants crawled around Carmelita. "Do they look like lions to you? Don't be afraid, ants are our ancestors. Sometimes a thing looks scary but it's not."

She doodled in the dirt. She made her doll a boat from a large leaf, and a chair out of twigs. She fanned her with a small bird feather. Carmelita ate a morsel of a berry. Then Winona laid her down for a nap wrapped in a scrap of pink satin from Livy.

A small brown bird rested on her shoulder. Winona sat still when the baby cottontails popped out next to her on the mossy grass. She held her breath as the rabbits hopped right by, ignoring her it seemed. *She* knew *they* knew she was there. She didn't move to scratch the itch alongside her nose or to brush the daddy long legs off her leg. She didn't move when the large grey animal with glowing eyes stood in a thicket, before it turned away.

She sat so still in her brown and green play clothes that a feeling bubbled up inside her of things being right. Like she was *planted*, like she belonged here. So, when the tiny sparrow perched on her small shoulder, she wasn't surprised. *Ahéheé, thank you, for visiting me.*

A black butterfly flew by, the yellow design on its back like a lady's shawl. A monarch butterfly, tan and rust and black-and-white with polka-dotted wings, lit on Winona's sleeve.

Maybe it thinks I'm a flower.

"Butterfly wings are collectors of the sun, *se me knductrs*, Doc Cleary says," Winona told the sleeping Carmelita, "their wings heat the same all over."

She tucked the satin blanket more closely around her doll.

"Once upon a time," she began, "there was a butterfly who was really a beautiful woman who could fly. She collected sun for the fairies in the flowers…"

Chapter 18

Bee wer ov beez. A hand-lettered sign in a childish scrawl was taped to the door of the hogan, facing the late morning sun. Above the door, near the end piece of one log, hung a perfectly formed beehive swarming with activity.

Hank spied Winona in front of the house walking slowly around an oak tree, its huge above-ground roots forming a knobby circular step. She saw him and called out. They started towards each other.

"Wait," she said, and broke into a little run, ending in a triumphant if wobbly cartwheel.

"Well done, Winona."

She looked pleased. A small bee rested on her knee for a second, then lifted lightly back into the air.

"Are they bugging you?" He smiled at her.

"Well...they're beeing. Are you beeing, Dr. Cleary?"

He looked at her then, in her summer play clothes, her child's face calm and serious in a way he'd not seen before. Winona, having spent most of her young life in Wisconsin, was in many ways the most Navajo of the Yazzi children. "I'm trying."

He squatted down next to her, his eyes level with hers. "This is for you. I brought it from Chicago." He placed a small leather pouch into her open hand. Multicolored marbles fell from the pouch and glinted in the sun.

"Oh...the worlds!"

"The worlds?"

"*You know*," she said patiently, "the ones you see when you dream."

They were both seated on the grass now. "*Ahyéhee'*, thank you." She put her little hand into his large one. "Sometimes there are fairies in the apple trees."

"Are there now?"

"Yes. They come when the lambs are born, and the flowers are new. They were here when Beulah was her old self. They have white wings and white dresses made of petals. They have bare feet and sit in the trees very still. Fairies are in the cherry trees too, but their wings and dresses are pink."

"And what do they do, *mavourneen*?"

"They're dreaming mostly…about other times."

Hank stroked the hand clasped within his own. "Did you know there are little people in Ireland too?" Winona looked up at him. "They're called the *Sidhe*. Fairy folk are in the wind, in the hills, and in the fire. A whole enchanted group of them live in lakes and rivers, and in the sea."

"First Man and First Woman came up through a lake, surrounded by the sacred mountains," Winona said.

"A long time ago, in Ireland, you could move into the world of the fairies after a storm or by stepping out of the woods." He smiled at her. "Leprechauns are some of the little people. They hide crocks of gold at the end of a rainbow."

"Rainbows give protection to *T'áá Diné*," Winona offered.

They sat in companionable silence. A yellow and black bee bumbled close to the ground like an overloaded cargo plane. A breeze stirred in Yazzis' yard.

"Is Beulah home?" Hank asked.

"No," Winona replied, as they got up from the ground. "But," she said hopefully, "Livy's here." And as he rose to his feet and straightened up, Hank saw her walking from the direction of the garden, out of a patch of shade, a spill of sunlight caressing her face.

Livy wore a loose sleeveless dress, a faint pink orange like the early hues of sunrise. She had taken off her shoes and was walking barefoot in the grass. As she came closer, Hank could see the dusky shell color of her arms and legs and the skin on her face.

"It's a luminous day, isn't it?" he said.

"Yes. And hot."

"Do you think it's going to rain?" Hank was noticing how one corner of her mouth did not come quite up with the other when she smiled, the lilting sound of her voice.

"I hope so. The ground is gasping for water."

"You look," he hesitated, "good." He took a white linen handkerchief out of the pocket of his shorts, wiped the sweat from his forehead.

"Thanks."

He sensed a careful courtesy, as though she might be weighing the memory of his sudden departure from the café before he'd gone to the city.

"How was Chicago?" she said.

"Oh, a lot of people…. It was good, saw some old friends. I almost made it to Wrigley Field for a Cubs game, but not enough time." Livy moved to sit down under a maple tree. "Let me help you." He put out a hand.

"I can do it," she sat down cross-legged, smoothing the thin material of her dress over her lap. Hank settled for seating himself on the ground nearby, keeping a little distance.

They sat in light dappled by the maple leaves. "How's the fire department?" he ventured.

"Great!" She smiled at him. "We checked the hoses and equipment yesterday, and we're going on a practice run next week."

"How's the man out on the lake road?"

"What man?"

"The one on the fire squad with you."

"Good, I guess. His wife's expecting."

The conversation had taken an upswing. "I heard you're part Irish," he said.

"Yeah, my mother's grandfather. I've known for a long time, but I've been thinking about it more recently." She shifted her weight. "Tell me about Ireland."

"Ireland. It's beautiful. My father liked to tell the story about the Irish guy who picked up a handful of Irish soil to take with him when he died. But St. Peter says to him 'You can't bring anything into heaven with you.' So, the guy had to drop the bit of earth. Then when he got *inside,* he found out heaven *was* Ireland. The whole place was Ireland!" Hank spread his arms wide. "We're an understated people, we Irish." He winked at her.

"I see." She smiled back at him.

"Ireland. The stories, the poetry…the smell of a peat fire…the music. I love the *sean nos*, the old songs, sung without any accompaniment. When my grandfather lived in the old country, he was a fisherman in Galway Bay, and he made four-man currachs, the boats they used. Sometimes he went out to sea in a larger boat. It was backbreaking work, hauling in the fish, and they didn't come back in until the boat was full."

Livy was leaning on her elbows stretched out on her back, watching Hank's face. She gave him an encouraging look.

"The first time I went over it was May. I was young, barely twenty. The heather was beginning to bloom, bushes of yellow flowers. And the cherry blossoms, and violet and white daisies, holly trees, and cedar trees, and that famous tree that creaks with the wind." He had walked everywhere, only the wind and steeper hills slowing him down. In the early seventies in Ireland, bicycles were too dilapidated and fragile to ride around on, and cars were generally few and far between. "I remember getting my clothes stolen by a tinker while I was taking a swim and being shot at near the border with rubber bullets by the *gardai* from the North.

"My people lived on a little island off the west coast of Ireland— an island by an island. I went fishing with my cousins. We caught pollets with a net, lobsters, and crawfish in cages off a trawler. I saw seals and sharks. We had lunch cooked on the trawler over a gas burner. The mackerel were swarming in the streams by the end of May, and we ate mackerel for high tea."

Livy looked at Hank, animated and flushed. This was a man she had not seen before.

For his part Hank basked in the pleasure of his memories. At the same time, he felt the presence of the woman next to him, her body, the way she draped the back of one arm in the grass over her head, her gaze, her listening. Her scent wafted to him on the warm air—jasmine, and something else, something indefinable. Like oranges. Or maybe the *feeling* of oranges.

The July day was in full bloom, quiet, dreamy. Hank had that funny dislocated middle-of-the-summer feeling—people off, not working— as if the whole world had taken a time out, like time suspended. What were Neruda's words? *Let us build an expendable day without winding the hours....* He lay down on his side, head propped up on one elbow, watching Livy who was looking up into the branches of the tree.

"I'll tell you a secret," Livy said, her expression serene. "I enjoy this weather…it suits me." She sat up. "What does it mean to be Irish, to you?"

"Ah…well," he said. "It has something to do with being a little crazy."

"Come on." She looked impatient.

"Well, there's Ireland, and then there's the Irish. There's the country and then there's the people. Being Irish is bound up with the sad and glorious history of the country."

"What do you mean?"

"It's in the DNA, I think—the sadness. *An Gorta Mor,* The Great Famine—from 1845 to 1850 - was what really broke our hearts. Before had been centuries of struggle and poverty, and lesser famines. But *An Gorta Mor* was agony.

"The potato crop was plagued with a fungus. There were eight million people in Ireland in 1845. A million starved to death. Hundreds of thousands died of famine-associated disease. Another million and a half had to emigrate, to scatter outside Ireland. It was our diaspora. Almost half the population lost in five years."

"If the potato crop failed, what could have been done?" Livy sat facing him now, her face serious.

He studied her for a long moment. "There was more to it than that. It was an artificial famine. Despite the blight on the potatoes, there was plenty of food in Ireland to feed the people, but it was exported by the British government. The potato crop failed repeatedly all over Europe. The difference was other countries closed their ports to protect their people. Ireland's ports were not closed."

"*Dios mio.*"

"They write about the laissez-faire economic policy of England at the time, things like that. In the end, it had to do with priorities, and Irish lives were not a priority." He paused. "We can work on forgiveness, but we have to remember."

Tears welled up in Livy's eyes. For an instant, Hank regretted bringing this story into the middle of their summer day. But it was a story he needed to tell her. "There was a long history of persecution before the famine, of course—religious and ethnic. Even in the early twentieth century, we Irish were still portrayed as monkeys in British and American newspapers and books."

Livy moved closer. She sat still, her knees drawn up, bare feet on the grass, arms hugging her legs.

"For the first time in hundreds of years," Hank went on, "there's money in Ireland. But as the poet said: 'Being Irish, he had an abiding sense of tragedy which sustained him through temporary periods of joy.' For so many, especially the old people, there's the habit of sadness. It's the long carrying of the sadness in their hearts."

"The carrying of sadness...." Her eyes were on him. "Maybe that's why the Irish in the Republic can't really get into the peace accord with the North of Ireland. They might have to give up being sad."

Hank stared at her. "You might have something there. Did you ever wonder what else rides along on our genes, besides how tall we are and the color of our eyes? ...how much sadness, and anger, and faith?"

They were silent. Then Livy said, "I never thought about it that way." She rose, stretching her arms and legs.

"God, Livy, what a story for a beautiful day!"

"It's okay, Hank. I wanted to hear it."

He wasn't so sure it was okay. She had lost her peaceful, relaxed expression. She looked bereft. *We like good times too*, he wanted to say. Instead, he said, "Let's go for a walk."

Winona appeared again, walking around from the other side of the farmhouse. She tagged after them out to the country road, trying to whistle—Old Harry had taught her, but her whistling was sibilant and erratic these days because she had recently lost her two front teeth. Hank and Livy's eyes met over her head, and they had a hard time not laughing. They were glad of the diversion.

Out on the road, alone again, they fell into step. "President Clinton's a consummate Irishman, when you think about it," Hank said as an afterthought, "charming in a circle of people, given to excess."

"Are you like that?"

Hank smiled. "I have potential." He cleared his throat. "That's a lovely dress."

"My dress?" She appeared startled. "Oh. Thank you."

"How are things going, as far as...the baby?"

"So far, no go," she said, without breaking her stride. "They're going to take a look at my tubes in a couple of weeks, make sure they're open, and that my uterus is normal."

"I want you to know I'm pulling for you. Waiting can be tough."

She looked up at him. "*Gracias*. I'm fine. I've got Alex, and Alice, and Elrita. And Mary."

"Mary?"

"You know. Mary, the Blessed Mother." They slowed their pace on an incline in the road. "I like Mary. Such a strong, sturdy woman-saint. She was really a *compasina*. I mean, she lived in a cave after all, had her baby in the middle of a bunch of animals. A lot of my *gringa* friends in Chicago were adding her in as a goddess, you know, to give her her due as the mother of God. The Church basically having laid her out as such a wimp."

Hank's mother, who had prayed the rosary daily to a pale lady in a white gown and blue veil, was probably turning over in her grave. Hank was enthralled.

"I wanted to visit my old church in Chicago," he said, "but it was locked. It was...I felt...let down."

"Too bad."

"My old parish was run by Franciscans. They say the Dominicans are the teachers, the Jesuits the thinkers, and the Franciscans the lovers. 'You'd be so Franciscan,' my sister said one time, 'if you weren't so complicated.' St. Francis, the saint of simplicity, the crazy saint – the one for me!" He chuckled.

"Elrita says the Franciscans brought Christianity to the Navajo," Livy said, "or tried to."

"Well, they're the agapé ones, overflowing with love," he said, "like that revolutionary, Jesus." They reversed their steps, heading back to the farmhouse.

"Jesus is cool," Livy said. "I think of him as the big brother I never had, as a kind of Jewish Brown Beret."

Back at Yazzis' the house and the blue spruce cast long shadows on the ground. "I have to get back to the café," Livy said. She ran inside to see Elrita. Then she climbed into her car and leaned out the open car window to say good-bye to Hank, smiling her lopsided smile.

Hank ached to lay a finger on the corner of her mouth. He leaned in towards her, feeling the heat of the metal chassis of the car, which had sat in the sun most of the day. The engine was running.

He wanted to say something so she'd stay a little longer. He put his hand on the car frame. "Twenty-three deer came right up to my cabin early this morning, Livy, bucks, does, and fawns."

She looked at him. "Suffering and sweetness," she said, just before she backed out to the road, "the Brazilians say they're woven together for the whole journey."

Chapter 19

Lonnie Two Rivers walked past the fast food place next to the motel in Harass. Tall weeds grew up around the restaurant. It had been a long time since anyone had driven in to the *Great Food Drive-In*.

He wore a metal necklace and, despite the warmth of the day, a jacket. He passed the El Dorado Cadillac, painted yellow tan with rust spots dotting its body like pox, parked in the same spot at the motel it had been in for weeks. One rear tire was flat under its bedazzled hubcap. A blue Chevy that hadn't been there last night sat in the diagonal space in front of the unit two doors down, fuzzy dice dangling from its rear view mirror.

He followed the cement walkway with its chipped green paint around to his room in the back. Next door to Lonnie's, mud-caked work boots stood outside the units. The guys working construction out by the highway had the day off. Later they'd wake up, sit out of doors for a while on the motel's metal chairs, line up their empty beer bottles along the outside wall, maybe offer him a beer.

In his room, he slipped a can of insect repellent out of one jacket pocket, a box of crackers and an orange from the other. He shrugged out of his jacket and shirt and kicked off his shoes. He turned on the wall fan and flopped onto his bed.

The maroon carpet bore the perfect dark imprint of an iron, and there were holes in the faded mustard-colored draperies. He was sick of the cigarette burn on the sink, the noisy old wall fan. Tired of lying on his sunken, full-size bed watching TV reruns through his toes at night.

Lonnie got a special rate in exchange for cleaning the rooms out back. Once a week he'd change the bedclothes, halfheartedly straighten up the bathrooms and vacuum the sallow carpeting. The Deep Sleep Motel was the kind of place where rooms lacked security locks because guests kept ripping them out of door jambs, and feuding lovers threw the remote controls for television sets against the wall.

One time the owner had asked him to nail a two-by-four across the door between two adjoining rooms.

Some day he would have real money. He liked to sit by the railroad tracks watching the freight cars roll by, company names emblazoned on their sides – *Santa Fe, Southern Pacific, Norfolk Southern, Canadian Pacific* – and imagine all the places he'd go when he had money.

In the meantime, he needed to get a new job. The old lady was no use to him for dough, sitting there in the trailer stuffing herself, all larded up with fat. Neither was the old man any more. Lonnie had left the Casino job three months ago. Since then, money, or its lack, had become a vexing problem.

His eyes came to rest on the tall spears with their barbed points standing in a corner of his room. They'd been handed down by his ancestors. His spirits lifted.

He was going to show Rufus Yazzi how a real Indian caught fish. And get a chance to check up on Beulah. He hadn't seen hide nor hair of her since that day by the fruit stand. He didn't think she'd spilled the beans to anyone, but he wanted to make sure, nose around Rufus.

There were other uses for spears. For instance, if you knew a man, a mean old man, maybe related to you, so mean and nasty. But still so straight. A white man's Indian, who wouldn't look the other way when you skimmed a little off the top at the Casino. What did it matter? "Them big-league Indians and their white buddies, they don't need all that money," he had told the old man, "*I* need money." Well, people pretty much got what was coming to them.

Rufus turned off the road leading to the little lake. He'd been taking care of horses and the chaff inside his sweat-soaked shirt was itchy and uncomfortable.

At the edge of the forest, a turkey vulture soared and glided on its six-foot wingspread in the afternoon sun. He loved the way light moved out of doors—how it drew you in, led you to follow it with your eyes. Leaving the road, he walked over the loam of the earth floor. Silver dollar plants grew wild alongside the path, translucent in light filtering through the trees. He spotted chips strewn around the trunk of an old pine, further up a large pileated woodpecker with its brilliant red crest.

Rufus was meeting Lonnie. When it got dark, they were going out on the lake to spear fish. He reached the rope bridge over the creek—a trickle flowed in the creek, tiny pale flowers lingering at its edges. The trail became hilly, then an opening of blue, and the path wound down to the water.

The lake gleamed in the sun. The color of cornflowers close to shore, further out it became cobalt blue. It lay nestled in the sandstone basin carved out for it long ago, leafy trees casting shadows around its perimeter.

Rufus found the thick rope attached to a branch which hung out over the water. He peeled off his sticky clothes and—with a running leap—swung into the air on the end of the rope, up, then down into the cool and wet of the lake. He came to the surface like a dog, spluttering, then dove aiming for the lower depths.

He floated on his back for a while, the air on his wet body, watching the play of light and color overhead. Then he swam to shore and got dressed.

Lonnie stood near the outcropping where they'd agreed to meet. Rufus waited, Navajo fashion, for Lonnie to recognize his arrival.

"Hey, dude," Lonnie said, "you ready to spear some fish?"

"For sure…I got a fishing license."

"Oh yeah?" Lonnie mumbled, "might come in handy."

"It's okay to spearfish, right?" Rufus said. "I mean, I didn't know if it was legal or not."

"Hey, man, the *Supreme Court* said so. They *gave* us Indians back our own rights."

"On the reservation and on open land too, huh?"

"As far as I'm concerned." Lonnie crouched down next to the water. The sun was beginning to set. Pink clouds appeared over the treetops to the north. "Let's get the rowboat."

A weathered rowboat was pulled up on the bank under some bushes. Everyone, the older kids who trekked to the lake with their fishing poles and the occasional adult angler from Alma or Harass, knew where it was kept. No one remembered who the boat belonged to originally, but everyone used it.

The two boys rowed the boat across the lake, silhouetted against the sky. The lake was without a ripple like a gray mirror in the fading light.

On the island, they turned the rowboat over on the shore and walked back into the woods; tucked among the pine trees was a shed, a blanket of soft tan needles covering its roof. They lifted a canoe, painted red and edged in white, out of the shed.

"It was my father's," Lonnie said. "It's a birch bark canoe. He made it out of white cedar ribs. He used black spruce roots to sew the pieces together, and spruce sap to keep it from leaking."

"Cool!" Rufus said.

"Yeah, a real Indian canoe. And it tracks real good."

They squatted down to wait for dark. Fireflies started to come out. Stars became visible in the sky; a wobbling star revealed the presence of a planet.

"What's happening with Beulah?" Lonnie said.

"Not much."

"She hardly shows her face any more—what's going on?"

"I don't know, she stays home a lot."

The lake lapped against the shore, shading to plums and violets. An owl hooted softly, something else rustled nearby. Rufus felt tingling at the base of his spine. "There's supposed to be spirits in the little lake."

"That's what the old Menominee say, so I guess it's true." Lonnie shifted on his haunches. "A Menominee caught a muskie here in 1949 that was 69 pounds. The mighty muskellunge! A few years later someone caught a northern pike almost four feet long. Don't think they grow that big any more."

The night became black around a sliver of new moon. "It's time," Lonnie said.

He and Rufus stripped off their shirts and carried the canoe to the water's edge, their muscled bodies an easy match for the weight of the boat. On the water, Lonnie secured a wide basket—like torch atop a curving pole to the front of the canoe. Rufus sat in the back holding the barbed spears, almost as tall as the teenaged boys. The burning torch cast bright light over the black water. In the cooling air, the torch gave off a smoky scent. The lake offered up smells of vegetation and fish from its recesses.

"Now we wait… for the torch to lure them to the surface," Lonnie said, "a little luck and we land us a meal!"

Both were bare-chested and wore shorts. Lonnie had donned a breech cloth over his shorts for the occasion. He stood in the canoe with a spear angled down towards the water—one hand balancing the spear against the bow, the other drawn back along the shaft— gazing intently. Then he lunged, driving the barbed point into the water. When he drew up the spear, a small-mouthed bass wriggled on the end.

Rufus missed at first. But when he saw a silvery fish swimming up towards the torch, his body poised, waiting, and he thrust the spear downward in one fluid motion.

They brought up walleye, muskie, bass. Intoxicated with daring, excitement burst inside them like small firecrackers. They felt eight feet tall, like they could do anything on a night like this.

Finally, Rufus said they'd caught over the daily limit.

Lonnie gave him a flat look. "Oh yeah? *We* have? Might as well catch some more then." He ignored Rufus, spearing more fish before they paddled to shore.

Back on the near side of the lake, they pulled on pants and flannel shirts and started a wood fire. Lonnie cleaned the scales from a bass with his hunting knife. He took a straightened wire hanger from a scrap of flannel and skewered the fish lengthwise, then re-wrapped the end of the wire in the flannel. They cooked the bass whole, tantalized by the aroma of the sizzling fish, the fire throwing out sparks from its spluttering juices. They were ravenously hungry.

After they'd eaten, the older boy lit a cigarette. Rufus liked the smell of the tobacco smoke.

"Sometimes I hunt for deer with my bow and arrows in this woods," Lonnie said. He paused. "How's it coming with the chicks?"

"It's coming." Rufus hadn't spent time alone with a girl yet, but he wasn't about to tell Lonnie that. "...thanks, Lonnie."

"For what?"

"Showing me your people's ways."

"Oh...yeah. Right." Lonnie stared into the fire. His head swung from side to side.

They were quiet, their faces warm from the fire, backs cool from the woods around them. Then Rufus said, "There's a dance at the nursing home Saturday night. I'm playing tapes for them, if you want to come."

"Will Beulah be there?"

"She might." He wondered why Lonnie was asking about his sister.

"Well, I could come by, bring some tapes I guess. I just got the new one by Assandass."

"Assandass! I don't think the old folks would be too hot for that cutting-off-of-hands stuff, or that neo-Nazi stuff. Especially not Old Harry."

"Maybe they'd go for the Acorn Zippers," Lonnie said.

"Yeah, maybe."

An east wind picked up.

"Think it's going to rain?" Rufus said.

"The robin's song changed today," Lonnie said. "It's different when rain's coming." They stood up, and he kicked dirt into the fire.

High above, light from stars born five, ten, or a hundred years earlier bent as it came towards Earth. In the distance, lightning formed geometric patterns, rising from the horizon like a Jacob's Ladder. Out on the dark lake road, before the animals turned away into the woods, their flashlights caught a skunk, white stripe running down its black body, and a pair of wolves with eyes the color of rubies.

Chapter 20

When Alma County Nursing Home was built by German immigrants in the late 1800's, they graciously included a chapel, a library and, on the upper floor, a small ballroom. It was Elrita's idea to have a midsummer dance for the residents.

The week before the dance, staff cleared cardboard boxes from the ballroom, dusted cobwebs, and cleaned the tall French windows and oak floor until they shone.

On Saturday morning, Elrita and Beulah dragged a potted palm into one corner, set a buffet table with polished silver and napkins, hung streamers, and blew up pink and white balloons.

Saturday afternoon the Home was charged with excitement. The ballroom had been declared off limits until the dance and, since many residents had never even seen the room, this only served to heighten anticipation. Men and women of the generation that fought the big war, traded ration stamps, and planted victory gardens, daydreamed about the dances and sweethearts of their youth.

In their rooms, old people made sure to have a nap before performing a careful toilette. "I fear I've fallen into a most regrettable state," they moaned, examining thinned or thickened bodies in a mirror. But all who were able planned to come. Women who once wore their tresses in upsweeps and pompadours, coaxed thin aureoles of hair into poufs and waves, bathed with Ivory soap, laid out their best dresses, and drew nylon stockings from scented recesses of dresser drawers. Men shaved or groomed whiskers, smoothed and slicked down what hair they had, and found the suits they usually wore for funerals at the backs of their closets.

By six o'clock in the evening, the dance was underway. The smell of freshly cut grass came in through the open windows, mingling with the scent of White Shoulders and Old Spice. Light from out of doors reflected facets of the cut-glass chandelier in the middle of the ballroom ceiling. The old people looked at the colored streamers and balloons, the chandelier, the shiny wooden floor, the teenaged Navajo boy arranging cassette tapes near the front of the room, and at each other. They were skittish, slightly in awe of the occasion.

"Nice to see you all gussied up," Mr. Willy said to the Ms. Barries, just as though he did not see them every day, apparently ungussied, in the hallway. He shied away from being the first to venture onto the dance floor. The Ms. Barries stood uncertainly by the chairs set up along the walls, unwilling to sit when they might be asked to dance.

But Rufus had come prepared. The first tape he played was *Moonlight Serenade*.

Ahhh...one could almost hear the collective sigh.

"Clear the decks and batten down the hatches," Old Harry, wearing a blue suit, grinned to the fellow next to him, and broke the ice by inviting Ms. Barrie the younger to dance.

"Oh my...oh me, oh my," she said and then accepted.

Mr. Willy proceeded to ask Ms. Barrie the elder, who wore a flowered red dress, "May I have this dance?"

"Don't mind if I do," she said, and soon they too were out on the floor.

The sounds of Count Basie, Harry James, Jack Teagarden, and Les Brown filled the old ballroom. Rufus played them all. Waltzes, fox trots...once he even played a Strauss waltz. Every so often he threw in a Wisconsin polka. The old folks liked the Acorn Zippers, said the music "reminded them of jitterbug." A few hardy souls even tried to dance to the Zippers.

Individuals made requests: *A Sinner Kissed by an Angel, Kissin' Bug, Ooh Maybe It's You.* An old timer asked for *Tain't What You Do It's the Way That You Do It,* sat tapping out time on a window sill, the green marble handle of his cane resting in his lap. They sang along with their favorite tunes. Louie the cockatiel perched in the vicinity of the potted palm, fluttering red and yellow feathers when the music swelled. A woman in a pastel dress wandered happily at the back of the room. Even the sour woman with the rouged cheeks swung her cane in wide arcs outside the group of dancers like a geriatric Ginger Rogers.

The buffet table was laden with finger sandwiches of chicken salad, bowls of cucumbers and carrots, pasta salad, punch, lemonade, and a large urn of coffee. Elrita had wanted light food, so the residents would have energy left over from digesting to dance. But Livy had insisted on sending over large containers of her macaroni salad from the café. "They're going to work up an appetite, Elrita," she said. For dessert, there were wafer-thin cookies and a cake Elrita had baked, decorated with white icing and fresh strawberries.

Music overflowed the ballroom, floated out through the elegant windows into the summer night, onto the balcony where old men were savoring a cigar, over the Home's small graveyard, over fields lush with vegetation. *You must remember this...a kiss is still a kiss, a sigh is still a sigh...as time goes by....*

Dancers swayed to the music, achy bones and joints forgotten. On this night, old eyes saw their way. A few individuals tilted precariously at times but, from a distance, they could have been any group of dancers.

In other places in the world, computers measured time in one-billionth of a second, and atomic clocks constructed time based on the movement of atoms. But in the ballroom, across a wave of time, Alma dancers moved to their own internal rhythm.

Old Harry was having a ball. He noticed the Indian kid when he came in, his air of bravado, the wily look about him. *That one looks like a member of the banditti. I'll bet he's had his brush-ups with the law.* But Harry was having too much fun to bother thinking about the kid, and he forgot all about him.

He had a wealth of dance partners – women happy to find someone not only alive and upright, whose parts were working, but able to get around the floor with some pizzazz. Harry liked how they felt in his arms, dressed up in their finery, and how they smelled – like flowers in a garden. He observed the old-time etiquette, his hand on his partner's back, leading subtly but firmly, both as light on their feet as they could be.

The Vagabond King Waltz began to play, and Old Harry moved out onto the dance floor with Ms. Barrie the elder.

"This one's my theme song," he grinned wickedly to the couple next to them, who had no idea what he was talking about. He overheard Mr. Willy ask Ms. Barrie the younger to dance.

"I dasen't," she said. But then she did, and the two of them were doing a polka around the floor, both turning stop-sign red—one from exertion, the other from blushing.

Partway through the evening, Harry got to play his sax, and that was so sweet he felt like he'd died and gone to heaven.

He brought Daisy a glass of lemonade. She wore a cream-colored lace dress. Her cheeks were pink. She sipped her lemonade, and then he took her by the hand and led her to the dance floor. Bing Crosby was singing *Moonlight Becomes You.*

Everyone's smiling more and more, he thought, looking around the dance floor, getting looser, looking younger. Maybe we're getting younger and younger as we dance the night away.

"I like a slow tempo that *moves* instead of dragging," he said to Daisy.

"So do I, Harry," she said. Her hair smelled like roses.

Later on, he finally sat out a dance by himself over near the potted palm. Daisy looked better than when she first came to the Home. She still tended to be quiet, but her face had filled out, and she had a sparkle in her eyes which hadn't been there before. Harry fancied her eyes sparkled more when he came around, but he didn't know for sure. Mrs. Yazzi's boy had done a good job. Not too hifalutin.' Of course, he lacked patter between numbers, but that was okay. He'd done a good job, even mixed in a few Indian tunes for variety.

A song running through Old Harry's head suddenly found its lyrics in the back of his mind: *Daisy, Daisy, give me your answer do. I'm half crazy all for the love of you....*" Harry, who spoke most of his words, sat silent. He moved one thumb over the knuckles of the other. Was it too late?

"Last dance of the evening," Rufus called, and the sweet strains of *Stardust* began to play.

Harry, stiff now, struggled to his feet and walked across the room to Daisy. He gave a courtly bow. "I'd like to have the last dance with you."

When Lonnie arrived, dancers of various styles and sizes were moving around the ballroom floor. He stood inside the doorway surveying the room. Rufus was on the far side at a table with a tape deck, sorting through tapes.

Lonnie adjusted his crotch, looked around for Beulah. An unsettling mixture of resentment and sexual longing thrashed around inside of him. Truth be told, Lonnie didn't have much success with females his own age, a year or two out of high school. They seemed bored with him, turned their backs almost before he could get started with them. He had better luck with younger girls, ones about Beulah's age. The way Lonnie looked at it, Beulah had spurned him. He wanted to touch her again, maybe *have* her this time, and he was mad as hell.

Lonnie liked to dance. He and guys he knew from the Casino had done the punk and heavy metal scene, and now they were mostly into rap and electronic music. He'd come to the nursing home to find Beulah, but Rufus had been going on about this big band thing, so he was going to check that out too.

The people on the dance floor were geezers, some so decrepit it was a wonder they could walk, much less dance. An old guy in a blue suit looked like he was having a gas attack, he was smiling so big. And the dresses on the women…whoa! Lots of big full twirly skirts… and jewelry, lots of jewelry. Two old ladies, one in a red dress, were squabbling on the sidelines. The music was corny, but he stood listening a moment longer before going over to Rufus.

"This is something else, huh?" Rufus said. "I think even Doc Cleary is coming."

"Word!" Lonnie said. He looked around impatiently. "So, where's your sister?"

Rufus looked startled. "She went home to take care of Winona. Our father's working tonight."

The cassette in the tape deck finished playing, and the old people clapped politely for a band leader long since dead, whom they saw in their mind's eye as clear as day. Rufus put a new tape into the player. "This music kind of gets under your skin, doesn't it?"

"Yeah, kind of makes your skin crawl." Lonnie felt irritated by Beulah's absence. Rufus seemed at a loss for words.

Lonnie had a glimmer he'd overstepped himself. "Not so bad, I guess. The music, I mean."

Rufus's face brightened. "Do you want something to eat? My mom's about to serve the food."

"Nah…well, maybe." He hadn't eaten all day.

Lonnie sidled over to the buffet table and loaded a plate with food. When he saw a woman with the same beautiful posture and glossy black hair as Beulah standing by the table, a gut feeling told him to avoid her eyes. He stayed just long enough to wolf down some sandwiches and lemonade. He put down his plate and turned to Rufus. "I'm out of here, dude."

The hell with Beulah, he thought. *The bitch.*

Chapter 21

Hank stopped off at the dance on his way home from a house call. "Livy coming?" he asked Elrita.

"Her extra waitress for Saturday night is having car trouble, so Livy might not make it."

He stood off to one side against a wall, eating a chicken salad sandwich. He imagined Livy arriving later in the evening, smiling, maybe a little out of breath, what he would say to her, what they might talk about.

"Did you know it's a Blue Moon out tonight?" he said to Elrita between swallows of his sandwich. She shook her head. "People think when there's two full moons in one month, the second one is a Blue Moon, but that's not right. It was originally based on the Gregorian calendar, and a Blue Moon is *really* the *third* one in a season containing *four* full moons, so that all the other full moons will fall at their proper times in the year." He looked at Elrita expectantly. She regarded him politely, but in a manner that suggested he'd told her more than she needed to know.

In my head again. *'Full Moon and Empty Arms'*—they ought to play that one for me. A glass of the *poteen* would go down well, but certainly there's none in the punch.

Alice looked downcast. Alex was out of town - once in a while she disappeared to Madison, then came back refreshed, glad to be home. Elrita enlisted Alice to pour beverages.

The residents, even notorious ogres and the addled, were on their best behavior. "How do you do?" they said and, "Pleased to meet you."

Alice's lovely brow smoothed. "A fine *soiree*," she said to Elrita and Hank, "the *fleches d'amour* are flying tonight."

"What?" Elrita said.

"Don't you see? So many are flirting shamelessly. Such *rapprochement!*"

Hank looked around. It was true. Residents who ordinarily cut each other off in the dining room to get the last biscuit, deferred to one another in charming ways.

"May I sign your dance card?" a portly gentleman said softly to an equally plump lady as he handed her a plate of cookies.

The younger Ms. Barrie batted her eyelashes as she turned to the handsome man beside her and said, "The lavender is lovely in the garden this year, isn't it?"

Hank leaned back up against the wall of the ballroom. One of his patients, a green-handled cane resting on his knee, brushed crumbs from his beard, Molly the tabby curled up in his lap. A couple men were talking about the new woman, whose name had turned out to be Daisy. "She's still in her sixties," one said, "…a beautiful girl. God, she's got beautiful skin. She doesn't weigh over a hundred pounds. She was a dancer at one time. She's in my exercise class."

He noticed Old Harry slip out of the ballroom. When Harry returned, he carried a worn black leather case. He stepped up to speak to Rufus. Rufus nodded and put on an Ellington recording. Old Harry opened the case lined with maroon velvet and took out a saxophone. He changed the reed and fiddled with the mouthpiece. When the music got to the tenor sax solo—*All Too Soon*—Rufus turned down the volume, and Old Harry pulled up a chair. "*A tempo*, boys," he said, and sat in with a band playing over half a century earlier.

As Harry played, Hank felt his fatigue slide away. "Look at him," he said to Rufus. "It's humming! He's purring! He's still got his chops, even at his age!"

When the number ended, there was loud applause. Harry walked over to Hank. "Hi ya, Doc. Did I pass muster?"

"Harry, man, you were more than alright!"

"Just one of the gentlemen of the ensemble," Old Harry said, barely able to contain his glee. "I'm approaching Methuselahood, so I figure I might as well enjoy myself before I get my ticket punched!"

"You were terrific," Hank said.

"Thanks. Well, you know, the bands had maybe a dozen and a half musicians, and it was fun to play around with the time signature. It was like when you go to put the electric plug in the wall outlet, and you got to fit the small prong in one side and the big prong in the other. But you can't really *see* the difference, so you *feel* it, feel the edge of the metal going in. You sort of want to *find out* if it's gonna blow the circuit, or light up the room.

"That's the way with the music. You just let loose into it and find out what happens – see what lights up." He paused. "It's harder to do that…play around," he said in a more subdued voice, "when the other guys are set." He waved a hand in the direction of the cassette player. Then he recovered his buoyancy. "But I had more fun than the law allows."

Rufus had dug up tapes of old ballads somewhere, and about nine o'clock he played *Stardust*.

One of the more courageous widows invited Hank to dance. "How about it, Doc Cleary?"

They *are* short on men. "I'd be pleased," he said and found himself out on the dance floor.

How did this happen? He hadn't danced in years. He looked at his partner. He felt that initially she'd relished the honor of 'dancing with the doctor,' but now she smiled at the pleasure of the dance itself, at the music, at him. She had a faraway look on her face.

The widow's eyes refocused on Hank. "This song was playing when I met my husband at the canteen."

He felt a surge of warmth for the worn woman in his arms. "It's a beautiful song." His arms and body remembered holding Sarah on a dance floor before the cancer.

Laughing with her on a dance floor, her breasts soft against his chest, her slender hands in his, as she teased him about his hair. "Even dressed up for a dance, that Irish hair of yours sticks up all over!" Now he ran his fingers through his graying reddish hair, smiling.

In the middle of the room dancing, Hank watched Old Harry and Daisy and other couples, some his patients, circle around him. An image of Livy flashed before him, moving about the café, her eyes bright. He felt a pang of longing for things he had given up hope of having.

Sarah had come into his mind so gently. For the first time since she'd died, he was remembering her without pain.

Chapter 22

"You guys gonna order?" At Livy's Bar and Café five old guys, breakfast regulars, sat at a round table near the window leaning back in their chairs. Livy knew she sounded crabby, but she couldn't help herself. It was August, and she wasn't pregnant. She was used to making decisions and having them happen, doing what she wanted. She was tired of waiting.

Now the fertility doctor wanted to biopsy the lining of her uterus to see if it had the right kind of "secretions to support an embryo." *My body can support a baby*, she thought, *and my body no es contento with all these invasions.*

In the kitchen the back door stood wide open. Outside one of the Willy boys unpacked a watermelon from a cardboard box and threw it into the waiting arms of her young waitress, who hoisted it onto the counter. The aroma of eggs and corned beef floated nearby.

"Your order is up," Livy snapped at the girl, "and when you come back make up some lettuce salads. The ham went bad, throw it out," she added.

The teenager's face took on a baleful expression, which finally caught Livy's attention. *"Lo siento!"* Livy hugged the girl, "I'm sorry!"

Livy placed a two-pound can of tomatoes in each hand and lowered and raised them, her eyes on the fields stretching out beyond the back yard of the café. She washed her face and neck with cool water and tied her brown hair back with a piece of red ribbon. She pulled hot rolls fragrant with yeast from the Garland oven. Then she left to pick up Winona.

The carnival came to Alma every year in August. It occupied a meadow, a half-acre just outside town, where the grass was cropped short for its arrival. A small carnival, family-owned, it had no sideshows, shooting galleries, or games of chance. But it had seven rides including a train called "the old special." Not *carnaval*, but Livy liked it.

As Livy and Winona made their way through the woods to the meadow it was hot, an over-ripe summer day, clover browning around the edges, the whiny hum of cicadas filling the daytime air. Trees and bushes still held onto all their needles, cones and leaves, but everything was just past green.

"You're a sight for sore eyes!" the carnival owner said to Livy.

"Hi," Winona said.

"Hi yourself." He grinned down at her.

"Hey, Ben," Livy said, "What's happening?"

"Oh, you know, back again...." He mopped his brow. "Like a little old steam bath out here, isn't it?" A cicada flopped onto the grass beside them. "A prehistoric remnant of a creature," Ben said, "they should be heard only, if they have to be, and not seen."

Only a couple women with small children strolled around the carnival. One of the women had the rounded belly of pregnancy. Would that *ever* be Livy?

"Not many people coming out on a day like this," Ben said. "Heat index up to 105, I heard," she murmured.

"Hot enough to be killing the fish," he said.

Winona wore a lightweight top, but over that she had put on Oshkosh jean overalls. Her brown cheeks were pink with excitement and warmth. "Rest," Livy told her. Livy bought cool drinks and a crispy funnel cake dusted with powdered sugar, from Ben's wife who ran the concession stand.

In the shade of a tree, they sat sharing the funnel cake. Livy considered Hank Cleary.

A Chicago guy who loved Ireland. Muy Guapo, handsome...y complicado.

"Mmmm..." Winona said.

"*Si*, delicious." Livy rested her arm lightly around the little Navajo girl's shoulders.

They looked around at the rides: the small planes in primary colors suspended on three wires; the tubs o' fun or barf buckets as the older kids called them; antique cars in hues of pink, army green, bright red, yellow orange, dark red, lavender, and blue; the combination ride with motorcycles, fire trucks, open-air buses, boats and race cars; the Ferris wheel; and the merry-go-round.

The owner ambled over again. "I'm forgetting myself," he said to

Livy and Winona. "Welcome to the carnival," he gave them a bow. "My grandfather started it fifty years ago, for no other purpose than for play, for children to be children, and for children...and people...to play. All the young children my father and grandfather put on the carnival for are older now, but they don't forget. *The seasons they go round and round,*" his weathered voice softened a little, "*And the painted ponies go up and down.*"

"That merry-go-round was made by Parker Carrousel Factory," he went on, "out of cast iron and aluminum, not out of plastic and fiberglass like the newer ones. The animals were made from a wooden mold in the old days, so they have a lot more details."

Livy and Winona studied the zebra, the pig, the tan dog, the large white rabbit beside a reindeer, a rooster with yellow running legs, a pink elephant side by side with a brown donkey (the "presidents"), the baby horses, chariots, and full-sized horses—some rearing with molded manes flaring, others with heads down.

Winona looked thoughtful, as if she might be wondering which animals moved up and down or trying to recall how fast the ride circled around. Real baby ducks quacked nearby. "I'm daydreamed," she said to Livy.

Around the center of the carrousel hung mirrors adorned with white filigree and blue. On the canopy, triangles the color of orange sherbet alternated with large ovals containing paintings of a blond turbaned man, a pirate, a woman, and an Indian with a fish behind his neck.

"The carrousel," Ben waxed lyrical to Livy, "has music, sculpture, art, painting, and movement." He ducked his head then, embarrassed at his expounding. He turned to Winona. "Do you know why the rabbit and reindeer are right next to each other?"

She looked quizzical.

"Because they both go around the world in one day."

The Louis Armstrong melody playing in the carnival meadow ended, and the owner switched on carrousel music. The tinny music, a blend of organ and mandolin, signaled that the merry-go-round was starting up.

"Do you want to ride?" Livy asked Winona.

Livy saw her finger the pocket of her Oshkosh overalls, feeling for Carmelita, but Winona had forgotten her today. "*Oh!*" she said in Navajo, "Yes!"

She ran to the merry-go-round, held her chin in her hand for a moment, then climbed fearlessly onto the back of a prancing and rearing white horse forever frozen in time. A carny worker in a Garth Brooks T-shirt and missing all but a few teeth, pulled the lever and the carrousel began to rotate.

Every time Winona's horse came around to the side of the carrousel where Livy stood, Winona carefully lifted one hand off to wave, and Livy waved back. Once when Winona disappeared from view, Livy saw another pregnant woman enter the carnival grounds leading a toddler in a blue sun suit by the hand. The muscles of her chest tightened. *Otro!* Another one!

Then Winona's small face reappeared, flushed with pleasure, eyes searching for Livy.

So Livy waved again and smiled.

When the ride ended Winona jumped down, calling "Did you see me, Livy, did you see me?" She tripped running and fell hard onto her knees.

Livy wiped her tears and rolled up the legs of her overalls. Winona's knees had shredded skin but were mostly intact and not bleeding. "You'll be okay, *m'ija*," she said. "I used to skin my knees all the time when I was your age."

She gingerly touched the blue-violet bruise blossoming on her own skin, where she'd bumped her shin on the fire truck the last practice run in their turn-out gear.

Older children began to show up at the carnival. "Time for calliope music," the owner announced; he pronounced it KAL-ee-ope. He sat down at the keyboard and the sound of steam whistles began to puncture the air.

"Gadzooks!" Winona said. "That's what Alex says sometimes."

"What?" Livy bent over to hear better.

"Nuthrwrdz," Winona said into her ear, "too noisy."

After a ride around the carnival perimeter on the train, they stood in line for the Ferris wheel. It was only a twelve-seater, but they both loved it. Livy knew Winona had saved it for last.

Ben helped them onto the red seat, and they placed their sandaled feet on the faded blue footrest. He latched the safety bar over their laps.

"The world's fastest Ferris wheel," he said, as he did every time, he started it up, "able to make the old feel young, and the young feel old."

The Ferris wheel lurched slightly, just enough to thrill the pits of their stomachs, and inched up. Up and forward, and down, and up again, through the warm summer sky. Their seat rocked slowly in the still air. When the Ferris wheel stopped to take on new riders, they rocked more and Winona clung to Livy's hand, especially when their car happened to be at the top. But Livy suspected Winona secretly hoped for other riders, so they could sway and rock again before they had to get off.

"How many times have we gone around?" Winona asked. "I don't know, *m'ija*," Livy said.

From atop the Ferris wheel, Livy saw the carnival spread out before her. She could see the pregnant women moving on the ground below. A small gust of wind blew by. The seat rocked, and then, supported by the struts of the large wheel, steadied and balanced itself.

She pressed the palm of her hand on the flat on her belly between her waist and breastbone. She felt a sense of power.

She laughed deep in her chest, tasting the wine of her laughter.

"All right," she said under her breath, rolling her eyes heavenwards, "*sea como fuere*, it's your call."

Chapter 23

Summer had dried around its edges, become blurry, lost its outline, like a woman who had spilled herself out giving birth to many children. But it had rained last night and there was moisture in the air.

Hank and Joe left Joe's old farm truck out on the road and took the path down to the lake. When they reached the creek, it was swollen, and cream-colored mushrooms with orange centers had popped up around it. They set their fishing gear on the ground and bent down to pick watercress for their sandwiches.

Hank had been spending time alone at the little lake. On his days off, he walked the three miles from his cabin with a walking stick he'd fashioned from a fallen branch. He really didn't need his *shillelagh* on the gentle inclines, but he liked the feel of it in his hand. Other times he jogged. Over the road and the ravine, onto the woods trail, and down to the lake, enjoying the rhythm of his own breathing, like the measured pants of a dog, and the good ache in his thigh and calf muscles afterward. He needed time to not think.

The little lake had never owned a proper name; it was just known in Alma and Harass by what it was. He rested there, grateful for the water, the air, the trees and the sunshine.

But he liked overcast days, their inwardness and containment. Sometimes sunny days felt too expansive, like the full light pulled you out of yourself more than you wanted. There was an attractiveness to grayness. Gray, and night, brought out a subtle beauty. Sounds became important.

He and Joe stood looking up at the cloudy sky. There was a sudden crush of leaves in the woods, and then a deer, not the whole animal, but the line of its back and gray-white spots through the leaves, and it was gone. At the forest edge near the lake, a short high-pitched sound distinguished itself. A hummingbird hovered, red throat plumage and the sheen of its beating feathers caught in a stray cast of light.

On the bank of the lake, they settled by a fishing spot they liked, fairly deep, where an old fallen tree was submerged in the water.

Joe put a can of moist dirt and Canadian crawlers under a tree. Hank tied hooks to their lines with the easy clinch knot Hank's grandfather had taught him long ago. He showed Joe how to spit on the knot and use the lubricating saliva to tighten it. "You don't want to put a line in your mouth any more, not after it's been in the water, that's a good way to get Giardia."

Hank took a minnow from the live bait bucket, put a hook through its back so it could still swim, and handed the bucket to Joe.

Joe lost his grip and the live bait pail dropped to the ground, water sloshing over its edges. He rubbed his fingers together.

"You okay, Joe?"

Joe didn't answer right away. A white person's question, Hank thought – not asked at home where the words weren't needed, and not at work where Joe's condition was of secondary interest.

"I can't feel my fingers so well," Joe said.

"What does Warren say?"

"Not much."

Hank placed his tongue between pursed lips, blew out a long breath. "I'm sorry." High time to put a bug in old Warren's ear.

They sat near scrubby evergreens and skinny birches, poles out over the water, fishing lazy, hoping for Northern or bass. They'd fished together before, relaxed but with little conversation.

"Still warm," Joe said, "a little cooler though."

"Maybe they'll bite better. In this kind of light bass'll bite on anything that looks like a frog."

The wind blew raindrops off the leaves onto their bare arms. Close to shore waterlilies, spread in a spiky bloom yesterday in the sun, were cupped today. Water gliders skated near the submerged tree. A dragonfly rested on the water, its huge green-gold wings extended out from its spotted red thorax. Hank wondered how it could balance.

"You know what Alex said to me the other day?" he said. "What?"

"I told her I'm working out again, you know, running in the woods trying to get back in shape. She says 'Good for you, Doc.' I believe her exact words were 'it's good to blow your gaskets out every so often.'" He grinned. "Then, she just gives me this *look*, and tells me something she read on a billboard somewhere – 'Eat right. Work out. Still die.' Nice, huh?"

Joe remained silent, and Hank remembered Elrita telling him

Navajos do not like to talk about death for fear of speaking it into existence.

He changed the subject, talking in a quiet voice to not alert the fish. "What is it about women, Joe? They're so…desirable, but they're frightening. The power in their smiles, their voices! They open up something inside you that you can't quite name. They *know* things. They've got this way of looking at you like they're looking way down into you."

"I know." Joe had a tug on his pole, and played his line a minute before it went slack. "Women have the power among the *Diné*. Every person is valuable, especially children. But lineage is through the women. Your clan is from your mother's side, and women own the line. The children belong to the women." He paused. "Navajo men cannot look at their wives' mothers or talk with them."

"Why?"

"That's just the way it is among our people. Women have the power."

Hank readjusted his hold on his fishing pole. "Women are bewildering to me. Sometimes I can't even remember the specifics or generalities of conversations I may or may not have had with them, except for patients of course." He smiled faintly. "Take Livy, for example. I was in the café the other day and she seemed glad to see me." He'd ordered grilled cheese and a bowl of soup, the café redolent with the smell of fresh bread baking, and diners eating long ears of sweet corn dripping with butter. He'd been in a good mood. "She sat down at the table and we talked. But then she started to look weary and, before I knew it, she looked *mad*."

"What did you talk about?"

"We-ell…I told her about delivering Mr. Willy's niece's new baby, her fifth, a healthy nine pounder! I made it just in time."

He had been thirty miles away and almost out of gas when Mr. Willy's niece had gone into labor. August was a lousy time to have a baby anyway, the mothers crabby and overwhelmed, blown up with puffed ankles and hands, waddling in and out of the clinic all summer. Women coping okay before, maybe not exactly happy, but at least hanging on, lost it. Mr. Willy's niece was no exception. At her last checkup she'd said, "Doc, my bladder is up around my eyes. If I have to go one more week before this baby comes, I think I'm going to throw you and me off the side of the ravine behind the Dairy Queen."

But he'd driven the distance, turned off at the tire and bible store, and got to the house in time to catch the baby, to guide its head and body through the birth canal and unwrap the couple extra feet of umbilical cord wound around its back.

Now Hank turned to Joe who sat silent, although he could sense the other man's careful attention. Joe has so much bearing, he thought, such natural dignity.

Actually, it had been worse than he told Joe. He'd heard Livy mutter *no seas pinche* under her breath as she rose from the table, a phrase he recollected from his Chicago days that meant "don't be an ass."

"Give her more time," Joe said.

"I have been giving her time. I don't believe she even *thinks* of me, that it even *occurs* to her that I'm …."

"Maybe bring her a gift –"

"A gift?"

"*Oh*, yes. Something that suits her."

Hank had a bite then, netted a small bass. He unhooked the fish, slipping it back into the water. "Joe, we've known each other a while…"

"Sure, Hank."

"I'm lost, man." He fumbled for words. "Out on a line, without a net." He studied the dark pools of Joe's eyes. "I stepped off the path, I'm not sure when. Maybe after my wife… was gone, maybe before that. I'm trying to find my way back."

"Sometimes you need to walk over uneven ground to find your way. You're turning on the path even when you cannot see it." Joe paused. "When I grew up on the reservation, my father made me wrestle a tree to develop strong muscles. Train yourself to be ready for any sudden attack, he told me. We took snow baths in the winter, and we did strenuous exercises and ran fast every morning. Today I'm a strong man, and mostly healthy." He touched his wrists. "I've created many songs, for riding, walking, planting, growing, songs of protection and harvesting, for horses and sheep, for love and romance, to greet the sun in the morning and bid it farewell in the evening. So, I am wealthy."

Hank couldn't recall his father giving him any concrete pointers. *Da used to say, Hold tight, me boyo, and Keep your nose clean.* "Sometimes it's hard to make sense of it all."

"Once Rufus and I found a nest with one egg and two baby birds.

More babies than eggs, but always an egg," Joe said.

"I don't understand."

"I don't either. But there's a spirit out there, and in here," he tapped his chest, "that does."

They fished then, listening to the birds, and the water against the bank.

When he spoke again, Joe said, "I was close to my little father – my mother's older brother. He was one of the code talkers in World War Two. They sent secret messages based on the Navajo language. Our words were translated into English and the first letter of each word used to spell out the message. Without the Navajo, the marines would never have taken Iwo Jima. The intelligence work they did for this country helped bring down Hitler. But I think hardly any of the other GIs – mostly white guys and black guys then – ever really knew it."

He scratched his head. "You're like that for us, Doc. You understand the code, so when one of us needs to get patched up, you know how to do it."

"But I don't think anybody knows who I am either."

"We do, Doc. You're our doctor."

"That's what I mean." Hank rubbed the back of his neck. "What happened to your uncle?"

"The instanding wind left him."

"In the war?"

"No. After the war, in Shiprock. He worked in the uranium mines. Cancer." Joe gazed at the lake. "I read at the bookstore," he said after a while, "that when the first radio wave radiated from Earth out into space, it became eternal. At home," his voice grew softer, "between the Sacred Mountains, the old people called radio 'the wind that talks.'"

Hank thought about language, words spoken and unspoken, heard and not heard. He thought about radio, the comfort associated with the human voice. And then of Livy's voice, the warmth of it, and the comfort.

The sky cleared a little and pale afternoon sunshine filtered down to them. Out on the lake, bathers floated in inner tubes from truck tires, motionless, only their naked arms and legs visible around the circle of the fat black tubes.

"I need to go," Joe said, "I'm on the night shift again at Harass."

"Okay."

"I'll drop your tackle off outside your cabin. *Haagoinee.*"

"Thanks. *Haagoinee.*"

The Navajo culture was one of silence; he respected the strength of that. He felt honored by the gift of Joe's words today, by what the other man had shared. Joe. His friend.

Hank walked along the shore until he found the old rowboat. He shoved it into the water, giving himself over to the rhythmic pull of the oars.

Out on the island he wandered around. Behind the shed he stumbled on something hard in the grass. He kicked aside pine needles and dirt with the toe of his boot, revealing the glint of metal. Half-buried in the ground lay a spear flecked with rust. The barbed end had rusted in a concentric pattern the color of dried blood.

I thought the tribe used bow and arrow for deer these days. Hell, I've seen too many injuries this summer. He headed for the boat.

Back on the other side, Hank reclined on the embankment looking out over the blue-green lake. He thought about Livy.

Her spaciousness of spirit—she was so impassioned. How intensely she wanted a child!

He had assumed it wasn't in the cards for him to father a child. Now, despite the craziness of the world, and in spite of his Irish DNA or maybe because of it, he wanted to leave something of himself behind. Livy was brave and stubborn, traveling back and forth to the hospital in Madison this whole summer. She didn't have to do it this way. *He could give her a baby.*

He thought about touching her, stroking her dusky skin, kissing her breasts. He felt himself go hard.

But maybe she only wanted a baby, not a man.

What if she didn't want *him*? She seemed to reach out to him. Sometimes he felt like she saw him, other times like she didn't see him at all. *How will you know if you never ask her?*

Swallows flew in and out of the bluffs, their paths through the air graceful and sure.

Hank's body relaxed. What did Yeats say? *For peace comes dropping slow…*

His mind drifted. The lure of something forgotten.

He was out of doors, seated on a stoop in a grassy place behind a house. There were other people in the house, but no one outside with him. In the corner opposite him on the greensward, on an elevated platform like a stage, actors in beautiful costumes were putting on a play, engaged in the old art of telling. 'Am I the only one to see this?' he asked himself. When they were through, the players climbed into a river and went away.

When he woke, he remembered the dream in every detail.

Now his body became looser. Then a breeze. Just barely a breeze. Not a breeze really, but a faint, ephemeral shift in the air. Like the tailwind left by a small insect, or an infinitesimal settling of quarks in matter. Some shift in his relations with the world. He felt vague alarm.

Almost before he felt it, and certainly before it began to flood his brain, all was gone: the event, the feeling, the memory of the event. He was back lying by the little lake. The flies were biting.

He began to walk home.

Near the lake he noticed a crevice in the sandstone, almost hidden by trees and bushes. He slipped inside, into a grotto of moss, about seven feet tall and twice as wide across. Shelves of rocks on all three sides completely covered with soft green moss, except for ferns visible on the ground above his head, around the perimeter of the cavern. He was enchanted. A shrine to moss.

In the woods, a tree lay in the fork of another tree, as though resting. Further along, a fallen tree split by lightning wrapped around a standing tree; they creaked together in the cooling air. A small dark animal skittered off the trail.

It seemed to Hank as though all his life he'd been a bridge person, his arms stretched wide to hold people and things together. This had entailed a certain loneliness, an accumulation of loss, a numbing of desire. What would it be like to let others extend their arms to him? Be off to the side? Perhaps, ironically, more of an actor in his own life.

He reached the clearing on the far edge of the woods. The crimson sky over Alma turned deep purple. He continued walking in the twilight.

I'm not a flim flam man. It's just I thought I was wandering, and all along I was playing both ends against the middle.

Chapter 24

After the evening meal, Elrita and Beulah sat on the back steps of the Yazzi farmhouse under the tall blue spruce. Facing them, the chalky outline of the moon rose in the day lit sky. The sun climbed down behind them on the other side of the house.

Beulah had consented to the healing ceremony. When Elrita first brought it up, Beulah had shrugged her shoulders, but then slowly nodded.

She and Joe had talked about Beulah in bed last night. "It's time, Joe."

"*Oh*," he said, a catch in his voice. "She must be cared for so closely."

Less poverty here, not so much drinking. Still.... "Would it have been better if we'd never left the *Dinétah*, do you think, never come here?"

"I don't know...." His voice trailed off.

Elrita would have preferred to be home for the ceremony. In the canyon *where the water comes out of the rock*, where the Holy Beings taught the *Diné* how to live, the place to restore harmony to mind and spirit. But they lived here now. In Alma, this green, growing place. There were hills here but no mountains, green earth but no red sandstone. So, she'd sent to her clan in Arizona, mailing them postage out of her nurse's wages, asking for the things she needed for the dry painting: red sand, black earth, white sand, blue clay.

She and Rufus had created the sand painting beside the hogan, out of sand, ground-up minerals, and seeds of various colors. Around the perimeter they placed the four Sacred Mountains, each a different color, and designs within to show the story of the Holy People, and in the sand, they painted their trouble. Rufus added an over-arching rainbow. Elrita cooked a good dinner for her family, to give them strength for the night ahead. She herself had eaten lightly.

She was grateful it was turning cool this evening. Since they'd come to Northern Wisconsin, her family had grown used to hot summer days followed by cool refreshing nights. This summer it had stayed warm, even at night, and it was dry. There were still green leafy trees, and large swaths of green in the fields and meadows. But the corn plants were short with dull yellow leaves, and farmers in small churches across Wisconsin, heads bowed over sunburned necks, prayed for rain.

Now she sat holding the hand of her afflicted daughter in the softening sun. Maybe they ought to have stayed in the protected place set aside for them by the Holy People between the Sacred Mountains.

Elrita was seventeen when she knew she would be a *hataalli* like her father, and his grandmother before him.

She had gone with her family to a dance on the reservation that lasted five days. On the final day, the rhythm of the drums throbbed inside her. She could hear her own pulse beating in her ears. Suddenly a light seared her to the core. Then she fell away from herself.

The only one she'd ever spoken to about it was Joe, the first time they lay together. "A kind of sickness came over me," she told him. "I dropped to the ground, like I fainted, but I was awake, floating, out of my body. I was in another world. My father and others held me and stroked my face until I came back."

Her father told her about her great-grandmother, who had been a medicine woman. How, when she was young, she had taken the Long Walk to New Mexico, forcibly deported from her homeland with other Navajo. How, when her great-grandmother returned to Navajo country, she became a famous *hataalli*.

Elrita loved, too, the stories the Franciscan priest with the light in his face told, about the holy man Francis, who turned back his first night at war, and gave away everything for love. The joy he found in the tiniest insect or the tallest tree, that he taught the birds to pray. How he was a brother to all creation. Like a Navajo.

They gathered in the clearing next to the hogan. Beulah sat in the middle of the sand painting. Elrita, Joe, Winona, and Rufus formed a circle around her. The night sky was bright with stars and a full moon shone overhead.

Elrita looked around at the members of her family. They wore silver and turquoise necklaces, and belts adorned with turquoise and finely worked silver. Joe and Rufus had flat silver bracelets inset with oblong pieces of turquoise, and turquoise and coral earrings dangled from Winona's ears. She and Beulah, like Elrita, were dressed in long-sleeved velvet blouses, with full satin skirts ending at their ankles: Winona in a red velvet blouse and sky-blue skirt, Beulah a green velvet blouse and brown skirt, and Elrita's blouse indigo, her skirt purple.

Elrita smoothed her long hair, pinned back in a chonga knot at her neck, and stood up tall. She took in her family seated in the circle another time. Rufus' dark brown eyes bright, watching, a gourd rattle resting in his lap. Winona, who had never been to a ceremony before, composed, looking at Beulah, her little face solemn. Joe looked tired—from irrigating crops every day, then going to work on the line at Harass. He gazed at Beulah too, and on his face was tenderness and pain.

Beulah, her black hair plaited in a braid down her back, sat bent over like an old woman. Her eyes were half-closed, hooded. She looked like she felt safer inside the circle, not so much like a scared animal.

Elrita remembered Beulah as a young child, smiling. How they put salt on her hand when she was a baby and gave candy out of her hand so she wouldn't be stingy. Irene Tso had made tiny Beulah have her first laugh, so Irene had to provide the food for the feast that night. She'd brought over a whole sheep to roast.

A faraway train made a mournful sound. What a small group of Navajo gathered for the ceremony, Elrita thought. These four people who loved her would be *T'aa Diné* for Beulah this night. They and the creatures around them—the sheep who were like family, the sorrel horse, the nest of rabbits in the hedge, the deer in the nearby woods - would be enough. Then Elrita felt the presence of her father and her great-grandmother, and all the *hataalli* who had gone before. She could see the beautiful, lined faces of the Navajo elders, half smiles on their lips, and hear their voices like singing.

She whispered a prayer to St. Francis and to the spirits of her ancestors. She checked the four *tsaá* baskets sitting at her feet: two contained medicine bundles tied with yucca, one held prayer sticks, and another turquoise, shell, and jet. She lit dried sage and purified the space.

She waited. A night bird called, the leaves murmured in the trees, an owl whoo-o-ed. The smoky scent of sage wafted in the air. She watched each person steadily until all were watching her.

Then she began to chant.

She followed the ancient Navajo rituals. She sprinkled Beulah with corn pollen, and sprinkled pollen on the ground. She thanked the Good Spirit for his gifts. She did hand trembling over Beulah to ask the Spirit for a diagnosis of her problem. She sang the Blessing Way. Joe beat the basket drum with a stick made of yucca, and Rufus played the rattle. Again, she sprinkled Beulah with pollen, and sang the Beauty Way songs. "'When you were born, different colors and different kinds of winds entered through your fingertips and the whorl on top of your head.'"

The moon moved across the sky, and the constellations changed their positions around the North Star. Winona lay her head on Joe's knee.

Elrita sang the Night chants. The drum and rattle stayed with her voice. Beulah sat quiet and still, more upright, her face serious.

Wind blew up and lightning zigzagged off in the distance. Elrita came to the most powerful songs, by which *hózhó* is restored to a person: the beauty not separated from good, from health, from happiness, or from harmony.

> *Hózhóogo naasháa doo*
> *Shitsijí hózhóogo naasháa doo*
> *Shikéédéé hózhóogo naasháa doo*
> *Shideigi hózhóogo naasháa doo*
> *T'áá altso shinaagóó hózhóogo naasháa doo*
>> *Hózhó náhásdlíí*
>> *Hózhó náhásdlíí*
>> *Hózhó náhásdlíí*
>> *Hózhó náhásdlii*
>>> In beauty I walk
>> With beauty before me I walk
>> With beauty behind me I walk
>> With beauty above me I walk
>> With beauty around me I walk
>>> It has become beauty again
>>> It has become beauty again
>>> It has become beauty again
>>> It has become beauty again

Power flowed through Elrita out over the center of the circle. In the air the musk of something fertile and rich, fecund, old, older, turning on hind legs…limbic memory…almost out of time. She heard someone's voice moaning. The sheepdog howled. The coals banked in the shallow pit outside the circle glowed red.

She gazed at the heavens. The light of the stars, traveling through space at tremendous speed, bombarded her body. Flashes, sparkling, the cells of her body picking up starlight. Her body transformed by that light…and Winona's…and Joe's…and Rufus'…and Beulah's.

There was a moment of stillness, as though the earth held its breath. Even the drone of the cicadas seemed to cease.

She went to the Place-of-Melting-into-One above, and deep into the inner world everyone has but few travel to. Her prayer became wordless.

Elrita came back to herself in the clearing by the *hooghan*. Despite the coolness of the air, her blouse was wet under her arms and her skirt clung to her bare legs. A soft orange light bathed Beulah's body. Tears escaped between her eyelashes and trickled over her high cheekbones, then fell to glisten on the velvet of her blouse.

The day star was rising and the full moon setting; the ceremony had lasted until dawn. All the Yazzis stood up and stretched, yawning, even the children stiff after the long night. The sand painting blew away in the wind.

In the farmhouse kitchen, Beulah did not look any different to Joe or Rufus or Winona; she looked just as dreary as before. To her mother, she also appeared the same.

But Elrita's shaman eyes had seen something else in the starlit circle beside the hogan. Something dark and twisted lifted out of older daughter's body, balancing in the air above her. Torturous, like a tangle of ashes, biding its time.

Chapter 25

On the last Friday in August, Hank walked home down a back road. The afternoon was glorious, clear and bright.

That morning in between regular patients, he'd diagnosed a rotator cuff tear, treated poison ivy, removed a fishhook from an embarrassed angler's leg, and sutured the chin of a toddler who'd fallen against the family coffee table. Beulah Yazzi had come in again with a headache. He'd been glad to hang up his white coat for the weekend.

Livy's Bar and Café was having a fish boil tonight. The concept of boiling fish did not especially appeal to him; he preferred the modern Irish cuisine, fish poached with fresh herbs for brief minutes, served with new potatoes and butter. But he looked forward to the fish dinner, cold beer, and time with Livy.

Hank was talking to himself as he walked along, a sort of pep talk. *Take a swing at the bat, you boreen! This time be more careful about the subject of pregnancy!*

On one of the isolated farmhouses along the stretch of road, a dog stood motionless atop the roof, its tail a comma in the air. A stranger, a man in a jacket, shorts, and fluorescent orange socks, pedaled by on an old single-speed bicycle.

Someone else was on the little-used road. As he approached the recycling plant, Hank saw a solitary figure in the distance. It was hard to tell if the person was moving towards him or away. The figure seemed to stop walking, and then start up again; it stood still as the man on the bicycle passed. A peculiar sort of color imagery, like a photographic negative, seemed to envelop it, a trick of light perhaps. Sunlight played around the individual's head like a diadem.

Coming nearer, Hank saw that, in addition to stopping and starting, there was an odd, measured rhythm to the person's gait.

Closer still, yet before either could clearly distinguish the other, he perceived that the other walker was a woman, of indeterminate age, wearing a nondescript navy dress, her hair wispy around her head. She carried a medium-sized bag over one shoulder, which appeared to weigh her down and put her off balance.

A little way off, the woman paused, apparently having spotted Hank. She seemed to be talking to herself. *Can't make too much out of that, I've been having a bit of a lacuna myself.*

There was something familiar about the hesitant woman. Not until he was almost upon her, did he realize that the lone figure was Silent Margaret. He was shocked; he'd never seen her anywhere but the bookstore.

When she reached him, Silent Margaret stopped and stood perfectly still, like a wounded deer. Her eyes seemed to fix on a point above his left ear, somewhere off in the middle distance. Her face wore its usual blank expression.

Her mouth worked. She seemed rent with feeling.

She wants to tell me something. He knew immediately. He did not prompt her.

She struggled. Then came the peculiar chanting voice. "Good afternoon."

"Hello," Hank said. He was taken aback by the formal greeting, and how difficult it had been for her. *We're going to be here a while.*

"Rufus," she pressed on, with a passion in her voice that surprised him, "Rufus…he has…I think…he sees the letters backwards."

For a moment, her face held an innocence and vulnerability that made him remember an earnest boy who, in a time when his father was drinking heavily, took the alleys to school instead of the sidewalks. Probably no one would have ever confronted the boy in the street.

His father's imbibing, or the extent of it at least, was kept within the family, a secret of sorts. But, for a mercifully brief period, the sidewalks out front were too much for Hank to bear.

Now, eyes wet, he regarded the woman standing before him on the road. "Thank you, Margaret."

In his cabin, Hank kicked his running shoes out of the way and rooted around on his bedroom closet shelf. His sock drawer contained only rolled-up socks, white linen handkerchiefs, and a blue crystal rosary tarnished between the beads and missing the crucifix. Finally, in his bottom dresser drawer, under a hardbound copy of the life of Albert Schweitzer, he found what he was looking for—an old letter.

In his early twenties, before Sarah, there had been a woman. A free spirit, an actress friend of his sister Tara. He stretched out on his bed to read.

Phrases leaped up off the unfolded page: *you...like the comet everyone was talking about last week...flash over my horizon...an unfamiliar joy.* Then *I love you...want to tell you...can you love me?* A risky letter.

He had never mailed it.

He soaped up in the shower, letting the hot water stream over his rangy body for a long time. *Livy.* He dried himself with a soft old towel, its faded print spelling *failte*. He pulled on clean blue jeans and a green tee shirt. *Livy.* He found the blue gilt-edged bottle of cologne Tara had given him for Christmas and splashed some of the woodsy scent against his neck.

He felt a pleasurable combination of elation and fear. *How do you bring yourself to someone when you're in this state?*

He grabbed up his jean jacket in case it got cold tonight outside the café. Then he headed out the cabin door.

Chapter 26

"*Buenas noches.*" Hank stood in the doorway of the café kitchen, his reddish hair almost scraping the lintel. He leaned his body against the doorjamb, thumb hooked in the loops of his blue jeans, affecting a casualness he did not feel.

Inside the kitchen Livy, wearing an orange halter top and shorts, dark brown hair pulled off her neck, was orchestrating the components of the fish boil. She moved from counter top to stove, her movements smooth and fluid.

"*Muy buenos!*" She whirled back to the chopping island in the middle of the room to face Hank.

"You're a maestro!" Hank said.

"More like a ringmaster in a three-ring circus!"

"May I come in?"

"*Si.*" She inclined her head. Her hands were full of chopped celery which she tossed into a huge bowl of shredded cabbage. "Some cooks allow you in, others don't. Anyway, most of the cooking is going to happen outside tonight."

Hank tripped on the threshold but held onto the paper bag he clutched in his hands.

"Great sign," he said. Livy had taken down the "BRATS AND CURDS" sign in front of the Café and hung one that proclaimed "FISH BOIL FRIDAY" over a line drawing of a steaming cauldron. He grinned. "If I didn't know better, I might think you've got a Lady Macbeth thing going on here! 'Double, double, toil and trouble, Fire burn and cauldron bubble....'"

Over her shoulder, she gave him a wicked smile. "Maybe I am secretly a *bruja*."

"Bruja?"

"A kind of sorceress."

"Ah...maybe you are."

"But I know the people in Alma," Livy said. "They love fish boils. If I didn't have them in the summer, everyone in town would drive to

Dick's Polish Smorgasbord or one of those other places close to Lake Michigan for their fish boils, instead of eating here. Besides, I'm ready for a *fiesta!*"

The lambent light of late summer afternoon played in the kitchen. Against one wall stood a six-foot-wide Garland stove with large gas burners and an elevated griddle plate. From its two double ovens came the aroma of baking cherries and pie crust. The music of the Gypsy Kings cascaded through the kitchen flowing over into the back yard.

"Salt!" Livy exclaimed, "You brought me salt!"

"I thought you could use it." He felt suddenly like a 17-year-old.

"Actually, I can. We use a quart of salt for each boil—for seasoning and to boost the temperature. *Gracias!*"

"*De nada.*" Hank felt lightheaded with relief, as though coming up for air after swimming under water. "I'm here to help."

"I could use more help." Livy waved her arms around the kitchen. "Can you peel and quarter onions?"

"I've done surgery, you know," he smiled, "I ought to be able to handle a knife in the kitchen."

"We'll see." She handed him a type of large knife he'd never seen before, with a wide blade near the handle tapering to a point at the tip, nothing like the skinny knives he used to cut up potatoes in his cabin. He started in gamely.

His eyes appealed to her. "Show me."

"Okay, *hombre*, this is how you cut with a French knife: rock it from front to back – use your wrist, see?"

"My defense is, I grew up in a dull-knived household."

"*Está bien, Está bien,* you've got it!" She gave him a dazzling smile. Ordinarily Livy didn't speak Spanish to him, but in her preoccupation and excitement, Spanish words were popping up in her sentences like castanets.

Tears slid down Hank's face.

"Peel them under water and they won't make you cry," Livy said. "The onion has a soft heart, it could have been a lily." She swatted a fly with deadly accuracy. She seemed to have a semi-Gandhi-esque approach. "If an insect loses its way and wanders into the kitchen, I coax it onto the swatter and escort it out the back door. But if they *invade* my kitchen, especially if there's more than one, I cut them no slack."

The weekend waitress poked her head in the kitchen from the back yard. "There's a crowd out here, they're just gonna race us tonight!"

Livy wrinkled her brow. "I hope I don't run out of potatoes. I bought the last of them at the general store."

"If you need more, I can go to the Pig in Harass. What's life without *praties*?"

"You're an Irish *caballero*?"

"No, but my pickup is fast." He gave her a courtly bow, the skinny peel of an onion hanging from one hand.

"I didn't think you knew Spanish."

"Oh, I picked up a little this summer." He'd secretly been studying Spanish in his cabin at night.

She removed cherry pies, juice bubbling through their golden crusts, from the ovens and placed them on the counter. When she rejoined Hank, sweat glistened in the curve of her neck. Tiny beads of perspiration clung to her upper lip.

He had a sudden desire to lick her neck, and to tongue and lick the drops of moisture on her lip. He felt like he could taste her sweat in his own mouth. His knees felt weak, a sensation he'd thought occurred only in cheap novels. For a moment, he could see himself and Livy from somewhere along the ceiling of the kitchen, standing together chopping onions.

It was hard to look at her too closely.

The smell of raw onions mingled with the clear almost-autumn light coming through the back screen door. The James Taylor music playing changed to Bob Marley.

"I'm not sure 'Soul Shakedown Party' is quite the song for a fish boil," Hank mumbled.

"That's Rufus…he set it up the other day."

"Then again, maybe it's exactly the right song for tonight."

"Hmmm…." She reached across him to grab another onion. Her bare shoulder brushed against his arm.

His body moved closer to her without even consulting his mind. He could feel her feeling him next to her. They were standing so close together he could have leaned down and kissed her. He caught a whiff of jasmine and orange, and another scent like dark cherries or a dark red wine. Below, mixed in with the others, a deeper smell, like a forest pool. *That's her smell, the smell of Livy.*

Her fingertips lightly touched Hank's arm. He watched her hand move in slow motion along his skin. The fine red hairs on his arm stood up. Heat, a warm glow, tingling, all contained in her fingertips, in his arm.

Their eyes caught.

Thoughts tumbled in his mind, then disappeared. He felt as though he were falling. He sensed something powerful and at the same time as delicate as blown glass.

Hank wandered into the back yard of the café. Small tables were set up, each with a squat candle in a colored glass holder, and a tub filled with ice held bottles of cold beer and pop. Alma people congregated around the tables talking, the cornfields stretching out in the background.

Well back on the gravel, a black metal cauldron sat in a metal strut over an open wood fire.

The brawny man tending the fire was talking to onlookers. "Settlers and lumberjacks used to do this a hundred years ago and we're still doing it. I've been boiling for a couple decades now." The water in the huge kettle bubbled fiercely, steam forming above it in the cooling twilight. "Nothing beats freshly caught whitefish. You're just in time for the first boilover. Redjackets been in twenty minutes, onions and fish ten – all about done. Water's hot enough; cedar's always a quick heat. Move back, now." He himself stepped to a safe distance. "Boilover!" he shouted, tossing kerosene into the fire. A burst of flame rose five feet in the air, slopping fish oil and salt onto the ground.

"Oh-h-h!" the hungry crowd responded.

The boiler and his helper lifted the slotted metal basket containing the food out of the kettle and carried it indoors. A buffet line formed and wound single-file around the yard and into the dining room.

Livy and her waitresses dished up chunks of whitefish drenched in butter, boiled potatoes and onions, fresh coleslaw, bread, and cherry pie. She waved off Hank's offer of help. "Eat," she said. So, he took a full plate and found an empty seat, and ate with gusto, washing it all down with a cold beer.

When a whoop from the yard announced the third boilover and another line of hungry people, he persuaded Livy to trade places. The customers, most patients of Hank's, seemed unsurprised to see their doctor loading up trays. "How are ya, Doc?" they said without really expecting an answer.

He caught glimpses of Livy while he served.

Finishing her meal, she gathered up dinners to take out to Old

Harry, Daisy, and Mr. Willie who'd arrived from the Home. Arms full, she gave a friendly kick in the butt to a teenager squatted down in the doorway to get him to move. Through the open door, Hank could see Old Harry charming everyone in sight. He and his entourage appeared to be in fine fettle. The old man kissed Livy's outstretched hand as she set down their plates.

On her way back from the yard, she knelt before a little girl. Hank looked up in time to see Livy hug the child, her eyes closed, her face filled with longing. His throat ached.

After the last customer left, they dragged padded chairs from the dining room to the back yard and sank gratefully into them. Livy put her feet up on a card table chair. In the dark the candles on the tables burned low in their opaque red, orange, yellow, and blue holders.

"That was something," Hank said, "I'll bet you fed close to a hundred people tonight. The only ones missing were the bookstore ladies."

"They're on the other side of the lake in Michigan this weekend, some kind of music festival." She leaned back and closed her eyes.

"Margaret didn't come either."

"No."

"Margaret," he said, "what do you make of her?"

"Margaret is a woman who won't talk."

Hank closed his eyes. The air smelled faintly of kerosene and fish oil. He remembered being with Livy in the kitchen tonight...no words, so alive.

Her voice floated to him again on the night air. "Are you sleeping?"

"I am a tiger who only seems to sleep. There were just enough potatoes..." He was feeling his way.

"*Gracias*, Hank." She swept her fingers through her hair and gave him a smile, the corners of her mouth askew.

"We bog-trotters have to stick together."

Livy rubbed her eyes, sliding her fingers over her cheekbones. "The French," she sat up, "serve five-course meals, each with its own bottle of wine; I haven't tried that yet. But here's the best: In Germany there's a restaurant that serves food in the dark! To accentuate the taste, I guess. They have blind waiters...I suppose it's easier to serve if you can't see anyway." She sounded unconvinced.

"That reminds me of the blind opera singer from Italy," Hank said.

"Strange—all those women attracted to him, knowing he can't see them."

"They're drawn to what they think he sees behind his eyes."

Her bare shoulders gleamed in the candlelight...beautiful. He wanted to tell her that he could see her kindness, her integrity.

"Speaking of eyes," Livy resumed, "my waitress from the high school is bewitched by yours. I overheard her talking about them the other day: 'Hazel,' she said and then kind of dipped her body in a swoon."

"Hazel, who is hazel anyway?" He winked at her.

"Really, your eyes," she said, "are probably my favorite color, for eyes. Blue green, like the lake, with hints of brown." Her own eyes shone like dark amber. Alongside her Tiger lilies glowed in the flickering light.

"Brown is my favorite, color for eyes that is."

"I'll bet you would have liked some Irish whiskey with your meal tonight."

"I might have at that. I like a wee drop now and again."

The North Woods air turned cooler. Hank gave Livy his jacket. "Whiskey," he said, "*uisce beatha,* the Irish call it, the water of life. Did you hear the story about the guy from Ireland who fell into the Chicago River in winter? He was doing construction work, mixing concrete on a board support, and he tripped and lost his balance. He was covered with ice when they fished him out of the river, and unconscious, so they lay him on his back and pour whiskey down his throat. They go to take the whiskey away, and his hands come up around the bottle, and he sits right up with it!"

"*Madre de dios!*" She pushed herself out of her chair. "How about tequila, and cherry pie?"

"You are a wilding!"

"*Pruébelo y le encantará.* Taste it and you'll love it."

He rose to his feet. He felt woozy but not from beer.

"*No.* Sit down and rest your heart, as my mother used to say."

When she returned, Livy had slipped on a soft wool sweater a shade darker than her halter top and carried a tray. "Hot black coffee, with tequila back and cherry pie. *Salud!*"

"*Slainte!*"

They bit into wedges of lemon, licked salt from their hands, and downed shots of tequila.

"How do you swing it all, Livy?"

"I just do."

Hank shifted his body in the chair. "I remember when I did my surgical rotation, the Attending said to me 'Lay that suture down perfectly.' Those surgeons – they were the most into playing God! But all docs are supposed to, you know."

"What?"

"Play God."

"Says who?"

Mouthfuls of strong coffee and sweet cherry pie. In the background, Emmy Lou Harris sang her heart out. "Sometimes it is a sweet old world, huh, Livy?"

"*Si. A veces,* life gets worn down at the heels, then out of nowhere, you get a new pair of shoes, v*erdad?*"

Beyond the yard, empty cornstalks gleamed faintly under the slim moon like ragged ghosts. The red candle on their table contained shadows within its flame. Hank had another shot of tequila. "The Irish," he said slowly, "believe in a kind of grand loneliness…I don't think I buy that any more."

Crickets chirped in the quiet. "Why did you bring me salt?"

"Salt suits you. I gave you salt because…you're the salt of the earth."

Her eyes met his. "No baby yet." Her husky voice was soft.

"I'm sorry, Livy."

"They're taking it step by step, but I'm tired of all the tests."

"Maybe you could go about it another way?"

"*Como?*" She caught the note of teasing in his voice. "What do you suggest, Dr. Cleary?"

"Something a little more hands on."

"Any particular specialist?"

"Someone closer to home perhaps." He reached out towards her, then he lay back. Stars dotted the dark veil of the Wisconsin sky. "All the stars in heaven are out tonight," he whispered.

"In South America, the sky is not like this," her voice dreamy, "the stars are in different places, and they open their eyes closer to the Earth."

They gazed up. It could have been eleven o'clock at night or three in the morning. She gave him a tentative smile, one corner of her mouth tilting precariously. From the café came a song about leaning out for love….

There was music beneath the music.

Chapter 27

In early September the heat wave continued. In the Atlantic region water was rationed and pastures withered, and the Midwest remained dry. A sense of dwindling rested lightly over Alma. No one felt sad about this. People were not paying much attention to things.

Rufus sat on a tree stump behind the recycling plant, a paintbrush in his hand. Before him, another stump provided a shelf for his portable easel and a cup of water. Large stands of pines and birches flanked the recycling plant, and there was a green and gold pond a little way down the road, but he liked to paint in back facing the more open vista. He stared at the field and western sky beyond the scrub grass, dreaming.

Sometimes when he left work, the sun was already lowering on the same scene, scattering colors with abandon. He painted these sunsets, trying to capture bands of violet and pink hanging low in a Wisconsin sky. And he painted the sunsets of Navajo country, sheer-walled canyons and frozen dunes of sand changing hues of rose, rust, and lavender against the backdrop of the Lukachukai Mountains.

Rufus had been ten when the Yazzis left the Reservation, but he remembered the Rez. Elrita and Joe didn't own a camera; his parents did not like to be photographed or photograph others. But Elrita talked about Navajo country, and Rufus had seen so many pictures in books he could see it in his mind's eye.

He painted dawn: the sun rising over the blue spruce, the Yazzi farmhouse and the hogan; the sun reflecting pink over double silhouettes of mountains, red sandstone stretched all the way across the horizon.

His paintings were stored in an unused closet on the main floor of the recycling plant: buttes and mesas, horses and sheep, the corn goddess, two holy people in blue with the mountains and earth on their gowns, and a large painting he'd created of two Indians standing by a canyon with a wolf and coyote, a rainbow coming like a waterfall out of the clouds.

He'd come to accept that clouds or sky could be blue and pink at the same time, some intermediate color. He was beginning to let his paintings suggest rather than represent. He tried to paint only what he saw.

Silent Margaret was the one who loaned him the books of paintings and did not seem surprised when Rufus tried to emulate the painters. Silent Margaret with the light around her had opened this door. With the little money from his job that didn't go towards the family income, Rufus had accumulated watercolor pigments. He'd selected carefully: burnt sienna, cadmium red, yellow ochre, ivory black, sepia, burnt umber, a red shade of blue, a blue shade of green, ultramarine, viridian, cerulean blue. He liked their names.

Now he ate quickly, sacrificing water to wash down his peanut butter and jelly sandwich, and placed a piece of white paper on the easel. He'd use the rest of his lunchtime before he had to go back to work.

Rufus was tired of doing extra work for Lonnie Two-Rivers. He'd started out wanting the Menominee boy for a friend. The white kids at Alma High School were curious about Rufus since he was not Menominee, but they didn't offer him friendship, and Rufus was not good at striking up the casual conversations they favored. A couple of white guys hung on the outskirts of the group like Rufus, whose natural thoughts seemed to be on other things from the crowd. Rufus didn't think to say "way," or "like, I care not." Lonnie was good at saying those things. But Lonnie had been kicked out of school, he'd left early, and Rufus didn't think Lonnie had *any* friends, Indian or white.

Lonnie had needed money so Rufus helped get him the job at the recycling plant, but Lonnie had turned out to be so lazy. He'd thought Lonnie would be an Indian brother, but lately he wasn't so sure. Lonnie seemed to be involved only with himself. Plus, Rufus did not like the way he talked about Beulah.

Lonnie wanted to be with girls, but he talked like they didn't matter. He kept asking, "How's Beulah?" But didn't really seem to care.

Rufus loved his sister. He remembered playing the rattle at the ceremony, Beulah in the circle all hunched over. She suffered still, her face sad, and did not confide in him. She spent time alone, not with boys or girls. But the holy ones had entered their images in the sand painting that night; he'd felt their healing power. He had hope for Beulah. He would not talk about her with Lonnie.

School started this week and Rufus would be working fewer hours. When he wasn't around so much to carry Lonnie's share of the load, he suspected the older boy would be long gone. Lonnie was probably inside the plant right now smoking a cigarette, goofing off.

Rufus worked fast so the paper would stay damp. He wanted to catch the play of midday light on objects in the field, more subtle, he thought, and difficult than the light of morning or evening.

Hay was rolled up in rows in the field before him. Not the Givenchy haystacks of Monet, like small huts in a village, but haystacks nonetheless, cylindrical like giant rolls of baling wire. Rufus wanted to show the nature of the September light sifting through the dry air and over the piles of yellow hay.

He loved the brilliant transparency of watercolor, although it prevented painting light over dark as with oils. He searched for the color of the sky, combining colors as he painted. Cirrus clouds stretched across the expanse of a sky almost the color of a robin's egg but touched with gray. He allowed three tints to run into one another, finding the color. Leaving part of the paper unpainted, he integrated the white into his composition. He dragged a dry brushful of heavy pigment across the paper, letting its grain show as a speckling of white spots like sparkles of light.

If Rufus altered the angle of his body or where he sat, just a little, the scene before him shifted. Form, depth, light, all changed. In school it was hard to hold still and difficult to concentrate on his books, but when he painted, he sat for long periods absorbed. He forgot about himself and his body. As though he were in another time and place.

Right now, he was aware of the time. It was 12:20; he'd have to go in soon.

In the distance, he heard thunder. Above the trees on the north side of the plant, cumulus clouds were banking. The light was strange. The air, already fragrant with the scent of pines, contained that almost-smoky smell that comes before a storm.

On the second floor of the recycling plant, Lonnie Two-Rivers was in fact lounging on an old sofa smoking a cigarette. At least when he worked at the Casino, he thought, it wasn't so boring. The springs were shot on the sofa, but it was comfortable enough to catch some shut-eye. He'd been out late the night before, and the day was warm.

He felt sleepy.

About this time Silent Margaret was walking home from her morning's work at the bookstore, along the back road that passed the recycling plant.

She liked the back road. Fewer people, quieter, and it wasn't paved like the main street in Alma, so she didn't have to step over the cracks. The direct route to her place led past the dairy plant, where the buzz of the generator made noise that tangled with her mind.

Margaret didn't *think* any of this – she just instinctively walked the long way round. Sometimes she felt as though she were missing a filter, like the sink drain in the storeroom of Pied-á-Terre. Sounds eddied towards her in chunks, unrestrained, nothing catching or diluting them to let only the small pieces of sound through.

She liked to walk by the recycling plant because on occasion she would see Rufus sitting behind the plant with his watercolors and easel. Taking a break from stacking paper boxes and sorting metal cans and plastic containers, his handsome face turned towards the countryside, eyes lifted to the horizon. She never interrupted him.

At times Margaret's mind rocked her body on the seat of a rubber swing in an empty yard. Thinking of Rufus *en plein-air* painting beautiful pictures smoothed things out for her somehow.

September 3. An odd-numbered day, that was good. What would Rufus see today?

She reached the stretch of the hilly back road that climbed to the recycling plant; the upper part of the plant came into view. The weathered gray building had been a family home she thought. Perhaps she had known the family, but she wasn't sure. Not much seemed to have changed on the outside the building was still two stories tall with the same shake roof. Maybe more had changed inside.

Now she saw something that ought not to have been there. She slackened her pace.

What was it?

She continued to walk along the road, stepping around twigs and stones. Then she stopped altogether.

Ahead she could make out a wisp of something, like the grayish trail from an airplane. But the wisp did not stretch across the blue sky. Instead, it rose vertically above the recycling plant like a faint pencil mark. The gray mark against the clear sky made her think of having a cigarette, the tendril of smoke from the cigarette's lit end when she reached home and took that first deep puff. Then Margaret knew!

And she began to run. Margaret, who had spent her life slowing down, ran. Uphill the quarter mile to the recycling plant, her smoker's lungs and middle-aged body forcing her to stop three times to catch her breath.

Thin smoke drifted from the windows, like dusky motes of sunshine. On the upper floor, something red leapt up and licked the wall inside a window.

Off to the side of the plant, at a safe remove, Lonnie Two Rivers was sitting up against a tree. There was no sign of Rufus.

Silent Margaret ran up to the Menominee boy, breathing hard, voiceless, her question written on her face.

Lonnie's hands lay limp in his lap, but he rolled over one thumb pointing to the open back door of the building. "He went back in."

She turned and was gone, running towards the recycling plant, and in through the back door. By now the red animal jumped and crackled, reaching its sinewy arms out a window of the second storey.

Chapter 28

The volunteer fire fighter who lived on the lake road was bouncing his new baby on his knee when he saw flames coming from the recycling plant. At 12:35 pm. the call went out to the Alma Fire Brigade.

Livy phoned Hank at the clinic a few minutes later. "It's a big one, Hank. There may be injuries, or worse." She hesitated. "Maybe you don't want to bring Elrita." He knew she was thinking of Rufus.

"I have to bring Elrita. She's the best I've got," he said, "and there's no one else here." He heard the old fire bell begin to clang, and in the background the sound of a large engine springing to life. "Be careful, Livy."

"*Si, gracias.*"

When the fire truck arrived at the recycling plant, the fire appeared to be contained to the second floor. The volunteers, wearing protective jackets, boots, thick gloves, and helmets, had responded in record time. They pulled flattened hose off the truck and ladders down from the top and sides. They inflated a large portable pool near the burning plant; the pond fifty yards south would be their source of water. Rapidly they worked to connect the hoses, draw up pond water, and fill the empty pool near the recycling plant. Water began to pump through the hoses up to the fire.

The man from the Lake Road was the unofficial captain of the team; everyone trusted his judgment. Hosing down the building from the outside was not enough, he decided. They needed to go inside to fight the fire.

The guy who worked in the filling station ran upstairs to the second floor carrying hose in a heavy coil over his shoulder. He signaled for water pressure. "Hey, Chief," he hollered down, puzzled. "There's white smoke up here."

The Lake Road man hesitated for only a second. The Alma fire fighters had scant experience protecting industrial buildings, but he had done his homework. "Cut the water!" he yelled. "Get the hell out of there, Kelly. That's magnesium!"

Just as Kelly gained the first floor, an explosion shook the air. An intense plume of white flame shot up. In one corner of the upper story the windows blew out, releasing thick white smoke.

"No one in the building without a self-contained breathing apparatus," the captain ordered, and the word was passed. He distributed the SCBA masks, which provided a seal around eyes, nose, and mouth, allowing air to be taken in as needed. "Damn!" the captain said, "water to magnesium is like a match to gasoline!" He turned to Livy. "Let's get some dry foam up there." Another loud explosion sounded from the upper floor. "It's going to be tough to knock down this fire."

Hank and Elrita arrived at the plant not long after the fire truck. The firefighter who was an EMT met them as they climbed out of Hank's dusty green pickup. "Doc," he said, "there's a boy lying out near the field. I just found him. I think you better take a look at him."

Hank grabbed medical supplies and his emergency kit from the back of his truck. His eyes met Elrita's. "Let's go."

Rufus was conscious, alert and breathing without difficulty. But diagonally across his face and neck was a long slender burn about three centimeters wide, as though he'd been burned by a skinny necktie. It began in the area of his left forehead and extended distally, sparing his eyes, but resuming over his nose, the right side of his chin and neck. Bulla like tiny fluid-filled balloons had formed along the linear wound. In a few spots the skin appeared pale and waxy; the burn was deeper than Hank would have liked.

Hank irrigated the wound with cool fluids to help stop the burning process; he left the bulla in place for protection.

"I tripped," Rufus sobbed. "I was trying to get to the front door, but boxes were blocking the way." Rolled-up pieces of paper stuck up from the waistband of his trousers. "Then Silent Margaret dragged me out the back way. She went back inside for my paintings, I think. Doc, she's still in there! Someone go get Margaret," he pleaded.

"Silent Margaret's inside," Hank said, but the EMT was already headed for the plant. Hank turned back to Rufus. "Do you know what burned you?"

"A piece of rope, I think, one of the ropes we bundle papers with.

It must have been smoldering, swinging loose by the front door. I didn't see it; it slapped me in the face." He began to shiver.

Hank and Elrita covered Rufus with blankets from the back of Hank's truck and gave him water to drink. Rufus groaned.

"He's in a lot of pain, Elrita." Hank hoped she'd remember that pain correlated with a more superficial burn, and less possibility of scarring. "I'd like to give him a shot of Demerol, *Azeé*, medicine," he said in Navajo.

"Yes, *Oh*," Elrita replied, tears in her eyes.

He gave Rufus 50 mg of Demerol IM in his arm. Elrita Yazzi stroked the other arm. "You are all right, Rufus," she said, "you're all right."

Silent Margaret was found collapsed on the first floor near a closet, unconscious. She was carried out over a strong shoulder and laid down gently on her back.

On his knees, Hank examined her. "Airway patent but edematous." Margaret's chest was inert.

"She's not moving any air, Hank," Elrita said.

"No pulse." His fingers on the carotid artery in her neck.

They moved fast: Elrita's mouth to Margaret's, giving her puffs of air, Hank kneeling beside Margaret administering chest compressions, in alternating rhythm with the breaths. *One-Two-Three-Four-Five. Breath, breath. One-Two-Three-Four-Five...* Hank palpated the carotid. "We've got her back." He scanned her body quickly. *No burns, no bleeding, no penetrating injuries.*

Margaret took a few ragged breaths on her own. She spoke through swollen blistered lips in a low, raspy tone. Her chime of a voice was gone. "Rufus," she said to Elrita, "...his eyes?"

"His eyes are fine," Elrita said, "and his hands." Hank's nurse seemed to be speaking to herself as much as to Margaret.

Something like beauty passed over Silent Margaret's face.

Then she gagged and struggled to breathe. Her eyes fluttered, opened again, and saw Hank. He knew she recognized him. For the second time in a month, she labored to say something to Hank.

He leaned down and put his ear next to her mouth to listen. "...going home," she said, "going home...."

She stopped breathing for a moment and then managed a shallow breath. "We're losing her again, Elrita." *Where's the ambulance? She needs intubation.* "Check her pressure." Suddenly he wanted this injured woman to live as much as he'd ever wanted anything.

"BP's 90/60," Elrita said, "pulse rapid."

Hank put his stethoscope on Margaret's chest. *V. Tach.* He positioned the sensor pads of the automated external defibrillator to monitor her cardiac rhythm. "She's in fib!" Years of training and experience kicked in. Hank took out the paddles and placed them on his patient's chest. "Clear!" he ordered, and his nurse removed her hands from Margaret's body.

He shocked her once with no response.

He repositioned the paddles and administered another shock. *Come on, Margaret.*

Come on, Margaret. Her body convulsed, but the rhythm of her heart did not stabilize.

As per protocol he tried a third time, the AED automatically increasing the joules of electrical voltage, to calm Silent Margaret's wildly beating heart.

In the end she never had a fighting chance. Small smoke particles had penetrated deep into lungs already damaged by years of smoking. Carbon monoxide and carbon dioxide had displaced oxygen in her bloodstream. The toxins released in the fire proved lethal.

"Let her go, Hank." Elrita was speaking to him. "It's her time."

He looked at his nurse. Slowly he removed the paddles from the dead woman's chest. He closed her eyelids. He touched the odd face that no one had probably touched for a long time.

Elrita stroked her hair. Then she rested her hand on Margaret's brow in a posture of prayer.

Hank Cleary sat back on his heels and closed his eyes, chin sunk against his chest.

The fire in the recycling plant was coming under control. "I think we've got the throat of it," the Lake Road man said to Livy.

Half the building had been destroyed, burned away, and lay open to the air. In the other half, heat had shattered glass, melted fluorescent light fixtures, and scorched walls; charred paper and cardboard littered the floor. A stench of burned flesh made Livy wonder how many mice or other field animals had met their untimely deaths.

One of the volunteers kept a hose trained on the portion of the shake roof still in place. Despite the crew's best efforts, embers still smoldered on the roof, flickering into a low flame every so often.

The fireman with the hose was on the pudgy side and hadn't been doing his weight-lifts.

His arms were tired. He lowered the hose to ease his aching muscles and blinked his eyes which felt gritty and irritated. At that moment, a gust of wind tugged at the roof, lofting embers into the bushes on the uphill side of the building.

Leafy bushes grew up along both sides of the recycling plant. The ground was strewn with dried grass, pine needles and fallen branches; nearby were white birches with wildflowers scattered at their feet, a little further on the pine trees. All in all, a pretty sight. If the fire had spread south down the hill Silent Margaret had ascended with so much labor, it would have encountered the pond along its way. As it was, the uphill side of the plant was not only a feast for the eye but also a feast for the fire. The dry brush caught in minutes and the fire jumped from the bushes to the birch trees, and towards the taller pines, poised to leap into the dense forest canopy. The topography of the terrain was like a ladder for the hungry flames.

When the tired fireman lifted his eyes, the fire was already eating the brush, but it was on the far side of the building so he didn't see it. Livy spotted the fire as it jumped into the first birch tree. She and the Lake Road man had just shared a joke and relieved laugh together.

"Oh my God!" Livy said, staring.

The captain followed her eyes. "We have to save the woods," he said grimly. "The last thing we want is a crown fire, with these pumps and only pond water. Divert the guys from this damn plant except for hosing the roof."

In the plant the fire had abated, become subdued and died, almost of its own accord, as though it had tired of the game. By contrast the woods fire was doing an energetic dance, skirting the tall pine trees, flirting with their perimeter.

"Reyna," the captain said brusquely, "call Harass for backup and then go get a hose." Thunder sounded and lightning forked in the distance. "God, if it would only rain."

The fire made its leap into the canopy of trees.

"*Madre de dios!*" Livy exhaled.

Thunder came again, closer this time. Flames leapt to a second pine, and then a third.

Rain, rain... The word ran through everyone's head.

And then it did. A large thundercloud parked itself overhead and released scattered drops, then pouring-down rain, a torrent of water. The fire hissed and crackled. But it was outdone by the benediction of rain.

Within a quarter of an hour, the fire in the woods was extinguished completely and the ruins of the building sodden. The sun came out.

Hank went in search of Livy. He found her with the other volunteers sitting on an old tarpaulin they'd thrown on the wet ground. They looked bone-weary.

"What a tinderbox!" someone said. "I don't think they even had a sprinkler system."

"Good thing in a way," the Lake Road man said. He dipped his helmet into the rainwater in an upturned wheelbarrow, then splashed the water over his head.

The twenty-year-old who worked at the general store sat with tears running in rivulets down his grimy face. "He saved me." He pointed to the Lake Road man. "My leg slipped through one of the wooden floor boards upstairs."

"That fire was a beast."

"Fucking awesome."

A few of them coughed up globules of dark sputum. The overweight volunteer who had a pig farm out near Yazzis was quiet. Kelly from the filling station lit up a cigarette.

Livy, her face smeared with soot and sweat, stood as Hank came towards her.

"She didn't make it, Livy."

"Who? Who didn't make it?"

"Margaret. I did everything I could." His skin felt tight over the bones of his face.

"Oh, Hank." She took his hand. "And Rufus?"

"Okay. Burned, on his face. But he'll be all right."

"His face? Not his face!"

"Not all over. It's a narrow band on his face and neck." *Like a caul*...the thought came into his head unbidden. "How are you?"

"I'm okay," she replied.

"Well, I'm going to take a look at you and the rest of the team."

"You," he said to the pig farmer who'd had a clump of hair singed off in the back of his head, "You," he said to the kid with abrasions on his leg, and "You," he said to the coughers. "I want you guys to get checked over again in the ER in Harass. If anyone has fever, headache, or chills that lasts more than a couple of days, come see me in the clinic."

"Aw, Doc," they protested but he knew they would if he said so.

"I have to check Rufus and Lonnie, and write some medical notes," he said to Livy. "I'll be back."

"Lonnie?"

"Yeah. He's fine, scared but fine."

He and Livy stood leaning up against each other resting. In the near distance they heard the sound of the ambulance siren.

Hank pulled a pad of lined paper from his glove compartment. He would travel to the hospital in his truck so there would be enough room in the ambulance for Rufus, Lonnie…and Margaret. Rufus was stable, but his burn was on the face and bordered on third degree; he might need transfer to the University hospital at Stevens Point. Lonnie would need 24-hour observation for smoke exposure in the hospital at Harass. There was nothing more to be done for Silent Margaret. He hoped the medical personnel on the ambulance would let Elrita squeeze in next to Rufus; otherwise, she'd ride with Hank.

He sat on the bed of his pickup. At least one of the firefighters would probably have poison ivy from thrashing around in the bushes, he thought randomly. He held the pad of paper in his hand. *How do you summarize a human life?* He began to write.

9/3/99

S: 43 y/o female, smoker, exposed to noxious gases in recycling plant fire Hank paused, then added *when she entered to help a friend. Pt. unconscious for unknown amount of time before being removed from building.*
O: Unresponsive. No burns or penetrating trauma. Airway patent, but oropharynx edematous.
No pulse or respirations. CPR begun. Pt. resumed spontaneous respirations x 3-4 minutes, BP 90/60. Cardiac: S1, S2, rate 140. Cardiac status then deteriorated rapidly. Pt. developed ventricular tachycardia closely followed by ventricular fibrillation. Cardioversion attempted x 3 without success.

Assess: Cardiac arrest and pulmonary failure secondary to smoke inhalation
  Pt. pronounced dead at 1:17 p.m.

  H. Cleary, M.D.

Chapter 29

After the fire, Hank and Livy collapsed together in his cabin, sprawled on the sofa, stockinged feet up on the coffee table, wrapped in the wool of a Connemara blanket. By unspoken agreement, no fire was lit in the large stone fireplace.

Livy pulled the blanket more closely around her shoulders. Between it and a flannel shirt of Hank's buttoned up over her own light clothing, she was finally warming up. Despite her bleary state, she took in the room around her—the books, music, walls the color of cream, photographs of the Chicago skyline, and one of a fair-haired Sarah in hiking clothes outside the cabin.

"How are you?" Hank asked.

"My legs and back *estan dolencia*, like I've been running marathons!"

Hank's eyes met hers. Only Livy's head and brown eyes showed above the blanket. A smudge of soot crossed her forehead and dark half moons showed under her lower lashes.

His own limbs were clumsy with fatigue. He knew this deep tiredness as his body's letdown after the adrenaline release of responding to an emergency. He lay back on the couch.

He had built the cabin himself out of logs. He'd planed and buffed the interior to a gold-brown, caulked the openings, and sealed the wood with a clear finish so the grain showed through. Carpenter ants invaded the cabin every year in spring; otherwise, it was sound. He felt respite within its walls. He stirred honey into cups of hot tea, the sound of the metal spoon scraping the cups distinct in the quiet room. Mists swirled around the cabin and out beyond the porch in the darkening night. *Like ancient Ireland.*

He leaned over towards Livy. "We can hide out here together."

"Like we're in a fairy land," she said, "*muy fuerte, verdad?*"

"*Si*. We're missing the circles of stone, but there's oak trees enough to please the Druids. But take care," he whispered, "the fairies change their shapes and colors at every moment."

She put a throw pillow behind her neck. "*I think the fairies are co-madres*, our allies like the animals, trees, and stars."

"Hmmm…"

Wet leaves splatted against the roof of the cabin. "Margaret…" Livy said, "*pobrecita!*"

"Margaret rescuing Rufus was brave," Hank said, "but talking to me on the road the day of the fish boil – *that* was courage."

He went to the kitchen and returned with short glasses and a bottle of Jameson's. "Let's get back to our roots." He poured two fingers of whiskey into each glass, then slid his body back under the blanket. "My father's cousin told me we were descended from seals," he gave her a half-smile, "which may explain a lot. My father…the cascades of shining speeches, other times his tongue thick with drink and regret." He paused. "Then came Sarah...and then she was gone."

"I hadn't been in town long when she died. It seemed like it happened so fast," Livy said, "then you went to Chicago. When you got back, you looked pale and didn't talk to anybody. Your patients used to come into the café and say, 'We know Doc's not doing so good. He's not telling jokes when he checks us over.' You were *solo* here in the woods."

He bowed his head and closed his eyes. "I was stunned and tired," he said in a low voice. "I felt at the edge of crazy."

"Oh, Hank." Livy angled her body towards him on the couch. "In some parts of the world mourners are considered legally insane for a year. They can swear, break promises, wake people up in the middle of the night, change their minds repeatedly, even be angry at the one who dies. Don't you know we're all just a couple of odds down from the next person?"

"Livy…." He turned to her. "At some point, who knew when, undetected, one of her ovaries went haywire - it grew huge, intruding on her bowel, bladder, kidneys, and abdominal wall. The chemo killed her other ovary. It was terrible for her. There was nothing to do. She died in three months."

He took a swallow of whiskey. The ovaries that had rounded her breasts and sent surges of hormones through her body, had turned on her. They could no longer make love. No more sudden romps between the sheets. They had mourned the death of sex. "Sometimes I would get this need for her," he hesitated, "for her body, and even if she wanted to, for me, she couldn't. It hurt her, and she was too weak."

"So, what did you do?"
"What do you mean?"
"About sex?"
"I...did without."
They stretched out along the couch, limbs intertwined.
"My head is spinning," Livy said, resting against his chest. The smell of smoke lingered in her hair. He stroked her back, her breaths became slow and deep, then her body went limp against his.

He slipped her down on the cushions and covered her with the blanket. Her arm dangled over the side of the couch, and he tucked it up under the cover. He watched her sleep, her mouth slightly open, dark hair down over her eyes. She made a few soft bubbly sounds.

He pulled an old comforter and down sleeping bag from the front closet and spread them out on the braided rug alongside the couch. He curled into the warmth of the sleeping bag, his head whirling.

A car shimmied out on the highway. His eyes became heavy.

Livy muttered unintelligible words. He heard her say Rufus' name, once she cried out "lift the hose!" Then she became quiet.

"My *San Patricio*," he murmured.

Chapter 30

The news of Silent Margaret's death at the recycling plant traveled fast. A fire fighter's wife phoned her sister who waitressed at Livy's Bar and Café, the breakfast regulars at the Café passed the word in the general store, Kelly at the filling station told customers. By noon, everyone in Alma knew that Margaret had died.

Hank and Livy had set out early for Pied-à-Terre, hoping to tell Alex and Alice before they heard through the town grapevine.

They didn't talk much, a layer of something gone between them. Hank felt as though he knew Livy from a long time ago and only now come to recognize her. Cows in the fields and clouds looked different, defined in odd shapes, the horizon askew yet clean with lines sharp and inevitable.

"We brought up the sun." Livy had one sock on inside out.

He pulled her to a stop on the road. "Man, it's a beautiful day!"

"¡*Soy una mujer*! a woman!" She straightened, the back of her hand on one hip.

"¡*Claro*! You are!"

They walked on. "Do you know we've traveled a million miles since yesterday?" he said.

"You and I?"

"*Si,*" he regarded her warmly, "*and* we've traveled a million miles in space."

"In Alma?"

"In Alma we're...outside of all that. I mean here on Earth."

Alex and Alice's living quarters were above Pied-à-Terre. Hank and Livy climbed the wooden stairs in back of the bookstore.

"I've never been here before." Livy sounded surprised. "Neither have I."

On the weathered frame landing sat a metal mailbox and milk pail, both painted red. A dark green ivy plant on top of the milk pail cascaded and trailed and wound around the mailbox and banister. The brass knocker on the door was a buxom goddess. Hank hesitated.

"Venus of Willenbrand," Livy said, pounding the goddess against the door.

After a decent interval they peeked in the window, through a lush indoor garden of hanging plants, many in bloom. They made out a chaise longue with a shiny wine-colored coverlet, but no bookstore ladies. Around front they found Pied-à-Terre unlocked as usual, but a black-bordered sign was taped in the bottom of the display window: "CLOSED DUE TO DEATH OF SILENT MARGARET."

They walked back through Alma, past the café, general store and gas station, and onto the back road leading to Silent Margaret's.

"Do you think we'll be able to uncover the names of any family members?" Hank asked.

"We can try." Suddenly Livy pointed. "*Mira.*"

Hank's eyes followed hers. In the direction they headed, a dark haze covered the sun. Above their heads the sky was cloudless, sunlight yellow, but in the distance—over the remains of the recycling plant, the sun shone full and round and orange through a lingering haze.

Silent Margaret's small, rented house was hidden away at the edge of the woods. Old-fashioned snowballs spilled from bushes under the windows; no other vegetation adorned the front of the house.

Just inside the front door, a navy jacket and grey winter coat hung on hooks, above a pair of galoshes. The little house, even in the absence of Margaret, felt like an island of silence. A great stillness inhabited it, as though time had stopped, and the house was waiting for Margaret.

They slipped off their shoes.

"The house smells clean," Livy whispered.

"She must have done her smoking outside."

The living room was sparsely furnished. On a low table a half-dozen books: dog-eared copies of *The Glass Menagerie* and *Of Mice and Men,* and large books with photographs of paintings, their bindings carefully mended. On the wall behind the couch, a print of the Sacred Heart – Jesus of the wavy locks, red drops draining from his pierced heart. "*Sangre de Cristo,*" Livy's husky voice came from behind him.

A spindly plant in one corner had slipped a tendril into the water dish of the plant alongside it, forming a kind of root-leaf, tuberous and pale. An unusual cactus displayed a fresh white bloom, near a framed photograph of a doe-eyed Central American child. There were no other photographs.

In the other corner of the room was a prie-dieu. The shelf above the kneeler held a jelly glass with violets, and two holy cards of *Teresa of Avila* and *John of the Cross* placed in exact alignment.

In the middle of the ceiling, hung a spiral bronze-colored mobile. Livy's rich flesh tones lent color to the room as she moved about; when she stood underneath the spiral, it seemed to be reflected in her skin, and something of her reflected within it.

On the kitchen table, bills, a thank you note from the Christian Missions for sponsoring Esperanza Soto, and a teacup hand painted with a lime and forest green bird sitting on an apple branch in blossom. Campbell soup labels paper-clipped together in a drawer, straight pins stored in a curtain, a cross on the wall above the kitchen sink, but no indication of relatives. Hank had read somewhere that Catherine of Siena was probably anorectic. In the cupboard—pasta, popcorn, cereal, peanut butter, noodles, beans, tuna fish; in the refrigerator—milk, eggs, margarine, jam. The diet of the poor, but not that of an anorectic.

In the bedroom, a piece of embroidery with the words "Watch and Pray" over the single bed. A pair of slippers, two changes of clothing on hooks, scuffed oxfords beside a bottle of shoe polish, a particleboard dresser. Silent Margaret's imprint so strong they felt like intruders going through her drawers, for clues to her people.

The bathroom (soap, toothpaste, aspirin, over-the-counter allergy pills, no makeup) revealed nothing, except his and Livy's puzzled faces in the tiny oval mirror above the sink.

The most notable thing about Silent Margaret's house was what it did not contain: clocks, closets, mirrors, a telephone, photographs, letters, cards, or obvious souvenirs. In death, Margaret held onto the secret of herself.

"Nothing, Hank," Livy said, "not an inkling."

"I know." A feeling of emptiness: not barren, more subtle. Hank had the same feeling once before, when he'd visited the cell of a Trappist monk in Kentucky. Austere, yet something of fierce integrity. He felt humble. He turned to Livy. "Everything is of a piece here."

A tinkling sound, a sweet light sound so faint they barely heard it, came to them on the wind. Out of doors, in back, chimes sounded delicately. Nearby a metal rocker, beside it a coffee can containing sand and cigarette butts.

"What must her life have been?" Hank's eyes sought Livy's.

"*Ella estaba loca por Dios*," she said. "She had her heart set on God."

Then a louder sound, like the cry of a young child: a slender grey cat rubbed against their legs. Livy filled a saucer with food. "*¿Tu eres el familiar de ella, gato?*"

They stood together outside Silent Margaret's back door. Before them was an apple tree, beginning to bear fruit. Beyond, Margaret's stretch of woods.

"A dark woods," Livy said.

"Yes," he said, "but lovely."

Chapter 31

On the third day after she died they buried Silent Margaret in the town cemetery, a rough green place not far from the carnival meadow.

The weather forecast had been right. Under a clear high sky, the September day was mild, and the old Alma graveyard was drenched with light, as though time had folded back in upon itself and spring had come again. Livy angled her neck to look up, shading her eyes. "*Azul, azul*," she said, "very blue."

The people of Alma sat on folding chairs facing the freshly dug grave, men wearing billed farmers' caps, a few in panama hats, women in dresses, encircled by the grave sites of their relatives and friends. Probably more company than Silent Margaret had ever had in life.

Alex and Alice served as next of kin. They sat in front, Alice in a long blue gown and fringed shawl, Alex in a starched white shirt and her good brown pants. The Yazzis, handsome and tall, were dressed in ceremonial clothing, except for Beulah who wore a sleeveless dress. The Lake Road man's wife nursed her baby in back, their other young children roaming close by. Beside Hank, Livy wore black and dark red lipstick.

A south wind blew across Silent Margaret in her coffin. The bookstore ladies had laid her out. Margaret, who had worn muted tones, was dressed in a purple caftan the color of ripe plums; she lay in a pretty box, a casket of wood with white satin lining. In death she looked relieved, as though she'd finally found a place quiet enough.

The minister had come from Harass because Alma did not have a church. He had a kind face, but he hadn't known Silent Margaret. How sad for Margaret, Hank thought, to have this man who never met her extolling her virtues.

The cleric's language was Midwestern, but he had an unusual manner of speech which affected his pronunciation of vowels. He either elided vowels completely or mispronounced them in such a way that the gathered people of Alma – desiring to be respectful on this solemn occasion – found themselves alternately sedated by the humming cadence of his voice or perplexed by a familiar word made foreign. The mourners politely ignored him, for the sake of decorum or because they weren't listening anyway. But when he intoned *everlusting* life for the third time, a wave of agitation rippled through the crowd.

The minister's wife and grown daughter wore cloche hats and had pleasant faces. They were large women, not unusual in this farm-fed community, but they too had an unusual characteristic. Both possessed a disproportionate body feature: enormous buttocks.

Hank had seen fine black girls striding down the streets of Chicago, their voluptuous asses riding high, presaging the mature women they would become. But even in clinical practice, he'd never seen anything quite like this. The posteriors of the minister's wife and daughter were beyond voluptuous. No matter which angle you looked at them – sideways, frontways, backways, you saw their backsides coming first.

Unfortunately, Livy noticed this distinguishing feature at the same time. An incredulous look passed over her face, she appeared mesmerized. At last, the absurdity became too much.

"The last shall be first," she said under her breath.

His Irish sensibility could not resist. "Get thee behind me."

"Butt of course." She began to shake with suppressed laughter.

Hank was lost. A strangled sound something like a sneeze escaped his lips. Livy emitted a low purr laced with mirth that seemed to come from her belly.

Differently abled! Hank admonished himself, but it was no help. *Damn!*

His and Livy's laughter became obstreperous. They were saved by timely fits of coughing from somewhere in the crowd. Hank laughed so hard, although inwardly, that tears rolled down his face. Livy herself laughed out loud softly, leaning onto Hank for support, but no one seemed to notice.

At last, he and Livy calmed and settled down. Out of the hum of the minister's voice, words made themselves distinct: "Be still and know that I am God."

Sam, who had been dozing at Alex's feet, eyes moving behind his lids, raised himself onto his haunches and wandered from one small knot of people to another as though searching for someone.

The cleric droned on. Hank tuned out. A gift he'd given himself since living in Alma: not listening to everything. This selectivity of attending. Growing up, he'd felt on standby with Da. And medical training: reams of lectures and information, every iota potentially important, or so it had seemed. Everything is not equally important, he had discovered. This minister, maybe he was an okay guy, but his excess words in the face of death had little import.

Silent Margaret – she was important. The Margaret who had been the speck of her father's DNA (who was her father?) and the speck of her mother's DNA (who was her mother?), helices whirling together forming tiny Margaret (did she already love color and shape, jump at sound, crave quiet?), this uniquely *Margaret* Margaret who had passed over. *This* Margaret, a human being, that unrepeatable gesture, someone Earth had never seen before and would never see again.

What will life mean when it becomes splices of DNA? He closed his eyes. *Cloning will flatten out the genes. The energy is in the wild gene. It's like trying to tame the sea.*

Hank regarded Margaret in her coffin. Her pale face was suffused with a warmth it had lacked in life. A subtle smile rested at the corners of her blistered mouth.

"My soul proclaims the greatness of the Lord," the minister was saying. Silent Margaret didn't proclaim much during her life, did she?

The Lake Man's children squirmed nearby. The toddler had spilled juice on his mother's blouse, and one small pink gym shoe rested on her lap. People leave their messes in your life, he thought, but you decide they're worth it. Otherwise, you live in isolated splendor.

He gazed at the markers and headstones in the cemetery, at the open grave carved out of the black Wisconsin soil. He thought of the cairns scattered around Ireland, the *killeens* in the sandy soil of Connemara, the Galway graveyard near the Ocean where his grandfather rested.

The green waves of Ireland, the face of his grandfather. Grateful, grateful.

They had cut the sod on three sides and rolled it back carefully after his grandfather's coffin was safely tucked inside. Like returning to the womb.

Livy stirred beside him. He felt a sudden fiery ache for her.

The cleric, talking on, gave a blessing. Hank made the sign of the cross over himself. He found himself missing the beautiful old rituals and blessings for the dead from his own Catholic tradition, but he wore the church like a loose garment these days. He offered a prayer for

Silent Margaret in his heart: *May she be light and have no pain.*

"I can't pray that way anymore," Livy leaned over to whisper into his ear, "asking God the Father over and over for things."

The minister's tongue darted to his lips. "What does it mean when God calls us before our time?"

If captions had appeared over individual's heads, they would have read: "I don't know," "God knows," "God's will," "Nothing," "Why?" "Oh."

His father, still stumbling out of bars when he died at seventy, before his time for Hank's mother. Sarah, burning like a nova that night before she died, a thousand thousand kilowatts of light.

Suddenly he sensed Sarah present, felt her near, as if he could just turn his head and see her standing there, looking out for him.

The smell of overturned dirt filled his nostrils. His eyes were wet. *The sweet pull of death, but we all want to stay, dear God, we say, please let me be here on this beautiful Earth a little bit longer. Death makes our lives real.*

The minister, as had become the custom, invited stories about Silent Margaret.

Alice began. "*Mes amis,*" she touched the corners of her eyes with a lace handkerchief, brushed a lock of auburn hair from her face, "Margaret was like a remnant, a scrap left behind, but there is a special place in the heart of the universe for remnants. Not all of us can be Josephine Baker walking a leopard down the *Champs Ellyses.*" People's heads came up. "Margaret was a grace note who embellished the music of our lives. Her spirit was ineffable." She took her seat to the mild bewilderment of the assembly.

Alex, grey hair slicked back carefully, had stayed in the background, grief weighing down her body, without words for once. Now she stood awkwardly, her face red and swollen. She spoke in a quavery voice.

"She didn't say much, you know," she said, in a vast understatement. "Once I said to her 'How is it for you, Margaret?' After a space, she said 'the din…the din.' That's about it, *n'est pas?*" Alex choked up, then found her voice. "Margaret didn't give a hoot in hell about twaddle. And she wouldn't want a meladrone now." At this she seemed to give the minister a warning look. "To the impercipient, Margaret appeared dull, but she knew…there's a torrent of beauty…."

Tears trickled down Alex's cheeks, she sat and buried her face in her hands. Alice rested a hand on the small of her back.

People didn't know Silent Margaret well, so no one told a funny story, and it seemed no more stories would be offered. Then young Tom from the general store rose gingerly, favoring his bruised leg. "Silent Margaret didn't talk, so you could talk to her," he said and immediately sat down.

The music was a potpourri. A farmer sang a lullaby from the Menominee who had shared it with his father some time in the forties. Alice rendered an Edith Piaf song, *Cri du coeur*:

It is not my voice alone you hear in this song...
You hear the sound of a new broken heart
The sound of love...dead or alive
It is also the voice of hope...

The Lake Man's wife led them in *Amazing Grace*. The minister sang along in a thin voice, and the assemblage dutifully attempted the high notes. By the end of the opening line two bell-like sopranos joined Alice's. Hank traced the sound to the minister's wife and daughter, both of them, huge hips swaying side to side, singing like angels.

Then Alice cleared her throat elegantly and began to sing an aria from *Rigolletto*. In a voice so rich, so pure, a deep quietness fell over the listeners. Each note hung in the air, clear and true, melting into the next, the words, one after the other, on wing with the music. A threnody that soared and shimmered.

When the last note sounded, no one moved for long moments. Then someone stirred. Maybe it was Winona, reaching out to touch Elrita's side. Or someone scuffled a loose stone in the dirt. Surely Alex touched Alice's hand. Joe straightened his back. The group, though still quiet, became animated.

The mourners put tokens in the casket.

Alex and Alice placed a small book of poems by Emily Dickinson into Margaret's folded hands, with one line marked in rainbow colors: "The wounded deer leaps highest."

The Yazzis sprinkled corn pollen around and into the coffin. Rufus, his face bandaged, carefully slipped a multi-hued watercolor alongside Margaret. Winona gave her white daisies, wilting from the heat of her hand, which she'd picked that morning. "Maybe she's the ghost of a flower now," she whispered to Elrita.

Livy dropped in a sprig of rosemary, and a tiny gilt and blue card that read "*Hasta siempre* – forever." As though it were necessary to translate for Silent Margaret, beyond words now, maybe where her body was free, with no more numbers to count, no more times to wash her hands.

Hank bent down and placed one foil star beside her.

Where sugar maples overhung the graveyard, sunlight honeycombed the mourners; the rest of the cemetery lay in full sunlight. Hank's eyes moved over Alex and Alice, and the Yazzis, and came to rest on Winona. She was sitting on the grass in a pool of sunshine, holding her doll. The girl appeared bemused, her young face raised to the light, like she might be daydreaming. Then she shifted position, and her eyes, dark and watching, met his.

Winona held Carmelita closely in her lap and cuddled against her mother's knee. She had been upset with Silent Margaret at first for going away, especially for leaving Rufus. Then she'd seen the tears of the grown-ups, and she felt sad.

Her eyes followed everything. The blues and greens and browns of the sky and the cemetery meadow, the cardinal and robin dancing red in the trees, small animals and more birds drawing near to the funeral, calling to each other. She saw the colors over people's heads too. Circles of light touched with pink, like daybreak over the farmhouse, or touched with yellow like the cornfield after school. Some she could hardly see, others were brighter, lifting and playing. Doc Cleary's and Livy's circles flowed together at the edges. Around the cemetery colors shone over the graves. A spill of gold glowed from Silent Margaret's closed coffin.

Her father, Rufus, and the Lake Road man on one side, Doc Cleary, the filling station man, and Alex on the other, took hold of the coffin and lowered it into the ground.

"Will she be scared of the dark?" she asked Beulah.

"No," Beulah said, "she's all right now."

The minister read from Ezekiel: "Wherever the stream flows...it will bring life."

When the last shovelful of earth was flung onto the coffin, a gust of wind blew up.

Overhead Winona saw a white bird gliding.

"A beautiful funeral," the townspeople said later. Those seated near the coffin swore that, mingled with the sharp autumn scent of marigolds, was the fragrance of frankincense.

Chapter 32

At Livy's Bar and Café, Harleys were lined up beside a flatbed truck filled with pumpkins. Inside, the motorcycle riders wolfed down cheeseburgers and bowls of chili.

"Everything okay for you?" Livy asked the bikers.

One burly guy with an American flag stitched onto the back of his leather jacket, flirted with her. "Could be better if you'd bring your pretty self over here and sit down with me." He ordered a beer and a bump to celebrate the new week and, fortified, stepped up his pursuit. "C'mon," he suggested, "I want to give you a ride!"

"Be a good boy," she poured him a cup of coffee, "I'm not interested in your engine."

"Whoa!" the buddies cackled and settled for ordering pieces of whipped cream pie.

Livy glanced up just as Mary Two Rivers walked into the cafe.

She wore a faded red t-shirt and black and white checked pants. She looked like she'd lost maybe fifty pounds, but she was still tremendously fat. She lumbered over and sat on a stool at the counter, her flesh spread around the stool. She would have teetered dangerously had her weight not served as an anchor against instability.

"What sounds good to you today?" Livy asked, as though it hadn't been a year since she'd seen Mary Two Rivers.

"The soup, I guess."

Mary seemed less crabby and more lively than Livy remembered. She wondered what had happened to Mary Two Rivers' husband. So much had been happening with the tribal casino lately. Charges about greedy DC pols trying to manipulate tribal elections for personal profit, rumors the tribe had been gulled, that capitol insiders had fleeced the tribe of millions of dollars, that gambling laws were being flouted. Shady dealings. Had Mary's husband been part of a con, a bad guy or a good guy in all this?

"How's your dog?" Livy tried.

"My dog got skunked last night."

Livy figured that was it for conversation, as Mary Two-Rivers was not known to be sociable.

But the Indian woman spoke again. "My dog, you know, only has two legs, because he lost a leg in a trap. And Lonnie, well, he fixed him a cart to get around on. It's a rough cart, not like the Yazzis woulda done, but it works. He never done somethin' like that before."

"That's good," Livy murmured.

Mary finished her soup and got up to leave. "I got to get home for my stories on the TV."

Rufus' skin was healing. He would have a scar across his handsome face where the burning rope had cut most deeply, but overall, his wounds were healing amazingly well. Hank had prescribed sulfa cream with twice-daily dressing changes, which Elrita did at home with Beulah's help.

All summer long Beulah had come in with complaints of headaches, but Hank could never find anything wrong. Her headaches had stopped, but now she complained of problems swallowing – again her exam was normal.

"I never saw Silvadene work this fast before," he said, examining Rufus. "I've never seen burn healing like this."

Elrita gave him a steady look. "I think it was the *calidra*."

"—*Calidra*?"

"*Oh*. A kind of poultice. Livy showed me. Her Aunt Angie is a *curandura*. It's a *remedio* from her aunt."

For some reason Hank's patients almost never told him when they used alternative medicine. He'd just been to the Home where Ms. Barrie the Younger no longer needed the diabetes medication he'd planned to start her on. She'd apparently managed to lower her glucose level by taking ginseng before every meal.

A farmer waited for him in the other examining room with respiratory problems from pesticides. "Leave the wounds open to the air now. You're doing a good job," he said to Elrita. He looked out his window at the changing leaves. For an instant he felt a mother's suffering for her son. "I know it's been hard," he said softly, "you are a true healer."

At Yazzi's farm, full-grown lambs bleated. There'd been a sun shower, then a breeze came up, but the sun felt hot through Livy's jeans.

She'd brought over more of her old dresses. Beulah liked them and Livy liked not having too many things, they just got in the way. She sat with Beulah under a maple tree flaming the color of a pomegranate, thinking about Hank. *El hombre sensitivo.*

Beulah studied the new old clothes. She sat upright in the grass, her black hair shining, skin burnished in the sunlight. Butterflies balanced nearby, a ballet of folding wings.

The teen-aged girl turned her dark eyes to Livy. "I think I might be a nurse like my mother."

"Oh Querida!" Livy cupped her cheek, the way you touch the face of someone you love.

Tears filled Beulah's eyes, but still she could not tell her story.

Livy opened her arms wide. She clasped the girl to her breast and gave her the words of an old Mexican saying: *Cry, child, because those without tears have a grief that will never end.*

Chapter 33

The autumnal equinox came and went. In America digitalized images in movies were seamlessly interwoven with historical film footage creating pastiches of fiction. A Wisconsin politician campaigned by driving a tractor around the state on back roads and expressways; no one ever caught up with him to inform him that driving a tractor on the highway was illegal. The moon rose during dusk for several nights in a row, giving extra light for farmers' harvest time.

Nights turned cool but days stayed comfortable and warm. Maples glowed red and orange. Apple and cherry trees were heavy with fruit. Yazzis gave Hank another lamb, the entrails already removed; he skinned and carved it and gave it to Livy for the café.

Alma was going to skip the annual bonfire, but piles of leaves waited to be burned or for children to jump in them. The scent of freshly cut grass mingled with the smell of autumn leaves. A disgruntled citizen released his boa constrictor out in the country, one of the White boys, probably the strange brother, whose mother used to drop them off at school wearing her nightgown.

The third week in October Mr. Willy choked on a chicken leg at the Home and died. He'd been sitting in the garden with Ms. Barrie the Elder talking about his plans for the spring garden. "He was telling me the longer you leave carrots in the ground, the sweeter they get," Ms. Barrie the Elder said. "I'd just said to him 'What can we say to laugh?' One minute Mr. Willy was laughing and talking, his eyes all lit up, next minute a surprised look come over his face and he keeled over onto a pile of leaves. Just like that! You know what he used to say?" She added thoughtfully, "'Don't be late. I'm ninety years old.'"

Hank raised his arm in greeting to Kelly driving by in his pickup truck, his girlfriend seated flush against his side. He'd had an easy morning in the clinic, mostly allergy patients, and the same rabbit hunter still refusing to wear ear protection because "he wouldn't be able to hear his dogs," continuing to go deaf in his right ear from the report of his gun.

Signs for the high school football team, the Redskins, were all over town: "Cheer For The Redskins" in construction paper letters in the window of the general store, "Warm Up A Victory" in the filling station, and brown placards shaped like footballs lining the street, with the name and number of each player and "Go Skins, Go" or "Go Reds." No Redskins were on the team; if they had been they would have called it something else.

Seeds of maple trees helicoptered around Hank to the ground. Dark yellow leaves floated golden in the sun like a flock of small birds. In front of a house, beside a jack-o-lantern, a miniature tombstone read:
HERE LIES TRU LOVE
GONE BUT NOT FORGOTTEN

At Pied-à-Terre, Alex was telling someone, "*Ni rien,* dear Georgia would not have painted it like that!"

After the customer stepped out over Sam, she turned to Hank: "What's with you? You look different, a better version, I'd say."

"I believe I am coming to my senses."

They talked about Mr. Willy's recent demise.

"Not such a bad way to go," Alex said, "when you think about it. Woody Allen says it's not that he's afraid to die, he just doesn't want to be there when it happens. The old guy was in his life right up until the last few seconds. It's almost like he wasn't there when it happened."

The Halloween window at Pied-à-Terre appeared plainer than usual, less artistic and exciting. It turned out Silent Margaret had decorated it every year, creating the swirling oranges and blacks, and the intricate Day of the Dead altar.

"Margaret was our window dresser," Alice said, "the special windows were *a la' Margaret.*"

The display this year contained fake cobwebs, a giant spider, a hanging bat, a glow-in-the-dark skull, Edgar Allen Poe books with illustrated covers, cut-out tin lanterns from Oaxaca borrowed from Livy, and a somewhat garish leaf tinsel garland dug up from another life. Dangling from the ceiling of the alcove, incongruously, was a fairy with big hair and large breasts. A man friend named Mike gave it to us, Alice said by way of explanation. In the center was a small *ofrenda* for Silent Margaret, made with Livy's help, surrounded by tiny candles.

"As long as you're honoring All Hallows Eve and *Dia de los Muertos*," Hank said, "you may as well add something for Samhain."

"—Samhain?"

"—The Celtic day of the dead, on the eve of the Celtic New Year which is November 1. The ancient Celts believed it was when the veil is thin between the worlds, and things happen at the edges."

"The Navajo talk about the South Corner of Time," Alice mused. "What shall we place in the window?"

"You could put an apple," he handed her the apple he carried, "fruit of the otherworld." He raked his fingers through his unruly hair. "On Samhain loose wild things are in the air you cannot see. For me, it has something to do with the Ur-self…your other self."

Alice set the apple carefully inside the window.

Hank helped himself to tea. He walked over by the grandmother clock. *In his dream last night, a man led him to a high place, just below him dark blue waves, the smell of the sea.* Back up front, he said to Alex, "More like fall, with the leaves coming down. Time change soon, we have to set our clocks back. What does that mean, really, time change?"

"Not much." She rearranged papers on the cluttered glass cabinet. "Space and time are as pliable as rubber bands if you get mass out of the way."

"Geesh, Alex, how do you know this stuff? I can hardly talk about it with anyone."

"I read."

Hank bent down and scratched Sam's ears, then stepped out into the deepening shadows to walk home. He passed a slender sapling, its yellow and orange leaves disproportionately large. At the edge of town, in the half light, he thought he glimpsed someone or something from long ago, but it was only Lonnie Two Rivers standing in the shadows.

Chapter 34

In his cabin Hank and Livy sat at the kitchen table deep in conversation.

"Once Sarah got furious with me," he was telling her.

"*Porque?*"

He stirred his coffee. "Let me tell you a story. When I was a medical student at Cook County Hospital, a nine-year-old kid came in who'd been critically wounded in a drive-by shooting. I had never seen a child that grievously injured. My heart was in my throat. I couldn't move. I was incapable of helping him."

"What does this have to do with Sarah?"

"In medicine we're taught to distance ourselves from emotional involvement with patients in order to help them, so we're better able to alleviate suffering. They call it professional detachment. What happened with Sarah, I think, is she felt the distance, not the help." Hank grimaced. "My mind created a distance from my feelings. 'I don't want you to tell me about the natural course of my cancer,' she screamed at me, 'I want you to feel my pain!'"

Livy's cheek rested in her hand, a Oaxacan ancestor gazing from her steady eyes. She listened so intensely it aroused in him an almost physical pleasure.

"Most of the time she was so *grateful*, for life, for *me*." He scratched his head. "I thank God, she said to me that last week, for being in this life with you. And *I* wanted to keep her, to hold her here with me.

"Everything had burned away from her by then - all the dross. Her body was frail, but she had this light shining out of her. I thought of the Celtic belief that our souls are not within our bodies but surround us. It was as though her whole personality fused into a single flame. When I looked into her face, I saw the essence of her burning there; you could see clear through her to something else, something pure.

"Little by little, she was consumed." His voice broke. "We would lie very still on the bed and rest together. In the end, she'd had enough. She loved me and I couldn't save her. I was going to save the world and I couldn't even save my wife!"

"Hank," Livy touched his arm, "we are bigger than what we do."

She sipped her coffee. "I lost a baby once," she said, tears in her eyes. She hadn't been careful. She didn't know what to do, and then the baby decided it wasn't her time to come into the world. "I wonder about that *nina*—who she would have been, the lives she would have touched."

Now she can't get pregnant. He took her hand. "In Ireland they wake the dead for three days, companion them over to the other side. Even then, the Celts say the soul can be reborn, come out of the happy otherworld and live once more—that the soul has the power to change its shape."

"The Indians here say that when you die, you go into the heavens and become a star."

"So maybe Sarah and your baby are stars?"

"*Si.*" Her brown eyes burned into him, the heat rose in her face. He caught her scent...jasmine, dark cherries, deep forest.

He felt a deep hunger. A loose helpless feeling. The feeling swelled in his chest, then rose to his throat.

Tears fell hot against his face. Deep sloppy crying loosened itself from his flesh. Racking moans wrenched his gut, huge engulfing sound, like the keening of his Irish ancestors over the centuries for all the sons and brothers and fathers lost at sea, for those who had died of starvation, in childbirth, for love, or for country. A chant of sobs poured out of him into the night air. A wild and beautiful lamentation.

Then silence.

Livy's heart stretched out to him and grew some more. Her heart held Sarah's death, and Margaret's, the deaths of her mother and great-grandfather, her unborn child, Hank's mortality and her own, all rooted and springing up within her breast.

She held her tongue between her lips. She placed her palm along the side of his face. "I *see* you!" Her eyes fierce. "You come from a long line of heroes and lovers. You are a Celtic warrior, like Cuchulain, come to the battle naked with only a sword and a shield that changes form." She closed the space between them on the couch and wrapped her arms around him.

Hank let his body slip down into her embrace. He let himself be held.

"You are one of the brave. You have *cojones*!" she said. "*Corazon*, you are a freedom fighter."

He was in awe of her. He unfolded his body, rolled off the couch, and dropped to his knees. He raised her hand to his lips and kissed her fingers. "I see *you* too," he said. "I want to hear about when you were a girl growing up in Pilsen, what really led you to Alma, what you dream about…"

"And I want to know the why and wherefore of Hank Cleary!"

He could not speak.

"Where my mother comes from in Oaxaca, they say 'What does your heart tell me?'" Her voice a croon, low and soothing.

"*Mo croi,* I want to walk to the ends of the world with you, do something together like have an insane life. I want to walk in all the showers of the earth with you unless there's lightning of course. For us to be like two sailing ships close-hulled in a strong breeze." He leaned closer. "I want to ravish you," he whispered, "and respect you."

"Ravish me with respect."

"You have enchanted me. Perhaps you are a *bruja,*" he felt a smile on his face, "or a fairy from *Lough Michigan*, Lake Michigan. A partly Mexican Irish fairy."

"—By way of Chicago," she smiled her lop-sided smile.

"I don't know where I'm going with this." Hank sat beside her again. "Yes, I do. You're my soul friend, my *Anam Cara."*

On his loft bed they lay. Bathed in sweat and saliva and tears, breath ragged, hearts beating, fingers urgent and gentle, arms strong, legs wrapped around each other, pelvises locked in mortal birth.

The night of the Harvest Moon, Hank and Livy drove out to Dick's Polish Smorgasbord on Lake Michigan for a polka party with music by the polka king Frankie Yankovic.

Neither of them knew how to polka, but they whirled and stomped around the floor anyway.

They danced all night long, the music oom-pa-pa-ing, the lake outside the open windows like an inland sea, waves crashing against the shore all wet and wild with longing.

Once they tumbled, breathless and laughing, onto the weathered planks in back of Dick's to cool off. He kissed her then under the full moon, and she tasted like cherries and beer and brine. And he thought, this is how he would like his life at the end, all sweat and laughter and deep pull at the core of himself. *Yes, I say yes to it all.*

Chapter 35

In early November, three hundred sheep walked over the edge of a cliff in Turkey. Rhesus monkeys in India, who had benignly lived in and around a Hindu temple for generations, began attacking small children in the temple environs. Without their permission, clones were made of a famous rock star and a South American writer; years later it would be found that the cloned creatures could neither create music nor write.

In Wisconsin it was unseasonably mild. People washed their cars and watered lawns in their shirtsleeves. Combines were getting the rest of the beans and corn. The Harass mall displayed charcoal briquettes alongside fabricated fire logs.

Canadian geese flying over Harass were mixed up. High in the sky they could be seen – chestnut brown and midnight black, slender necked – heading vaguely south. Their distinct honking call was heard, so they might be migrating for the winter, but the flock circled over the auto plant, then descended, seduced by the aerated industrial lake which never froze. The geese had forgotten about seasons and rhythms, they had forgotten where to go.

At Yazzi's the faint sound of singing came from the open door of the old wooden barn. Elrita Yazzi was working in the studio Joe had made for her in the barn, her hands stroking and smoothing clay. Wrapping her hands, pressing, kneading, over the face of a beautiful boy, a boy looking up, seeing something on a horizon not present in the sculpture. But somehow present in the clay, there in the rapt face of the boy.

Elrita hummed a long-ago, far-away tune. Through the window she glimpsed the ivy climbing the side of the house. Around her in the studio space were sculptures of bird girls, a small child, and in one corner a metal sculpture of Changing Woman covered with verdigris. Elrita was in a part of her mind that did not think, but with her fingers she remembered Rufus' face as it had been, smooth and unmarred.

The wind picked up, lifted the storm cellar door on its hinges, sent a refreshing breeze in through the open door. The chalky dank smell of the clay entered her nostrils. Elrita was a Navajo *yataalii,* yet the Franciscans had left her with a devotion to the heart of Christ, and so she prayed now as she sculpted.

For her son. Rufus had changed since the fire. The mark of suffering on his face. His paintings with more gradations of color, and deeper colors. He spoke now, when he did talk about his painting, about endarkenment. "The majority of the world is a dark world," he told her. He placed words around the perimeter of his drawings "to slow the viewer down, we need to slow down to the speed of life." He continued to like the impressionists, but he was studying Toulouse Lautrec, and his palette had gone from reds and pinks to darker shades.

Elrita prayed for Beulah, still with that wounded look about her eyes, and for young Winona, who Elrita knew would be a *yataalii* herself one day. And for Joe, whom she loved deeply, who loved her back, who believed in her love and accepted it fully – what more could anyone want?

She prayed to their Athabascan ancestors, who had come from Asia so long ago over the Bering Land Bridge to the Americas. She gazed at the statue of Changing Woman, daughter of Long Life Boy and Happiness Girl, brought up by First Man and First Woman. She thought about how Changing Woman is involved in the creation and regeneration of life. In her Navajo heart, she prayed for the essence of Changing Woman in each Yazzi life.

Elrita knew a woman who had learned to sculpt in a marble cave in Italy, not far from the cave where Michelangelo had worked. She'd told Elrita about sculpting in rainbow marble—veins within the stone displayed an astonishing variegation of color. Elrita had read that a sculpture by Michelangelo himself can be viewed from multiple angles, as it is always in the process of becoming. When she completed one of her own sculptures, Elrita felt such delight and wonder that she walked around her creation in hopes of seeing what it was becoming.

Now a soft gentle rain, called the female rain by the '*dine,*' began to fall. She smoothed the clay form with her strong hands, waiting to discover what it would become.

On this warm November day, so far from bleak it took your breath away, Winona was playing out of doors. She swung on the rope swing hanging near the hogan as high as she could. She spun cartwheels in the field.

She came upon a single large white flower on a bush as tall as she was. It looked like a morning glory crossed with a lily, with velvety soft petals surrounded by dark green leaves soft as the petals. The pink tip of her tongue rested between her lips. She knew this flower. The bookstore ladies had given her the word: Moonflower, a flower that blooms only one day a year. "*Ahyéheé*, thank you, for blooming for me."

She saved the treehouse for last. Her father and Rufus had built the treehouse in the arms of an oak tree, wide at the bottom, roots bending above ground. A ladder led to a platform with circles carved out for thick branches to continue their journey skyward. Open on all four sides, the treehouse was secured with wooden railings. You got onto the platform through an opening that became part of the floor after you climbed up.

Winona understood already that the top sometimes becomes the bottom, that what is above you can become what you stand on, and what you stand on become what boosts you up to the stars. She knew that Rufus too looked up and out, seeing things only he could see and feel. That she would live her life looking up through openings until there would be a vast opening around her as she lay dying.

She understood all this within her in the treehouse, although it would be years before it would come into her mind, one day in time, in Alma.

Alongside the ladder was a sign, hung recently, written in her best cursive: Boyz Kep Out. She stood with the length of her body resting along a branch. She did not need to put her arms around the tree, but she always did. In this position, she could look out from her bower and see in all directions.

She considered the fields and trees. More leaves gone from the trees, she could see the clouds better. Some birds around, woodpeckers tapping on trees, the dove who makes the sad sound, robins and cardinals, and a bird whom Winona thought was Silent Margaret's. Most of the flowers gone, except for a few daisies and roses. She had rose petals and pansies on her birthday cake this week, flowers you could eat. Now she was seven, she knew a lot more. How people did not always see the same thing, and that it was *reely s-o-o-*

o important to tell what *you* saw, as *exackly* as you could, and be *pacific*. So, she practiced words, like saying *i-land* instead of *is-land* for a small piece of land in the middle of the ocean.

Trees shifted and swayed in the warm breeze. California weather, Livy called it, sun every day, no rain. "60 degrees in November!" the grownups said.

Last night Beulah had told Winona that a bad thing had happened to her. She didn't say what, but said she was getting better. "In a way you're too young to tell this to," Beulah said, "but in another way you're older that I am, so it's okay. I had a dream about a dragon and now I feel safe: I know who I am."

Winona thought about the photograph she'd found in a book that belonged to her father's little father. It was of a bomber, an airplane people used to kill other people – she didn't understand that.

Wind blew around the treehouse. She shook herself. "I'm daydreamed!"

Alice had said Winona had 'a wild mind.' Winona thought this was good, but she didn't know why. Alice also told her, when she was cross, the story of the little girl with the curl in the middle of her forehead.

The female rain began to fall. "Rain, rain, come again another day…" Winona sang. After the shower, a beautiful rainbow swept across the sky. She loved the word Livy had for rainbow, *arco iris,* and how it sounded when Livy said it: r-ko-ee-rees.

Winona put on an old dress of Livy's, kept in a waterproof sack in the treehouse. She hummed a little tune under her breath. She thought about Rufus, how he looked now with the red line running across his face, and about all the things that he painted with his brushes.

She started dreaming with her eyes open. Stories came into her head, about little people, and other magical people, and people she knew. Her face became earnest, sweet, and grave.

In years to come she would write these stories down. She did not know that yet. Her mind and heart would grow for many seasons hidden from the public gaze, so she would became a woman who could see and say what was not being seen or said.

But inside her she knew that someday she would tell stories about Rufus and his paintings, about the things her father found in a piece of wood with his carving knife, how her mother could sculpt bodies and faces, and how beautiful her sister Beulah was. She would tell stories about the corn goddess, and about the time she and Beulah and Rufus jumped out of the barn loft, and she *knew* that Rufus was scared but she didn't tell anyone, about the tangle of wild roses in the secret garden behind the Home, and about Alma.

In the end, all her stories would be about Alma.

Chapter 36

The North wind blew into Alma. A lunar eclipse turned the moon pinkish red. After a scattering of snow, headless armless snow people popped up with spindly twigs sticking out of their sides. Overnight the leaves fell, littering the ground with red, yellow, green, and brown leaves from maple, oak, and linden, all in their dark wetness appearing the same color. Between the bare branches a new landscape opened up.

In Livy's Bar and Cafe, the smell of fresh coffee permeated the air, and the Andrew Sisters sang. Alma folks congregated in the cafe enjoying the new wood-burning stove.

Livy had outlawed the serving of black and tans at the bar, once she knew who the Black and Tans were – English prisoners, the dregs, she told customers, released to go to Ireland to kill off the Irish.

"That stove warms your cockles *and* your toes," Old Harry proclaimed over lemon cream pie. To the guys across from him he added, "I'd like to say something mildly perverse."

"If it's mild enough," said one.

"If it's perverse enough," said the other.

In one corner, crew cut, clean-shaven, and earnest-looking, in a long-sleeved white shirt, grey pants and a small, checked tie, a young man sat holding a Bible. He glanced around as though he were looking for people to save.

Hank talked with Alex. "Things seem familiar, and then they're not...do you think that the closer we get to moving at the speed of light, the faster we move into the future?"

"Beats me," Alex said.

"In some research lab scientists made pulses of laser light move 300 times faster than the speed of light."

"More-is-better syndrome," she muttered.

"I wonder what it all means." He looked around for Livy.

She was holding court with a group of Alma women. "*Si, si, pero* I think the story about the woman caught in adultery, and saved by

Jesus, is tiresome. It's just another story about a man rescuing a woman." There was a moment of stunned silence, as they took in this comment on the gender game as played by the Son of God.

Hank followed her into the kitchen. "Looks like summer's finally done daring winter to come!" Pots simmered on the stove. "Smells good in here - what're you making?"

"Pesole. I need to jazz up the menu. I'm adding spicy peppers and ginger. Elrita says they're good for healing."

He caught her up in his arms, nuzzling her neck. "*You* smell good!"

"It's body cream *Tia Angie* concocted, laced with rosemary. When I wear it, I feel like people near me will have a sudden urge to order the lamb or beef and wonder why."

"Livy," he whispered urgently, "you're so...juicy."

She was a wild type—a hybrid born of the Connemara Irish, themselves come from Iberia, and the Mexicans. A double mestizo, hardy as they come, tough but soft in the center. What would a bright Pilsen-born streetwise Latina say to all that? There was so much he wanted to ask her. Since he'd been young, he'd excelled, had the right answers. Maybe he was finally asking the right questions.

"The café's going well, isn't it, Liv?"

"I've been a waitress, and a taxi driver." She shrugged her shoulders. "This is the best – we've even got heat!"

"Did you have enough heat growing up?"

"*No,* but my mother warmed us with her heart."

"When Tara and I were kids and we'd go skating at the outdoor ice pond, we used to wait for Da to pick us up. There was a sort of wooden lean-to for shelter from the wind – no heat, nothin.' And, you know, he'd *always* say he was coming and, *every time* we'd think, oh, *this* time he'll come. Not right away, of course, but this time he'll come sooner rather than later. It'd be 15 degrees or 20, or 5, really cold with that good old Chicago wind—"

"*Entonces?*"

"—and then he wouldn't come. It'd be a half hour, then 40 minutes. All the kids were gone – walked home or gotten picked up by their parents. And my sister and I would be sitting there, our fingers and toes going dead inside our gloves and boots. Man, I'd have tears running down my face when those digits started to thaw after we finally got back home. It wasn't always that he'd been drinking either – or at least not that much – more that he had to tell one more story or joke to a crony, or stay inside the long bend of a conversation, or sometimes it was to have one more drink."

"*Carino...*" She touched his hand.

He felt like all the things deep inside that he wanted to say, didn't get to say, never said, he could say to her and whatever it was, it would be all right.

That evening Hank drove to the home of a fragile patient named Agnes. Near 90, she still lived gracefully in the small farmhouse she'd shared with her husband.

He found her sitting on her sofa, an afghan over her knees, sipping hot cocoa. He set his black bag down on the faded rug and accepted a cup of cocoa from her.

"Just a little short of breath, Doc," she told him.

He sat on the bench next to the old upright piano and listened to her heart and lungs.

He used his new portable EKG monitor to check her cardiac rhythm. "I think the indoor heat has kicked up your asthma, Agnes." His hand rested on hers. "Let's increase your inhaler for a while and try leaving your bedroom window open a crack at night." *This house needs a good dusting too, she needs someone to help her.*

He looked around at what she called her parlor, at the old family photos in ornate metal frames on top of the piano, the once elegant window dressings, the parakeets chirping in their cage, the soft glow of the fringed table lamp, the flowered sofa, her sweet face. "How's the pain?"

"All right." She hesitated a moment, then spoke softly, "I'm old, Dr. Cleary, and getting weaker, but my soul is getting stronger."

The goodness of such a life! It's an honor to be part of her story, to be able to lessen her suffering.

Chapter 37

Lonnie scowled. Thanksgiving week – the white man's holiday, not one for the Indians. Deer hunting week in Wisconsin, he'd miss out on that this year, and fishing season for the muskellunge.

He was heading out. He'd had enough.

He'd thought about just taking a car in Alma. Those people were so wide open, they almost deserved it. No one locked their doors. They left cars sitting in their driveways with the keys in them, so whoever wanted to use the car next could just get in and go. Instead, he found a beater dumped on the reservation, repaired it, hiked up the front wheels, and souped up the engine. He covered the bumper sticker which read "If you don't like demolition derby, you can kiss my taillight," with one from his grandmother which said, "Menominee Power."

Last week he'd stopped to help a stranded driver, then sped away, feeling good about having his own wheels, until that cop pulled him over and took his driver's license. But it had been easy to make another license in the copy shop in Harris. He forged and copied a state license in full view of the lazy clerk who was supposed to trouble spot customers.

He'd gone out drinking with some dudes from the reservation last night. It'd been fine until that white guy in the bar started mocking him, insulting his people, insulting the Menominee. The guy pushed and pushed, with his sly, mean words, until Lonnie finally had to jump him. And then, because the smart-ass was a *big* guy, he'd beaten the hell out of Lonnie, including giving him the blue-black shiner sprouting around his eye.

He glanced at himself in the car mirror: the black eye, dark hair slicked back into a ponytail, around his neck the bronze feather engraved with symbols that had belonged to his father. Damn! He hoped the border police wouldn't make a big deal out of the eye – they'd already be targeting him because he was an Indian.

He felt like hell. He'd ended the evening screwing the girl who stayed in the shack on the edge of the reservation. The shack stank of poverty, but the girl was all right, better than nothing. He could still taste the cheap wine and cigarettes.

A deer suddenly stood in the road just ahead of him. He jumped, then swerved the car to avoid hitting the fawn who walked behind its mother.

Animals! His grandmother's dog, now he was something. Tried to go Romeo on any bitch that moved, which ought to have been hard, him having only two legs and all. Lonnie grinned. *He usually had to kick that old dog out of the way climbing into the trailer. He didn't know what come over him, but he'd gone and made the miserable mutt a cart to get around on. The cart was rough, but it was a good one. He surprised himself when he done it.*

His grandmother'd be okay. She was too sick to help him anyway. He took a drag on his cigarette. *He'd never known his mother. She'd been a boozer, they said, had taken off for the city when he was just a baby. If there ain't nobody in your corner standing up for you, what're you gonna do?*

He stopped off at Pied-á-Terre on his way out of town, he wasn't sure why but felt like he wanted to see Doc Cleary. He stepped over the old yellow lab lounging in the doorway. The Bookstore Ladies were weird, but kind of classy. They asked him how he was.

"Dunno."

Then the pretty one with the red hair startled him. "Dostoevsky," she said, "find yourself in yourself." Lonnie didn't know what she meant, but he liked that she even bothered.

Time to move on.

He was tired of living in a rundown, seedy motel, no job, nothing to do in Harass or on the reservation. Tired of having time on his hands. Did other people ever have time on their hands? At least now he was doing *something*. Heading for Canada. He'd heard there were Indians there who bowed to no white man. Maybe he could fix cars or televisions, he was good at that, or win some money gambling and parlay it into something big. Those pasty-faced high rollers didn't have to be the only ones making a killing.

He was done with white men. Their lies, their constant talk about money, the dead look in their eyes. White women were not so bad – he could see it in their eyes, the confusion, the beseeching, the knowing of the lies.

In Minnesota he stopped for a beer. On television, women were leaning against cars and cleaning toilets as usual. On the road again, a car ahead of him sped up on yellow and almost hit someone walking across the road. He rolled down the car window and threw out his most raggedy t-shirt. A girl wearing a baseball cap, breasts spilling out of her skimpy pink top, stood and stared. He touched his middle finger where it bent the wrong way, from the time his grandfather crushed it to the ground with a rifle butt. *No.* He fingered his amulet. Sometimes it was like all that shone in him was under muddy water.

A lot of the time it still felt like things floated away from him, but his life had taken a turn, could be he'd gotten his mojo.

He was making time now. Clouds banked overhead, gunmetal grey, sunshine glinting around their edges. He lit his last cigarette. He liked to use up the last of something. Even Beulah. When he saw her dark eyes for the first time, he felt pure, like looking into a curving river you could see clean to the bottom of, but never know where it would end. He wanted the wildness and beauty inside those eyes.

A small truck with antlers jammed under the front grill taunted him by tapping the back of his beater a couple times. In the rear-view mirror, he recognized the asshole wearing the NRA belt buckle from the bar last night.

It got colder. He stopped hearing the sound of the car tires turning on the road.

Cars around him slowed down—what for? The road looked clear. He put his foot on the accelerator. *Thing is, you gotta keep on going, and go fast. It's like a game. You gotta roll your dice big.*

On the bridge the small truck passed him, sliding on the road. Lonnie braked suddenly to avoid hitting him. The beater skidded and spun towards the embankment.

He thought about his birch bark canoe, the proud Menominee, the woods and streams. Just before he went over the edge, a fierce and beautiful light swam before his eyes, a light he had never seen before but that he knew. He thought he heard a bell, then a faint high sound like music, only better, like the sound of the wind in the trees at home.

The car soared for a long moment before it catapulted down the embankment. Lonnie felt himself soar too, aloft in the cold clear air, high above, looking down on all the mess below. He held onto his life: all that it meant, or could have meant, then he let go.

The old jalopy bumped and flew, end over end, down the steep embankment. He was free.

Chapter 38

"The coroner said it was a contrecoups injury, before the car went over the side." Hank put a Christmas ornament on the tall white pine standing in the middle of the café.

"*Muy mal*," Livy said, "a *desperado*, but still."

Hank balanced on a step stool to hang a blue icicle. He felt sadness, and a tinge of fear, barely understood, as if glimpsed in dim light at the other end of a long corridor.

Mary Two Rivers had talked about Lonnie, but Hank hadn't ever gotten to know him. He remembered Lonnie lounging in his grandmother's trailer, feet up on a counter, his face without expression, yet somehow young and vulnerable, and he remembered how frightened Lonnie looked the day of the fire. A lost boy. Unknown, denied, unappreciated, what might have been....

"He could have been a brave warrior," Joe was saying. He and Elrita had stopped by with a wild turkey, the first he'd shot this season. Now they added ornaments to the tree.

"*Gracias!*" Livy said. "Hank's putting them in clumps, from wherever he's standing on the stool!" Hank made a face at her.

"Mmmm...the tree smells good." Elrita hung a miniature creche on a lower bough. "Do you think it will be cold this winter?"

"So far. Kids skating on the little lake." Hank placed a sailor Santa next to one of the Magi.

"Not much snow yet. Remember three years ago? Those six-and seven-foot-high snowplows stuck in the drifts?" Joe coughed. He'd been able to get off the line and switch to painting, which helped his wrists, but he'd started coughing. Hank suspected it was from the closed-in paint space.

Mince pies baking released an enticing aroma of mixed spices and raisins into the dining room. Elrita and Joe drank cups of hot mulled cider, then bundled up to leave. "Need to feed our animals." The two stood quietly, the colored lights of the tree glinting off their dark skin and hair; they looked older than a year ago, but peaceful and dignified.

"Merry Christmas," they said in Navajo, "*Yateeh Keshmish.*"

James and LaShondra phoned from Chicago, and Hank put the call on speaker phone. "Might've known we'd track you down at the café," James said, "how are things in Alma?"

"Oh, good, the best really." Hank could hear Bessie Smith singing in the background. "Livy…" He looked over at her, relaxed in jeans and a red sweater, reading through holiday recipes.

"I hear it in your voice, man. I'm glad."

"And the practice is better, I'm actually enjoying it these days. How are things there?"

"Sweet Home Chicago! It's the real deal." James paused. "Don't want to bring you down, man, but our old classmate McCready committed suicide. Financial strain, and some kind of frivolous lawsuit, I heard."

"Oh no! That's terrible!" Hank had shared long nights on call with McCready; like Hank he was always scrounging change for coffee. He'd sacrificed so much to become a doctor, to have it come to this. "Poor guy! How's his family taking it?"

"Really hard." Bessie Smith sang *blues…all around my head.*

James spoke up. Not enough winter in Chicago to kill the viruses, a little snow scattered around. Did Alma have a lot of snow? No, Hank told him, but cold. Did James remember all those cold Decembers making Rounds at County?

"It was a moment," James replied. "By the way, you ready for Y2K? There may be a computer meltdown at the turn of the millennium – it's got a lot of people riled up."

"Haven't heard." LaShondra wanted to talk to Livy. They'd never met, but Hank was getting used to life filled with surprises.

"I want to tell you about Hank," LaShondra said. "He's difficult at times, but – praise Jesus! – there's so much there to love."

"I know," Livy said. "You're a good *mujer*, LaShondra."

"Thanks. You go, girl! Have yourself a blessed Christmas, and a ring-a-ding New Year!"

Hank stared out the window. A flock of boys ran down the middle of the road sliding on the snow, arms outspread, like happy gliding birds trying out their wingspans. After they went by, a hushed winter quiet inhabited the café. Twilight gathered outside.

"Am I difficult?"

"Sometimes," she gave him her lopsided smile, "but I think you're worth it."

A thick glass candle bearing the image of *La Senora de Guadalupe* burned on the ledge near the bar, casting an unsteady light on gleaming bottles of tequila and rum. "It's too soon to decorate the tree," Hank protested. "It's only the twelfth of December—the Christmas season really doesn't begin until December 24 and lasts until January 6. The stores tell us it's over on the twenty-fifth, but they've got it all wrong."

"You're *muy catolica,* so Catholic," Livy said. "My customers like the decorations. Not all of them have happy memories of Christmas time—it does their hearts good."

Past Christmases came into his mind. A sorrowful Christmas this year for the McCreadys, he thought: an Irish wake, the drinking, the contradictions, everything woven into everything, nothing particularly clear. "Maybe you're right."

Hank looked around the café. The talking deer's head with the red nose, that Old Harry had bestowed on Livy, bobbled on the wall near an exquisite, embroidered tablecloth from Oaxaca. Snowflakes and angels appeared alongside surreal masks with faces of watermelon skulls, the weeping woman, or fish-women. Sprigs of holly decorated the tables and windowsills. A menorah sat in one window. Livy's Bar and Café had been transformed into a mélange of Wisconsin holiday and Oaxacan decor. It somewhat resembled a fifties' movie set, but on another level felt warm and inviting.

Livy sat poring over recipes for mole, the complex chili-based sauces often requiring chocolate. "Did you know Oaxaca is known as the Land of the Seven Moles?" she called, a hint of despair in her voice, "*negro, amarillo, coloradito, almendrado, rojo, verde,* and *manchamantel*. That last one literally means 'stain the tablecloth.'" She selected her mother's *mole negro* to make for Christmas; it would take hours, but it was the best. It had twenty ingredients, but she'd have everything in place—*mise en place,* Alice had given her the word. She'd use her mortar and pestle to grind the spices.

Hank moved the step stool around the tree and leaned out, tilting his head to get a better view of Livy. She'd taken to wearing glasses to read, which he found fetching. He teetered on the stool, arms windmilling to regain his balance.

"*Ese, ese,*" Livy laughed in his direction.

"This must be what the Irish mean when they say, 'on both sides between.' *You* are dangerous." Hank climbed down off the stool and walked over to her.

He sat down heavily. He raked his fingers through his hair. "My old classmate killing himself. One more senseless death...."

"It's a hard thing," she said gently.

Diamonds of colored light were reflected in her eyes from the Christmas tree—she was breathtaking. *She takes my breath away, then gives it back to me fuller than before.* The room became a kaleidoscope of color. He felt so dreamy that he checked the flue on the stove to make sure it was open. "I'm lightheaded."

"Maybe your soul needs to catch up." She poured him more hot cider. "Have you heard the story about the man on an expedition in the wilds of another country? He's traveling with *indio* guides when suddenly they stop. He urges them to go on, but they refuse. He asks why. They say, 'We need time for our souls to catch up.'"

Her voice grew husky. "I was dancing as fast as I could in Chicago, and it wasn't any good, so I came to Alma, and after a while there you were."

"I can't believe the likes of you wants the likes of me."

"You have a heart of gold," Livy said, "only you didn't know it. Ask Winona, she kept telling me, 'Doc Cleary has a heart of gold.'"

"No one has a heart of gold," he said. "My heart has been a cave. Things sheltered there, and hidden."

"*Carino,* your cave of a heart contains pure gold."

He stayed quiet for a moment, weighing her words. "Maybe you melted my heart and turned it into gold," he leaned toward her, "or spun my straw into gold."

They'd begun to get each other's rhythm. He could feel her pace, faster than his. She sensed his rhythm, slower, melancholy there even underneath mirth.

"*Feliz Navidad.*" He kissed the sweet spot on her neck.

"*Nollaig Shona,*" she said in Irish, "Merry Christmas."

Chapter 39

Wrapped in quilts, Old Harry and Daisy were taking a moonbath in the graveyard outside the Home. They leaned on a tombstone near where Mr. Willy had been laid to rest in the fall, visiting their departed friends.

Inside, they tiptoed around Louie, who fluttered his feathers but stayed quiet and did not give them away. The ballroom door on the upper floor opened easily.

Harry had traded his everyday blue pants for his good black pair. "This night comes every thousand years," he said. "We may not be here the next time. If ever there was a night for celebration, this is it! I'd play the sax this evening, but so many of 'em are already asleep. I would keep it wailing for you. I'd play 'Last Night When We Were Young.'"

Daisy smiled and touched his sleeve. She wore an old red feather boa of Livy's and glitter that Winona had sprinkled in her hair earlier in the day.

"My family couldn't afford a saxophone," he continued. "Metal was so expensive during the War, but I got hold of one secondhand."

"It was a romantic time though," she said, "my sister got engaged three times. She kept accepting engagement rings from men. Everyone was in a hurry to marry when the war started, but it was wonderful when it finally ended, wasn't it? Remember when we had balloons again after the war?"

"Yeah. And that great music. Remember Benny Goodman? I got along with him. Not everyone did, but it was okay for me. You know, the Nazis forbade jazz."

"Good heavens!"

"Daisy," he said all of a sudden, "you jazz my heart."

She gave him a puzzled look.

"I mean you start out with jitterbug, you have your rock and roll, blues, even classical. In the end it comes down to jazz. If you're lucky, your heart ends up playing all the notes."

Daisy took his hand and led Harry across the ballroom to where the moonlight shone in the French windows. "Let's dance."

"We'll have to make our own music. *I'll be seeing you…*" he sang softly.

"*…in all the old familiar places…*" she chimed in.

He blended his song to match hers. A change in key can make all the difference, he thought. "I can tell you were a dancer by the way you move. You move like a dancer."

"Thank you. The ankle I broke last spring hurts some, but not too much."

His knee joints jabbed. "My knees sound like popcorn." His balance wasn't so good either.

"We can still move on the dance floor and sing," she said, as if reading his thoughts.

In Daisy's bedroom, wrapped in quilts, they took turns dipping spoons into a bowl of butter pecan ice cream. "This is the life!" Old Harry said. "A night to make whoopee."

He gave Daisy her pill. For a moment he remembered her diagnosis, what a shot across the bow it had been. "Down the hatch, old girl."

He pulled out his pocket watch. "It's almost time. Time's almost up." His eyes misted over. The rose he'd given her rested in a small vase on the night table. He poured them each a glass of the sparkling burgundy smuggled in by a friend. "Did you know there's no sound after the flatted fifth? I don't want to hear the flatted fifth, Daisy."

"Shhh…I'm here."

They lay down on Daisy's bed, resting in each other's arms. The tabby Molly curled up at the foot of the bed.

"You are beautiful. You're my morning glory." He held her in the crook of his arm. She smelled like roses and baby powder. "I was carrying a torch for you from the moment we met."

"After the dance," she blushed, "after the lemonade and you played and you were so gallant to the ladies, then I set my cap for you."

"Your hair's so soft," he murmured. *If you find someone so filled with the milk of human kindness, who tells the truth, you never let them go.*

"Harry, I vouchsafe you my heart."

"It's good to be beholden to someone." He rolled carefully onto her, lifted her hips gently beneath him to fit the curve of her body to his.

She gave him feathery kisses on his neck. "Easy now."

"You too."

When they came together awkwardly, he bit his tongue, but it was wonderful. Then they surrendered to sleep.

At Pied-à-Terre the wind swirled the snow against window casements attempting to gain entry. Above the bookstore Alex and Alice were snug inside their boudoir.

They reclined on their chaise longue near the fireplace, sharing a crème brule. Tea candles around the room cast flickers of light on green plants overhead and trailing along the walls, and on a Monet painting of the cliffs of Etretat and the sea; blues, greens, reds, and pinks, moving in and out of light and shadow.

On a table nearby were a dozen red roses, cups of Darjeeling tea, dark chocolate on a prized Limoges plate found at the second-hand shop, and French champagne cooling in an ice bucket. An open book lay in each woman's lap. Everything they needed was within arm's reach, including each other.

Alice had made up the bed with fresh sheets, carefully creating the French corners her mother had taught her so long ago and placing a flannel blanket under the down comforter on this cold night.

"You've put up with my wanderings all these years…I needed to blow out my gaskets every so often, the hormones were raging, they're quieter now. My heart was open," Alex said, "Women came to me, wanted to be with me. I was in love with life, not them! *Pardonnez-moi, s'il vous plait*, my erstwhile self."

"Riven," Alice replied, her face pensive, "at times I was riven."

Sam and the yellow wolf-pup dozed nearby. Sam and the she-wolf had arrived at an agreement. How it came about no one in Alma could figure out, but in the end, Sam brought the little half-breed back to Pied-à-Terre. Now Sam woke and raised himself onto his haunches, then settled back down. The pup dreamed half-dreams. Alex put more sticks of wood in the small fireplace.

"Chilsy, eh?" She tucked the afghan more closely up around Alice and caught a whiff of lavender soap. "Better?"

"*Merci, mon chere, je suis bien.*" Alice wore a pink dressing gown of flannel and lace in the style of a 1920's trousseau, her auburn hair loose against the chaise pillow.

"Remember when we met?" Alex said. "I'll never forget – you were wearing a red velvet dress."

"And that night on the beach, when you played the harmonica?" Alice dimpled. "You were scintillating! After a while you said, 'Abide with me.'"

"And you have, amazingly."

Alice placed her hand on Alex's plain face. "You're crabby too, but you are my eudemonia—my happy demon. We know each other by heart."

"You gave up so much."

"*Je ne regretted rien.*"

"In the grand scheme of things, it's good, isn't it? A life with books, in Alma, not too many clichés or mangled sentences." Alex grinned.

"The beauty of language, a way to stay still." Alice continued her reverie. "You know what Mary Daly said? We're in the flow of tidal time."

"We're moving into the 'archaic future,'" Alex said. "Being with you is be-dazzling!"

"Freedom from unreal loyalties, the dear Virginia Woolf wrote. We have no time for them."

"We know what we know."

"*C'est bon.*" Alice's face lit up. "We'll keep throwing our lives as far as they can go. *Moment á moment.*"

Midnight approached. The young wolf-pup lifted his head and howled.

"Our *fin de siecle*," Alice said, "though hardly a *belle époque*."

"A maelstrom of a century! If dear Sylvia Beach had not published the grand Joyce in Paris, where would we be?"

"Margaret …" Alice mused.

"Livy told me the oldest goddess in Ireland was called the great silent one."

"*Mais oui.*"

With a flourish Alex popped the cork on the champagne. "To the new millennium. *A votre sante!*"

"*A votre sante!*" Alice's face is soft in the candlelight.

"You are *tres belle…*" Alex kissed her ear.

"Are you flirting with me?" By now Alice was in a state of dishabille.

"*Après vous.*" Alex swept aside the covers. "*Je suis a toi.*"

They held each other in the embrace that comes to those who have found each other.

Chapter 40

The cold air was clear and dry, the sun distant behind bare trees. On December 30, a rainbow encircled the moon. The next morning it snowed.

In the cabin, Hank and Livy sat in front of the fireplace eating pasta with basil and garlic pesto, and nibbling on tres leches cake, warmed by a crackling cedarwood fire. A tree creaked outside, its branches rubbing together in the wind like steps in an attic. At the edge of the clearing, two deer stood perfectly still. A red cardinal posed in the snow.

"The end of the year," Hank said, "the end of a millennium."

"Silent Margaret, Mr. Willy, and Lonnie, gone," Livy said.

"Accidents, illness…and old age. Apoptosis they call it – our cells programmed to die at certain points in time." He took a sip of coffee. "Earth is a garden planet, or at least it was, before all the toxins. Did you ever think that all of us are part of one big organism, like leaves on a plant? Maybe when we die, we're being pruned for the good of the whole."

"Maybe."

"An old Irish woman, a friend of my parents, used to say, 'If I don't see you next year, I'll see you in eternity.'"

She stirred sugar into her coffee.

"The times though, they are achangin'," he continued. "A single laser beam can now transmit the entire Bible in less than a second."

"Does it matter if people don't read it anyway?"

The sun began to bleed red across the sky. A flock of wild turkeys, ungainly, with pale pink legs, grayish heads, wattles, and brown and gray wings, crashed through the brush, then flew up into the trees landing one by one on the pine boughs making them sway. An old Beatles vinyl was playing, *I am the eggman*....

"I am not the eggwoman," Livy murmured. "No baby." Droplets of moisture stood on her lip. "Maybe my eggs are seared. Time after time…no baby."

He touched her shoulder gently. "*You* are magic."

He felt her deep inside. Into the shifting topography of his life, she had come like an epicenter over an earthquake. He remembered when he fell in love with her, the ache of longing, waking in the night, his spirit searching for her. He would feel himself lift up, out of his body, leave his cabin, travel in the sky, over the woods and the roads of Alma to the café, to lie beside her, at rest.

When they first made love, it felt almost like making love to a part of himself. But he was making love to *Livy*, to *her*! *Can anyone ever know who another person is?* Hank knew he would have to look at her, again and again, for the rest of his life until he could really see her.

The newness and strangeness of their love, like an ancient stone circle, pointing in an unfathomable direction, full of mystery. Lines from Neruda flashed into his head:

my words…climb on my old suffering like ivy
…become stained with your love.
you occupy everything, you occupy everything.

"I'm grateful, even for missing you when we're apart. Things could have turned out badly for me." He rubbed the back of his neck. "Yeats had a tower he retreated to. I'm glad I'm not up in a tower any more. What we have is like a spring of water flowing from one of the sacred wells in Ireland." Silence stretched out around them in the woods. They lay in each other's arms in front of the fireplace. He wanted to freeze the moment, like a spume of sea spray caught at the top of its arc, green-etched and pearl-splashed against the sky forever.

"The eve of the millennium…" he mused. "Do you know that most of the universe is dark energy? So, it's not in time."

"Maybe it's God," Livy said. "Sometimes I see God as my *abuela*, giving me courage for *la lucha*, the struggle. Or God is *una mujer agua*—water-woman, letting the water come down, taking away our thirst."

"Hard to understand." He cradled her head. "Where did we come from? Where are we going?"

"*I* think the *universe* is pregnant. The whole place giving birth all the time, everywhere. *I'm* not, out of my body," her face looked sad, "but in some *other* way maybe I am."

"Mo *croi*, you are!" He stroked her hair. "You, me, Alex, Alice, Old Harry, the Yazzis, Mary Two Rivers, Sam, the trees and wind moaning out there in the snow, we're all giving life, aren't we?"

"*Si, si, si.*"

They climbed the ladder to the loft. She pushed him down on the bed, her face radiant in the moonlight. His own face was wet. They touched each other in earnest, their bodies coming together. Then they fell back, loose-limbed, onto the covers.

"The millennium is just around the corner," he whispered.

"*Gracias a la vida.*"

"To life? or *dios*?"

"*Mismo*, the same," her voice drifted back.

"Livy," her name like music, "are we there yet?"

"We're on our way."

Chapter 41

In Alma all are in bed, in dreams.

Snow covers the fallow fields, the Hogan, the barns and the gabled farmhouse at Yazzi's. The moon creates diamonds of silvery light in the snow. The gigantic blue spruce, blanketed with white, shelters the farmhouse.

In the barn the sheep, milk cow, and sorrel horse have animal dreams. Seeds deep under the ground dream of spring. The beehive is vacant, its inhabitants gone to wherever bees dream in the wintertime.

Beulah and Winona have left breadcrumbs outside for deer, rabbits, and the birds who hid in the fragrant evergreens. Now all is still.

Elrita's eyes move beneath her lids. She is dreaming about Joe. She can't see him but feels deep and warm, so she knows she dreams of Joe. The wind blows. A young woman falls to the ground in the power of the Great Spirit. In a deep purple gown Elrita walks along a path with beautiful trees and water and animals all around, blissful. Day turns to night, the heavens fill with stars.

Beside her Joe dreams it's quitting time at the plant in Harass. The big boss leaves for the day. Joe stands high on a catwalk looking down on the line, where workers are reaching and tending to machines. Cars disappear under mounds of snow until they change into the buttes and mesas of Navajo land. A brindled horse stands, ears erect against the horizon. Joe wrestles trees in the snow. He sits out of doors before a wood table with green grass growing through its seams, carving beautiful, curled lines into the supporting legs. He looks down into the canyon between the Sacred Mountains, then he is on the canyon floor tending sheep. He hears a drum beating.

Rufus is dreaming, a furrow in his brow. A sense of loneliness, no one around, the landscape empty. He sees a dark figure opposite, like a shadow. It looks like him, but the figure is a girl. She too has a scar across her face, but her wound is part of her beauty. He is aroused. Danger and excitement. The girl waits. Rufus opens his arms and chest to bring her in. A rich explosion of luscious colors – red, gold, violet, chartreuse, maroon, magenta, dark gray, blue that burbles like a brook, strange and new colors never before seen. Sumptuous fabrics and textures – velvet, silk, brocade, fur, leather. His hands become iridescent. Monet whispers, "Forget the names of things."

Beulah no longer sleeps in the bedroom with the slanted ceiling, but on the ground floor not far from Winona, in a room with squared-off walls and ceilings. A prayer feather hangs near the top of her bed. She hums in her sleep. She is dreaming about the new boy at school. He looks strong, his brown eyes shiny, full of life. Beulah turns away and begins to run. Through the cornfields, sweating, her heart beating so hard it may come out of her chest. She's barely able to breathe. Someone is after her, on her heels. It feels like there is no place to turn. This time she stops and turns around. Lonnie stops too and stands a little way off. "Go away!" she screams. "Go away! Go away!" Anger fills her to the brim. He becomes a young, scared boy. "You can go away now," she says. She turns over and falls into a deep sleep, tasting the salt of her tears.

Winona dreams of people traveling by boat, plane, train or on foot. They talk to each other, people she knows and people she's never met, in fascinating and beautiful ways, as if by magic. She dreams she is a fairy. Winona knows she is dreaming. She doesn't know whether she is Winona dreaming she is a fairy, or a fairy dreaming she is Winona. She wonders if she is dreaming in her sleep or awake dreaming her life. She crawls through a hole in a fence. She can see the worlds. She is surrounded by a dark blue light. Lying on her back, she sees herself on the bottom of the curving Earth, looking down on the Milky Way. Earth does not let her fall.

At the Home, the snow lies deep over the graveyard and the secret garden. Old Harry snores in his sleep. He's beside the ocean. He's tempted to go in the water, but he wants to find the town, so he turns and walks on. A young man skates on a winter pond. Daisy skates on the pond, so gracefully it's like a dance. A song plays in the background. The man and Daisy join hands and skate in tandem. The ice where they skate is very thin.

Daisy dreams she's in an interior room. A veil of white lace covers her head and face. She is dancing The Firebird. She's young. Her limbs are lithe, her joints fluid, she moves easily. The ballet moves through her as though she is channeling Stravinsky, her body's rhythm one with the music.

Nestled under the eiderdown comforter, hot water bottles at their feet, Alex and Alice dream they are flying. Arms spread wide, leaving *les Etats Unis*, they fly out over the Atlantic. On an island, an old woman in gold and silver raiment tells them about the original beings.

Once upon a time, she says, all beings had four arms and two sets of genitals on the outside, but then they were split in half. They search for their lost other selves in order to be complete: male for female, female for male, male for male, or female for female. Over the northwest coast of France, they see chateaus, strawberry beds, rabbit hutches, fields of wild poppies. The Bretons call to them from the ground: "*Bienvenue, Mesdames!*" They are blessed with savior faire.

They alight in a small village, taste the *fruits de mer* – sea crabs, shrimp, prawns, oysters. Paris, the city of light! The Eiffel Tower, Notre Dame Cathedral, open-air markets with bright flowers and vegetables, the vast outline of the Louvre. The Parisians' faces are unsmiling, but the dreamers can see their tender hearts. They fly over the Left Bank and Montmartre, the arrondissements, the Luxembourg gardens, the Sorbonne. In the parlor of Gertrude Stein, they attend a salon. Writers and artists talk of Marcel Proust and books and art of the day. They both feel a pull towards Gertrude Stein. Over a rugged countryside, a special light bathes the landscape, subtle and dazzling. They know then they are in Provence. Paintings of Cézanne and van Gogh. Lush vineyards and olive groves. *Une experience magnifique.* They are filled with an incredible *joie de vivre.*

In the cabin loft, moonlight glimmers. Livy is dreaming about babies with quizzical Latin eyes peering out of Irish faces. Alebrijes with fantastical bodies of animals, birds, and insects inhabit the streets of Pilsen in Chicago. Her *abuela* rocks a little girl on her lap, singing, their fingers intertwined. She leans on her grandmother's breast. Her *abuela* becomes a woman in regal robes. "*Ay*," the dreamer says, "I know you. The dark *co-madre.*" She lolls on large soft beds of wonderful food, feels the skin of Hank's body. The green of the sea is in his eyes. Mexico. *Pasiones.* Mayan ruins. Danzon in Mexico City. Indigenous flutes, stalls of whole raw fishes, pork feet, cuts of cattle, cactus, mangoes, papayas, tortillas, chilies, maize. On *la playa* she eats ceviche by the water under a vast heaven of *estrellas.*

Hank drifts off to sleep. He holds a small child to his chest. Children call each other to come out and play, the way they used to. Outside his back door they're calling, "Yo-o, Hank." A clearing appears in front of his cabin. The women of Alma stand there: Livy, Elrita, Alice, Alex, Silent Margaret. Each speaks with beauty and grace, from her heart. They're telling him something. A rune? Secrets are revealed in the silence between the words. A dark radiance surrounds the women, though suffering is present. He's enfolded in dark vibrant energy.

Tremendous power. A spiral opens, becomes longer and reforms, like a moebius strip. Ireland. Stones her bone. Waters her blood. The sons of Mil come from Spain. Memories not his own. His nails grow long in the woods. D'anu – the eternal giver. A feminine land, men live in her folds. Rain on the wind. All the shades of green. Cows, sheep, donkey, mare, foal, roaming. The sound of a bird's wings like a gurgle of water. Currachs, water roils and spins and crests. High tide, the sea up to the back steps of the cottage on the small island. The smell of a peat fire. The old songs, only the lilt of the human voice, a land so steeped in poverty the instruments are gone. In the swirling mists the Innis Islands appear and reappear, trailing opalescent shadows.

Chapter 42

Looking into space is to look into time, at what happened a long time ago. The sun spirals within its galaxy, other galaxies spiral, planets swing.

On one planet, beings lower nets into clear blue liquid to catch finned creatures to feed on. Another planet is filled with five-foot-high creatures weighing hundreds of pounds who no longer roam but sit before a communications screen to find out what to think. On another, a race lives along a river that spans half the planet, constructing their forms in shapes that configure the meaning of their stories and themselves. On the cusp of the light galaxies, but resting in the shade of cosmic darkness, hangs a planet of particulate beings within the cosmic wave, all genders birthing, all the time. Further out on the edge is a planet all wild, springing spontaneously from within its core, vast, diverse, interrelated, lying close with the nearest warm thing, immensely happy, new.

All a fraction of created matter.

Beyond endings the vast majority of the cosmos is dark. Energy vibrates in exquisite balance. Something in that hidden space holds galaxies and galaxy clusters together, while causing space itself to fly apart.

A century seduced by its own blood draws to a close. The threshold of the new millennium is filled with the longing of a planet's people for another chance, to begin anew. They are all one now, and all alone. This night marks time in the history of Earth. It is a point of time floating within the universe.

The Eagle Nebula births a star. Hank and Livy's child decides whether or not to be born.

For hours the snow had fallen, creating a holographic world. Reflecting light and taking light in and refracting it like a pearl. Each frozen crystal singing. It fell at first so fine it could barely be seen, then thicker against the windows. Over the Midwest where the earth meets the horizon in a special way. Over the North Woods, the little lake, birches and pines, and bushes bowed to the ground. At an angle over the gas station in Alma and the auto plant in Harass, softening outlines, transforming shapes, muting sounds.

The snow stopped earlier on this New Year's Eve. Now it began to fall again into the quiet.

In his cabin, Livy beside him, Hank prayed into the silent dark. For Livy, for the women of Alma, for the woods and lake, the city of his birth, the worlds he knew and the ones he would never know, for what he'd been given in his life and what he had missed, for what he'd been able to do and what he had failed to do. He gave thanks for joy and for pain.

Wolves howled under the winter moon.

And the snow fell, watering the land, timeless with absolution.

About the Author

Maureen Connolly's writing appears in The New Guard, Write City, and The Country Doctor Revisited, among others. Her published poetry book is *Wing*.

Awards from Illinois Arts Council and Chicago Writers Association, Machigonne Fiction Prize, and grant from StoryStudioChicago. Her story in The New Guard nominated for a Pushcart.

She is a dual national of the United States and Ireland.

Printed in the USA
CPSIA information can be obtained
at www.ICGtesting.com
CBHW032111110724
11457CB00008B/214